I068050б

THE OMEGA CONNECTION

ALLAN LEVERONE

Copyright ©2015 by Allan Leverone

All rights reserved as permitted under the U.S. Copyright Act of 1976.
No part of this publication may be used, reproduced, distributed or
transmitted in any form or by any means, electronic or mechanical, including
photocopying, recording, or by any information storage or retrieval system,
without the written permission of the author, except where permitted by law,
or in the case of brief quotations embodied in critical articles and reviews.

This is a work of fiction. Names, characters, places, and incidents either
are the product of the author's imagination or are used fictitiously.
Any resemblance to actual events, locales, or persons, living or dead, is
unintended and entirely coincidental.

Special thanks to:

Kealan Patrick Burke and Elderlemon Design for the outstanding cover art,
to editor Dan Persinger for ensuring I dotted my "i's" and crossed my "t's" (or
is it the other way around?), and to JD Smith Design, for the formatting and
design of THE OMEGA CONNECTION print edition.

For Pam Stack: radio host, survivor, friend.

1

Tracie Tanner shifted in her seat, fingering her gold cross necklace uncomfortably. The necklace had been a gift from her parents upon graduating Brown University nearly ten years earlier, and its delicate construction and expensive price tag made the jewelry risky to wear in any but the most formal of settings.

This meant she had rarely gotten an opportunity to wear it. Tracie and formal settings were only marginally acquainted. As a veteran CIA covert ops specialist, she was much more comfortable in the field, with a gun in her shoulder rig and a combat knife strapped to her ankle, than in cultured company dressed in high heels and evening gown.

But tonight's dinner date qualified as a rare exception. The Congressional Steak House had been a Washington, D.C. fixture for nearly one hundred fifty years. A favorite of politicians and high-ranking bureaucrats, it represented a challenging dinner reservation for anyone not at least a cabinet-level member of the current presidential administration.

How Marshall Fulton—a CIA data analyst with no significant string-pulling connections of which Tracie was aware—had managed to score a table at seven-thirty on a Friday evening she had no idea, and Marshall wasn't saying. He offered her a dazzling grin when Tracie broached the subject, making him look exactly like a little kid who had just learned to ride his bike.

"You're not the only one with a secret or two," he said with a wink. His white teeth contrasted with the chocolate-brown of his skin when he smiled, instantly transforming a good-looking man into a breathtakingly handsome one.

Tracie laughed, losing at least a little of the discomfort that had plagued her since accepting the dinner-date invitation. She had only agreed to the date out of a sense of obligation after a chance remark during an extremely stressful night a few weeks ago. But she had come to realize that being alone with your regrets could be the worst thing in the world.

Marshall almost seemed to read her mind. "If I'm being honest," he said, his smile never wavering, "I wasn't at all certain you would accept when I asked you out."

"Really? Why not?"

"Well, we do make a rather…unusual-looking couple, even in a supposedly enlightened city like Washington, DC, and even in the supposedly enlightened year of 1987. I was afraid you might not want to put up with the hassle."

Tracie returned his smile. "That's how you would describe us? 'Unusual-looking'?"

"Well, you know what I mean."

She nodded. "You mean a Mack truck-sized black man walking around with a petite, redheaded white woman on his arm."

"Nah." Marshall waggled his eyebrows. "That's not what I meant. I was talking about a classy chick like you being seen with the likes of me."

The two shared a laugh and sipped their drinks. They hadn't even been shown to their table when they had observed at least a half-dozen people do comical double takes at the sight of them.

"Seriously, though," Tracie said. "You didn't really think I'd be concerned about the opinions of people I've never met, did you?"

Marshall's face turned serious for a moment. "No, not really. But I still wasn't sure you'd say yes when I asked you."

"I already said yes," Tracie answered quietly. "Remember?"

"Oh, I remember alright. I don't think I'll ever forget. But you have to admit, you were a little preoccupied trying to save the life of the U.S. secretary of state at the time."

"As were you," she reminded him.

He shrugged. "I was just driving the car. You did all the heavy lifting."

"You're not giving yourself enough credit. If it weren't for you risking your career by sharing classified information, and then following me after I specifically told you not to"—Marshall hung his head in mock contrition and Tracie laughed—"I would never have been in a position to save anyone."

"Still, it was a hectic moment and I'd certainly have forgiven you for changing your mind. You know, after having time to reflect on it."

"I was thrilled you asked me, Marshall. I haven't been on a real date in years, and to spend a few hours with someone who shares so many of my interests is wonderful."

And it doesn't hurt that you're so damned handsome, either, she thought. Big, strong and athletic—he had been a high-school football star more than a decade ago in his native Louisiana and looked as though he could still fit into his uniform—Marshall Fulton cut an imposing figure in a town filled with effete politicians, bureaucrats and analysts.

So, despite the fact she was still hurting from the death of Shane Rowley, the man she had met and fallen in love with a few months ago on an earlier assignment, Tracie had pushed her misgivings aside and agreed to the date.

"Besides," she teased with a smile, "this is probably the only time I'll ever get to see the inside of the Congressional Steak House. How could I pass up an opportunity like that?"

*   *   *

She decided the restaurant's reputation for excellence was well deserved. The service was prompt and courteous, if a little off-putting in its formality, the cuisine was delicious and the surroundings exquisite.

Without exception, the men were dressed in suits and ties and the women formal eveningwear. Tracie had felt ridiculously overdressed leaving her apartment in her only true formal wear: a full-length gown, midnight blue and studded with sequins. But now she realized she would have risked being denied entry had she elected to wear anything else.

They lingered over dessert and coffee, their lively conversation petering out to a companionable silence. Tracie realized with some surprise she was considering inviting Marshall back to her apartment for a nightcap. It wasn't something she did regularly—she hadn't dated seriously in years—but she was not ready for the evening to end.

They exchanged smiles and Tracie said, "I think we'd better consider bugging out of here. I've noticed the wait staff sending dirty glances our way, and I don't think it's because we look like Mutt and Jeff this time."

Marshall sighed. "You're probably right. We don't want to overstay our welcome and not be invited back, now, do we?"

At that moment a tiny ice cube splashed down in his water glass with a *clink*. Water sloshed out of the glass and spotted his tie, and he wrinkled his forehead in confusion. "What the hell?"

Tracie had noticed a sudden, unexpected movement out of the corner of her eye, a movement that would have gone unobserved by most. But even in this formal and romantic setting, even after a couple of drinks and the best meal she had eaten in at least a year, it was impossible to shut down the alertness and the observational acuity that had kept her alive over her nearly eight year career as a CIA covert operative.

The ice cube had been thrown by a young man sitting three tables across from them in the crowded dining room. He looked barely out of his teens, and he was sharing a table with another young man, roughly the same age, both of them dressed in rumpled suits and ties. They carried themselves with the arrogant entitlement of spoiled brats who had been brought up knowing nothing but privilege, and who felt they were untouchable no matter their behavior *because* of that privilege.

They were probably local college students, likely the sons of high-powered politicians or lobbyists or businessmen.

Marshall wrinkled his forehead and looked in their direction. As he did, the two young men turned their attention to their table, snorting in derision and making perfectly clear they had caused the commotion and didn't care who knew it.

Marshall cleared his throat unhappily and Tracie said, "Kids are stupid, aren't they?"

His anger seemed to melt away and he turned back to Tracie.

"*We* were never that stupid, were we?"

"Oh no, of course not. Not us," and at that moment a second ice cube whizzed through the air and struck Marshall on the side of the head. It then bounced off the table and skidded onto the floor.

He shoved the chair back roughly and stood, moving with surprising grace and speed for a man his size. Tracie could see why he had been a successful athlete in high school.

She could also see that things were about to get ugly.

She leapt to her feet, maneuvering her small body as gracefully as Marshall had moved his large one, and darted between Marshall and the troublemakers. He had taken one step in their direction, but she threaded her arm through his and began guiding him in the direction of the door.

She spoke quietly. "Stupid kids, remember? Let's get out of here and leave them to demonstrate their lack of manners to someone else, shall we?"

For a moment she thought he was going to ignore her, and then he looked down at the floor. Took a deep breath and winked. "Fine with me," he said. "I'm leaving with the prettiest girl in this entire place, and they're leaving with...well...each other."

They shared a laugh and continued toward the front door, Tracie thankful the two idiots hadn't managed to ruin the evening. They threaded their way through the dining area, moving unhurriedly, and exited onto the sidewalk, the cool air refreshing after the crowded stuffiness of the restaurant.

Marshall had parked on the street, at a meter a quarter-mile north of the Congressional Steakhouse, and the pair walked arm in arm, the sidewalk nearly deserted, the near-confrontation already fading into unimportance.

They were maybe halfway to Marshall's car when Tracie heard the sound of harsh voices, muted but distinguishable. The voices floated along the nighttime air from somewhere behind them. She knew instantly it was the pair of losers from the Congressional Steakhouse. She wondered whether Marshall had picked up on the fact that they had company yet, but his suddenly rigid posture answered her unspoken question.

Marshall slowed his pace and Tracie said, "Forget about them. They don't matter. Take me home and we'll have a drink and laugh at the fact that they barely have one working brain between the two of them."

Reluctantly, Marshall resumed walking. Tracie could feel the air being let out of the balloon of good feelings the date had engendered in them both. The two idiots had managed to ruin the evening, after all.

The night was clear and relatively quiet, at least for DC, and soon they could hear bits and pieces of muttered curses and punk threats:

"...stick with your own kind..."

"...guess she'll find out if it's true what they say about black men..."

Though he had continued walking, Tracie could feel Marshall's anger rising. The tension was building inside him, although he was doing his best to hide it from her. Soon it felt like they were moving in slow motion, walking through waist-deep water.

She felt exactly as she had in the restaurant when the damn fools were throwing ice: things were about to get ugly.

"...and the white bitch, she's a nasty little slut, isn't she..."

That did it. Marshall stopped in his tracks. They were directly under a streetlight.

He spun around, turning to face down the punks. Once again he moved with surprising agility. "I don't give a damn what they say about me, but I won't let them insult you," he growled.

Tracie wrapped her two small hands around his elbow and began pulling him toward his car. He was big, but she was deceptively strong and had learned over a career's worth of CIA training how to use leverage to move bigger, stronger bodies.

"Forget about them, Marshall," she said under her breath. "Besides, all you're doing by standing in the light is making a target of yourself. Do you really think they'd have the guts to come after someone your size if they were unarmed?"

He seemed to recognize the reasonableness of her statement and turned toward the car. He moved slowly, though, as if not totally committed to the present course of action.

Once she had gotten him moving again she reached up and pulled a diamond earring off her right ear.

Dropped it on the sidewalk.

Counted to ten.

The punks were almost on top of them now.

"Dammit," she said quietly.

"What is it?" Marshall asked.

"I dropped an earring."

"I'll go back with you."

"No. I've got this."

"You're not going to fight my battles for me. I can handle those two slimeballs with one hand tied behind my back. Besides, I know you dropped the earring on purpose." Marshall Fulton hadn't been a successful CIA data analyst for over a decade by being stupid, nor by being unobservant.

"I know you can take care of yourself," she said, and she meant it. "But what do you think is going to happen when the police get here and find a large black man standing over the prone, bloody bodies of two smaller white men? What do you think the end result of that is going to be?"

Marshall stopped, fuming. The fury and frustration radiated off him in waves. "This'll only take a second," Tracie said. "If you think I'm in trouble, come and finish it."

Without waiting for an answer, she began walking. The punks seemed surprised she had moved ahead to meet them, and for a second they stopped just outside the ring of illumination provided by the streetlight, the outline of their bodies vague and indistinct.

Then they stepped forward.

Immediately Tracie sized them up. The kid on the right was the instigator, the one who had thrown the ice back at the restaurant. He had one hand in the pocket of his suit jacket, likely wrapped around a knife. At least, she hoped it was only a knife.

The other kid was either unarmed or happy to let his friend handle the dirty work. Both his hands were visible, even in the dim light, and his posture—slouched and casual—suggested a rich kid who was accustomed to getting his way without ever having to fight for anything. He was a classic follower.

"Oh!" Tracie said, pretending to be surprised at the sight of them. "I didn't know anyone was there. I dropped an earring and I just need to…"

She took one step forward and then a second, pretending to sweep the sidewalk with her gaze but in reality keeping a sharp eye on the first kid. His hand was still in his pocket.

"You should learn to stick with your own kind," the leader said, seeming to grow bolder as Marshall stayed in the background. "Maybe you've never dated the right white boys, but Me 'n' Paul will be happy to change all that for ya…"

"Ah, there it is," Tracie said, bending at the knees and leaning forward as if preparing to pick up her earring.

The moment she began to bend, the first kid stepped forward quickly, removing his hand from his pocket. A soft *snick* told Tracie she had been right about the knife, and as he started to step around her and move toward Marshall a small blade flashed in the light.

She made a ball out of her fists, wrapping her left hand around her right, and drove them upward as he passed. The surprised thug tried to leap sideways but he was much too slow, and Tracie made solid contact between his legs.

The switchblade clattered to the sidewalk and the kid let out a shocked gasp before dropping like a felled tree. He landed on his side, moaning and swearing and thrashing.

Tracie turned her attention to the second kid, who had frozen in shock but was now advancing as if to rescue his friend.

She stood and in one smooth motion stepped toward the second kid and punched him in the throat. She intended to pull the punch, to hit him just hard enough to put him down, but she misjudged his forward motion in the half-light. He joined his friend on the sidewalk, choking and gagging.

Oops, she thought. *Oh well, serves the son of a bitch right.*

She bent and plucked her earring off the concrete. Stepped over the two downed men. Stared at the leader until he met her gaze. Then she smiled coldly. "The guy I'm with is twice the man either of you will ever be. And by the way, you should learn to keep your ignorant opinions—meaning all of them—to yourselves."

She turned without another word and strolled back to where Marshall was standing. He had watched the entire episode unfold in a matter of seconds, and his dazzling smile was clearly visible even in the darkness.

"That was fast," he said as she took his arm again and they turned toward his car.

She flashed him a grin. "I told you it wouldn't take long. That didn't even qualify as a workout." Then she examined her right hand and swore softly. "Ah, dammit."

"What's the matter? Are you hurt?"

"Worse. The second punk was wearing what looked like a gold necklace, and I guess I chipped a nail on it when I hit him."

"Well, that's better than the fate *he* suffered."

"Yeah, but still. The one time in my life I get a manicure, and I break a nail within six hours. Figures."

By now they had reached Marshall's beat-up old 1979 Buick Regal, and he unlocked the passenger door and held it open for her. "You could break every last nail and you'd still look damn fine to me."

Tracie smiled crookedly. "Flattery will get you everywhere."

2

Allan Nesbitt lay against the headboard on his fluffed-up hotel pillows, eyes half-closed, and breathed deeply. Raggedly. The cocaine and champagne he had been indulging in to excess were beginning to take their toll.

As president and chief executive officer of National Circuit Corporation, Nesbitt was due downstairs in the Washington Arms Hotel ballroom in less than thirty minutes for the board meeting/dinner that in reality was to be the triumphant annual celebration of the company's rebirth.

He was starting to wonder if he would be able to make it.

Founded in the late 1940s, National Circuit's original mission had been to provide vacuum tube circuitry, and later on, electronic components, for radios and television sets. As TVs exploded in popularity, the resulting surge in orders carried NCC through its first decade on a wave of ever-increasing sales, the resulting profits permitting research and development into new products on a massive scale.

Government contracts soon followed, including what seemed like a relatively innocuous agreement to manufacture miniature circuitry for a concept being pioneered by the U.S. military known as the "Global Positioning System." The experimental system utilized the concept of triangulation between satellites in constant orbit over the earth to pinpoint the location of receivers on the earth's surface.

Scientists theorized that once enough geosynchronous

satellites had become operational, it would be technically possible for commanders to determine the location of any soldier anywhere in the world at any time. And the positioning would be accurate to within astonishingly precise parameters—six feet or less—provided the soldier in question was provided with a special electronic device, similar to a tiny radio transmitter.

For more than two decades, the defense department GPS circuitry contract was responsible for just a small percentage of NCC's overall sales, even as satellites were launched and tests were conducted and various branches of the U.S. military began making use of the technology.

But four years ago, as NCC was suffering through its eighth consecutive year of declining profits and sluggish sales, a tragic event occurred that would single-handedly turn the company's fortunes around: the Soviet Union attacked and shot down a civilian airliner, Korean Airlines Flight 007.

September 1, 1983. The Boeing 747 carrying 269 people was on a flight originating from JFK International Airport to Seoul, South Korea after a stopover in Anchorage, Alaska. The mammoth passenger jet strayed into Soviet airspace and was fired upon by a Soviet Su-15 supersonic interceptor, with tragic and deadly results: Flight 007 crashed into the Sea of Japan, killing everyone on board.

The incident resulted in some of the tensest moments of the Cold War since the Cuban missile crisis. The Soviets accused the Americans of spying and even of attempting to provoke war, and the White House responded in kind, accusing the Russians of obstructing search and rescue operations, as well as of initially denying responsibility for the crash and then hiding evidence relating to it.

At first glance the event seemed entirely unrelated to the declining fortunes of a minor player in the electronics manufacturing sector. But everything changed in a heartbeat with President Reagan's decision to declassify the U.S. military's GNSS system, the forerunner of the modern GPS system, and to allow worldwide civilian access.

The civilian possibilities for the technology were nearly limitless, and as the patent holder for a critical electronic component in the GPS receiver, National Circuit would be involved in the production of every GPS unit manufactured. Almost overnight, the company was transformed from a washed-up relic sliding into obscurity, into a worldwide leader in electronics manufacturing.

That had all occurred four years ago.

In the tumultuous months following the KAL 007 disaster, even as NCC was being reinvigorated, company founder James Nesbitt suffered a massive heart attack and died, leaving day-to-day operations in the hands of his only son, Allan. Though groomed for the succession since early childhood, Allan Nesbitt had possessed neither the business acumen of his father nor the man's drive to succeed.

Allan would be the first to admit, even if only to himself, that the phenomenal success of NCC was due more to sheer, blind luck than to intelligent stewardship on his part, but nevertheless, he had found himself in charge of a hugely successful corporate entity, and the recipient of far more wealth than he would ever be able to spend.

That didn't stop him from trying. In the three-plus years of his tenure as CEO, Allan had blown millions on houses, cars, drugs, alcohol and women. Many of the women were the sort to whom love was nothing more than a financial transaction, often a short-term one of twenty-four hours or less.

All of which had led to this: Allan Nesbitt stretched out barely conscious on the bed in his hotel suite after overindulging in expensive champagne and sharing cocaine snorted through rolled-up hundred dollar bills—he knew it was a cliché but didn't care—with a high-priced call girl named Melani.

Allan was savvy enough to know Melani was her hooker name and not her real name, but he didn't care about that, either. As far as he was concerned, she could call herself whatever the hell she wanted. At fifteen hundred bucks a night, she was pricey, but Hooker Melani was one of the most beautiful and alluring women Allan had ever seen.

And the best part, the absolutely kickass part, was she had been a total surprise.

He had checked into his room earlier this afternoon, prepared to shower and dress and be bored out of his mind at tonight's self-congratulatory gathering of company bigwigs and ass-kissers, and instead had been greeted by the sight of the petite, fine-boned, vaguely Mediterranean-looking young woman dressed—more or less—in black leather short shorts, fishnet stockings, and a red velvet leather vest working overtime to contain her perfectly sized assets.

Melani refused to divulge who had hired her to be Allan's guest for the evening, and if he was being honest with himself Allan didn't much care who was paying her. He knew what rate she was charging because he asked her, and in his considered opinion—one he arrived at before even sampling her services—Melani would be worth every penny of…whoever's money had been shelled out.

So now, rather than being *bored* out of his mind all night at a white-bread company gathering, Allan Nesbitt was *stoned* out of his mind. He lay back and contemplated the suddenly daunting prospect of dressing and attempting to navigate the hallway, and then the elevator, to the downstairs banquet room.

He looked up at Melani through bleary eyes. "Good God, but you're beautiful," he muttered. "And the best surprise of my life." At least, he thought he had said it out loud. He was so toasted right now he couldn't be sure.

If he *had* said it, though, he was glad. It was the God's honest truth. Not only did she look better than anything he had ever slept with, not only was he receiving her services for free for the evening, not only had she filled him in on all of the things she would be doing for—and with—him tonight after the company gathering, but on top of everything else she had supplied the coke they had just finished sharing!

Of course, "sharing" might not be the most accurate description of the last couple of hours," he thought. He had inhaled a hell of a lot more of the drugs than she had.

Now that he thought about it, Allan couldn't exactly recall her ingesting *any* of it. Melani had sipped champagne and teased him relentlessly with her killer body, all the while encouraging him to snort more of the high-quality coke. Through his haze of confusion and impairment he began to think he might have used it all himself.

And that was okay, too. She was a professional, after all, and it was important she stay more or less sober, if for no other reason than to follow through on all of the things she promised to do the minute the banquet was over downstairs.

He lurched off the bed and staggered toward the bathroom, aware of Melani watching him through narrowed eyes. He attempted to smile at her as he passed. Based on her reaction, he guessed the smile more closely resembled a grimace.

"Be right back," he said, wobbling on his feet and trying not to slur his words. Even after a lifetime of practice talking while impaired, it was almost impossible to pull off. "I gotta pee."

Now that he was no longer flat on his back, Allan Nesbitt realized he really didn't feel very well. Maybe he had overdone it a little with the coke, although he had snorted more than this on plenty of occasions in the past and it had never hit him this hard.

He took one struggling step and then another, and he realized he was sweating like a pig. Perspiration rolled down his face like he had just run the New York Marathon despite the fact that he had turned the room's thermostat down so low he could see the goosebumps on Melani's exposed arms.

The hooker stepped back to let him pass, her expression indecipherable, and as he stumbled forward a crushing pain gripped his chest. It was as though some invisible attacker had wrapped a studded steel band around his heart and was even now tightening it mercilessly.

He dropped to his knees, suddenly unable to breathe, and then toppled onto his side. His chest was on fire and he felt like he was about to puke, and that would be the worst thing in the world because everybody knew after you puked you had to breathe—had to pant like a dog, actually—and Allan simply COULD NOT BREATHE.

He rolled onto his back and locked eyes desperately with Melani, the beautiful little dark-skinned call girl. She stood over him without moving, staring at him like a butcher eyeing a prime cut of meat.

With what little air he had left in his burning lungs, he gasped, "Call...ambulance...heart...attack..."

Melani didn't move.

"I...I...I..."

Melani didn't move.

He opened his mouth to scream, to tell the stupid goddamn bitch to call the front desk, to run and get help, to do any goddamn thing, but he still couldn't breathe and he had nothing left inside, and the pain was so goddamn bad and she wasn't moving and his mouth opened and closed like a trout caught on a fishhook, and the last thing he saw before everything went black and his goddamn heart exploded inside his goddamn chest was a tiny smile of satisfaction as it crept across the face of his killer.

3

Edison Kiley hated gatherings like this. He hated anything that took him away from his laboratory and the research and development work he so enjoyed, but he especially hated dressing up in a suit and tie and…mingling.

Even though the people he was being forced to mingle with were, for the most part, men and women he had known and worked with for years—decades, in some cases—his familiarity with those coworkers didn't make the torture any easier to bear. In some ways, that only made it worse. Hell, he saw these very same people eight, ten, twelve hours a day, five or six days a week! What in God's name was the point of getting together on their off time just to have a few drinks and tell stories?

The annual event was pretentious and ridiculous.

But it was also necessary, or so claimed the company big shots. "It's only once a year, Edison," they said.

"Our stock is flying high, Edison, we have a lot to celebrate," they said.

"You're vested in the corporate profit-sharing plan, Edison, you have to join us," they said.

So, here he was—reluctantly—necktie strangling him like a stylish garrote, the wool from his trousers causing his inner thighs to itch continuously, his eyes practically glued to his watch as he observed the sweep second hand, waiting impatiently for a couple of hours to pass so he could press a hand to his mouth in a false yawn and go home to bed.

But as distasteful as all of those things were, they didn't even qualify as the worst part of the night. The worst part was that the good-for-nothing CEO, Nesbitt—the young punk who had taken a quality company and done his level best to drive it straight into the ground after his old man died, only to be saved from his own incompetence by sheer luck—had yet to show up.

The damned fool was late.

It figures, Edison thought to himself. *He's either doing it on purpose, keeping everyone waiting so he can make a grand entrance, or he's face-first in a whiskey bottle and has simply forgotten all about everyone else.* It wouldn't be the first time.

One of the perks—if you could call it a perk—of being a thirty-year veteran of National Circuit as well as the R&D genius who developed the critical refinements to the GPS receivers that had saved the company's bacon, was that for the last four years he had been seated at the head table during this annual waste of time and money. Now he listened as the typical business-related chit-chat—stock and bonds, housing market, cost of living, not a one of them anything Edison gave a damn about—gradually died away and turned into impatient grumbling about their leader's absence from his own party.

"What's taking him so long?" The man seated to Edison's left was Chief Financial Officer Kirk Moreland. As far as Edison knew, Moreland had never set foot in the R&D lab; Edison doubted he even knew where it was located. The CFO leaned forward and looked past Edison as if he wasn't even there.

"Well, he's definitely not tied up working at the office. I don't think he's gone home later than two p.m. in the last six months." This from the man on Edison's right, longtime VP Chris Nuñez, who had been stuck in his position for years, thanks to Allan Nesbitt's bloodline. Nuñez undoubtedly made good money, but his lust for corporate power was so strong that even Edison, who tended to be oblivious to those types of things, could clearly sense it.

"Is he even here?"

"He's here. I saw him go upstairs to his room a couple of hours ago as I was paying the catering crew."

The financial guy shook his head. "The rest of us have to drive home after dinner and drinks, and His Majesty reserves himself a room at one of the most expensive hotels in DC."

"And you know who's paying for that room."

"The company," the two men said simultaneously, and then shared a chummy laugh.

The VP made a show of looking at his watch. Then he sighed. "I suppose I ought to go upstairs and find out what's taking so long."

Neither of the two men had so much as acknowledged Edison Kiley as they carried on their conversation with him seated between them. Instead of being annoyed, he was glad. He had nothing in common with either man and absolutely no interest in making small talk.

He did, however, recognize an opportunity to escape when he saw one, even if only for a few minutes. He decided to take advantage of it. "You gentlemen seem to be enjoying your cocktails," he said, surprising even himself with his smooth delivery. He wondered where *that* had come from. "I've known Allan since he was a boy. Why don't I go upstairs and find out how much longer he's going to be?"

The two men shared a surprised glance, eyebrows raised. It was obvious neither had expected to be addressed by the odd-duck researcher who had been employed by NCC since they were in diapers, and neither seemed to have any idea how to respond.

Edison shrugged. "Like I said, I've known him almost his entire life."

The VP shook his head, a small grin tugging at the corners of his mouth. He picked up his drink and sipped from it. "Have at it," he finally said.

* * *

The elevator was empty. Edison breathed deeply, able to relax for the first time since pulling on his suit a couple of hours ago. The temptation was strong to rouse Nesbitt from his drunken slumber—why else would he have gotten a room if not to party?—and then to hit the road. It would be a simple thing to wake the boss and then ride the elevator to the hotel's basement parking garage, climb into his Peugeot and head home.

He wouldn't do it, of course, but it was a pleasant little fantasy, and Edison amused himself with it as the elevator climbed to the fourteenth floor. After a disappointingly fast ride, it braked to a stop and the doors slid open, revealing an empty hallway.

Nunez had told him Nesbitt's room number was 1408. "Halfway down the hall on the right," he had added, as if maybe the head of Research and Development might be incapable of reading numbers on doors.

Edison stepped out of the elevator and froze as a room's door opened—roughly halfway down the hall on the right—and a young woman stepped into the hallway. She was dressed provocatively, in very short shorts, and her lace-covered legs looked impossibly long.

He froze. He couldn't have said why, but he felt a nearly overwhelming sense of danger radiating off the woman. He guessed she was late-twenties, maybe thirty, but was by no means confident in that assessment. The hallway was dimly lit, and Edison's visual acuity had been sliding downhill for years.

Something's happened to Nesbitt. The thought flared immediately, and it made no sense because from this distance he had no idea whether the young woman had even come out of Nesbitt's room. Still, he couldn't help how he felt, and he watched as the hooker—she was almost certainly a prostitute, the way she was dressed—glanced down the hallway in the other direction, and then swiveled her head and locked eyes with Edison.

A spike of fear coursed through him and he realized he had never felt quite as old as he did right now. *I'm being silly,* he thought, and he began walking slowly toward her along the otherwise empty hallway.

The woman tracked his progress for a moment with eyes narrowed to slits. Then she turned on her heel and headed off in the other direction. Edison had never been on the fourteenth floor of the Washington Arms before—had never been on *any* floor but the first—but he doubted there was anything at the end of the hallway besides a set of fire stairs.

Odd that the scantily clad young woman would choose not to use the elevator.

Then again, this whole bizarre little vignette was odd.

Edison slowed his pace as he became more and more convinced that the young woman had, in fact, exited Nesbitt's room. It wasn't hard to believe the CEO would have hired a hooker, but the vibe this woman gave off was distinctly dark. Dangerous. Edison couldn't put his finger on exactly why he felt this way, but it seemed critically important the woman not discover he was heading to the room she had just come out of.

He approached Nesbitt's room—as he got close enough to read the number he realized it *was* same room she had exited—at the same time the woman pushed through a heavy metal fire door at the end of the hallway and disappeared. It occurred to him that she could turn after the door eased shut and watch him through the narrow, wire-reinforced rectangular window and he would never know, but there was nothing he could do about that.

He stopped in front of Nesbitt's door and rapped with his knuckles, three quick knocks, the sound almost like a violation in the stillness of the hallway.

Waited for a response.

Nothing.

Knocked again.

Still nothing.

Now what do I do?

* * *

It took some convincing for the platinum blonde desk clerk to agree to disturb Allan Nesbitt. She flat-out refused Edison's request for a key to the CEO's room, and only reluctantly decided to accompany Edison upstairs to open the door after Edison had enlisted the help of his new VP friend, Nuñez.

Even after Chris Nunez's assurance that he would accept responsibility for any fallout over the invasion of Allan Nesbitt's privacy, the clerk made them wait while she enlisted someone to cover for her at the front desk. She wasn't about to hand over her room access key to anyone, so Edison was forced to cool his heels for several minutes before getting started back upstairs.

Nuñez, despite agreeing to bear the brunt of Nesbitt's wrath, disappeared back to the function room and his drink the moment the clerk's back was turned.

Edison didn't mind; in fact he preferred it. He hadn't been kidding about knowing Allan Nesbitt for decades, and he was one of the few people at NCC not intimidated by the CEO.

As he waited for the clerk, he considered what he had seen upstairs. While it wasn't hard to imagine Nesbitt hiring a hooker, it *was* hard to imagine him allowing the woman to remain in his room if he wasn't in there with her.

In fact, it was impossible to believe.

Allan Nesbitt was a loose cannon, and, at least in Edison's opinion, a man utterly unprepared to guide the fortunes of a company like National Circuit, but Edison didn't believe even Nesbitt was foolish enough to allow a prostitute the run of his hotel room.

More to the point, even if he *was* foolish enough to do so, where would he have gone? He wasn't in the function room, and an attention hog like Nesbitt wouldn't hide in the hotel bar drinking while a room full of sycophants and suck-ups waited just a few feet away to spend the evening kissing his butt.

Finally, the desk clerk emerged from a back office looking none too pleased. She swept past Edison, glancing his way with a curt nod, apparently an indication he should follow. So he did.

The elevator ride to the fourteenth floor was spent with the clerk voicing her displeasure. "Men like Mr. Nesbitt value their privacy, and it's against hotel policy to barge into their rooms uninvited, unless there's a serious emergency involved."

This time, Edison was thankful for the fast ride and he more or less ignored her, avoiding her wrath by nodding and murmuring bland words of agreement at strategic intervals. He was barely listening, thinking instead about the sense of danger he had felt upon seeing the young woman leave Nesbitt's room.

The elevator stopped and the doors slid open, Edison eerily certain the same woman would be standing at Nesbitt's door waiting for them, ready to do…something.

But of course the young woman wasn't in the hallway. No one was in the hallway, and the desk clerk marched down it like an avenging angel, moving much faster than Edison had earlier, much faster than his nearly eighty-year-old legs could carry him now. It seemed that, with her goal in sight, the platinum blonde was anxious to get this distasteful task over with and back to the safety of the front desk.

She stopped in front of Room 1408 and cast a dark glance back at Edison, then rapped primly on the door. "Mr. Nesbitt," she said loudly. Edison briefly considered telling her he had already tried knocking and calling out to him, then decided not to bother. She was clearly not going to be influenced by anything he did or said.

Her knock went unheeded and she tried again, and by this time Edison had finally caught up with her.

She glared at him one more time, apparently in the event he had somehow misread the earlier evidence of her displeasure, and then said, "You realize we're disturbing all the other guests on this floor."

Edison had no idea how to respond, so he said nothing.

The clerk savored her victory for a moment and then said, "Well, he's your boss, go ahead on in."

Then she slid the key card into the receptacle. The lock clicked and a green light flashed and she pushed the door open slowly, stepping back to allow Edison to pass.

Despite the sense of danger he had felt upon seeing the hooker leave Nesbitt's room, he was completely unprepared for the sight that greeted him just inside the door.

Nesbitt lay on his back, arms stretched out to either side as if beseeching God for help that would never come. His wrinkled dress shirt was partially unbuttoned, his necktie thrown across the messy bed. His sheet-white face was contorted in a rictus of agony and Edison could see he wasn't breathing.

Could see he would never breathe again.

He took one step into the room and stopped, and the impatient desk clerk tut-tutted behind him. "Well, is he in there?"

She stepped around him, saying, "What the devil's the prob—"

Then she screamed. The sound was high-pitched and persistent and reminded Edison of an electric drill being operated at maximum RPM. He had the absurd notion that he should warn her she was disturbing all the other guests on the floor.

Instead, he ignored her and bent to check Nesbitt's pulse. The exercise was pointless, but he did it anyway. Edison was surprised by the sense of calm he felt when he knew he should be panicking.

His knees had just hit the carpet when the muffled *whump* of an explosion drifted through the hotel, shaking the high-rise structure on its foundation. The noise provided a bass counterpoint to the shrill screams still being shrieked out behind him.

Explosion in the banquet room, Edison thought as placed two fingers lightly on Nesbitt's carotid artery. The thought was more or less random; there was no reason for it. The hotel was massive, the explosion could have occurred anywhere in the building, including from one of the floors above, but he knew it hadn't occurred anywhere else in the building. It had occurred in the room in which he had been sitting not fifteen minutes prior.

The desk clerk stopped screaming, her shrieks cut off mid-breath. She stood stock-still, mouth hanging open, like someone had flipped a switch to cut off the power to her brain.

Total silence fell for what was probably only three or four seconds but what felt like an hour. It was as if every single person left alive inside the building was holding his or her breath, exactly as the shocked desk clerk now seemed to be doing.

Then the screaming started from downstairs, the sound soft but clear. It built in intensity and was soon joined by the platinum blonde, whose brain seemed to have powered up again.

Edison stuck to his task. There was nothing he could do for the victims he was certain were strewn around the banquet room, but he couldn't simply leave Allan Nesbitt without confirming the man's death.

It didn't take long. There was no pulse.

Edison took a deep breath and calmed his shaking hands.

Tried again.

Nesbitt was still dead. The young woman he had seen exiting this room had killed him.

There was nothing more to be done here.

Edison stood, wincing at the pain in his arthritic knees. He reached for the desk clerk's elbow and began leading her out of the room.

He closed the self-locking door behind them and the clerk

said, "But Mr. Nesbitt, he's—"

"The police will want to know nothing's been disturbed," he said gently, and the woman looked at him wide-eyed and uncomprehending.

She turned for the elevators and Edison shook his head. "We'll want to take the stairs," he said. "We don't know where the explosion occurred"—although he thought he did—"and we don't know how much damage has been done. We don't want to be trapped in the elevator if the power goes out."

The woman continued to stare at him as if he had suddenly begun speaking in tongues, and Edison led her patiently to the doors at the far end of the hallway—*the same doors Nesbitt's killer went through,* he thought.

He only hesitated a moment before pushing them open and beginning the long climb down to the lobby.

4

Tracie Tanner hated meeting CIA Director Aaron Stallings at his home. Hated everything about it, from the sheer size of his palatial house in the DC suburbs—*just how does a career civil servant, even one as high up the food chain as Stallings, ever make enough money to afford all this?*—to the arrogant, dismissive attitude the boss affected every time he spoke to her.

The most galling part for Tracie was the knowledge that, as CIA director, Stallings had the leeway to dispatch a tech team to Tracie's apartment to install a secure phone line any time he wished. Within a matter of hours, this cloak-and-dagger bullshit could be dispensed with, and Tracie would have the capability of receiving instructions from her handler in a far easier and more efficient manner.

It was never going to happen, though. In an agency renowned around the world for Black Ops—ironically, what people *thought* the CIA was up to often went far beyond what they were actually doing—Tracie Tanner was, quite possibly, the blackest of Black Ops operatives, the most covert agent on the payroll.

Nobody at the agency—besides Stallings—was aware she had been rehired after successfully rescuing kidnapped Secretary of State J. Robert Humphries a few weeks ago. Nobody with any *oversight* over the agency—meaning the United States Congress—was aware she had been rehired, either.

Her handler was none other than Director Stallings himself. And Stallings was far too savvy to put his career at risk by discussing covert operations over a telephone line, secure or otherwise, when those discussions would take place with an off-the-books agent working directly under him.

CYA was the order of the day for government bureaucrats everywhere, but that truth was no clearer anywhere than in the CIA. And no bureaucrat was better at covering his posterior than Stallings. His long career was ample proof of that fact.

So for the foreseeable future, the current scenario was unlikely to change, despite the fact that for Tracie, driving to a meeting with Stallings was like enduring a root canal with no Novocain.

She doubted it was ever going to get any easier. But she had no choice than to put up with the aggravation, because it was either endure the distasteful CIA director or find a new job. He had made his feelings on that issue abundantly clear when he went against agency policy and rehired her after canning her for insubordination during the investigation into the Humphries kidnapping.

And, despite all it had cost her, she still loved her job.

She breathed deeply and knocked on the closed door to Aaron Stallings's home office. He had told her on the phone to enter through his home's unlocked front door and come directly to his office, which she had done.

Mrs. Stallings was nowhere in evidence. If she was home, she was upstairs, a situation for which Tracie was glad. It would have been difficult to make small talk with the wife of a man she detested—and who detested her in equal measure—without her disdain for him being obvious.

"Come in," came the order. Tracie opened the door and stepped through, moving directly to the chair he had placed in front of his desk. She sat without waiting to be asked. She had played this game before.

"Director," she said coolly, and for the first time, Stallings lifted his gaze from a mountain of paperwork covering his desk. Tracie had to admit, the man might be a distasteful worm, but he was a workaholic distasteful worm.

CIA Director Aaron Stallings—at least when Tracie was around—had the perpetual look of a bloodhound whose food bowl had been taken away. He was a large man, overweight, with fleshy jowls that had a tendency to jiggle when he talked, his features turned down in a semi-permanent scowl.

Again, at least when Tracie was around.

He stared at her for a moment and then surprised her by turning his attention to her hands. "Quite a nasty bruise on your knuckles," he said, narrowing his eyes and looking at the back of her right hand.

"I'll survive."

"How did you get it?"

"I slipped in the shower."

"Really. You wouldn't care to reconsider that statement?"

"Nope."

"It wouldn't have had anything to do with an altercation outside the Congressional Steakhouse last night, would it? Because according to witnesses, a petite young woman with flame-red hair, in the company of a very large black man, single-handedly laid out two young men without even breaking a sweat."

"I'm sure I'm not the only redhead in the DC area."

"The witnesses told authorities this redhead knew what she was doing."

"Look," Tracie said. "Hypothetically speaking, *if* I had been the woman involved, those two snot-nosed little punks would have had it coming. *If* I had been the woman involved, that beating would have happened only after they continually harassed a very nice man and then threatened me with bodily injury."

"If," Stallings said.

"That's right, if. But let's face it. *I* could never get reservations to the Congressional Steakhouse; it's one of the toughest scores in Washington. So it had to have been some other gorgeous redhead."

"Nobody said she was 'gorgeous.'"

"That's because it was dark out," she said, smiling sweetly. "Anyway, I doubt you called me here just to discuss my...I mean, someone else's...adventure last night."

"No I didn't," Stallings agreed. "But before we get to that, let me just say this: be careful. Use a little discretion. Publicity is something you don't want and we don't need."

"Understood." Tracie wanted to be angry with the director, but in this case she couldn't manage it. He was right. The first rule of covert ops was to stay under the radar. That was true in foreign countries and it was just as true here in the States.

In fact, given her situation, it was probably *more* true here. And she had come dangerously close to having her face splashed all over the news last night.

"Anyway," Stallings continued, "were you too busy *not* kicking two racists' asses last night to watch the news?"

"I saw the news. Which portion of it are you referring to?"

"The explosion at the Washington Arms Hotel."

"A technology company was targeted, correct?"

"That's right. National Circuit Corporation."

"The CEO died in his room just prior to the bomb detonating, if I recall correctly."

Stallings smiled. It was something he rarely did in Tracie's presence, and the effect resembled a cross between a half-hearted sneer and the expression of a man suffering extreme heartburn. "That's right," he said.

She bit her lip to keep from laughing at the sight. "Tragic, but it sounds like a matter for the DC police. It was probably a disgruntled employee or ex-employee. What's our interest in some crank blowing up the board of directors of a tech company?"

"Yes, it is a matter for the police. I'm sure they're knee-deep in their investigation even as we speak. And a disgruntled employee is one possibility. Industrial espionage is another."

Tracie leaned back in her chair, thinking. "That sounds like a stretch. I can understand companies trying to get a leg up on their competitors, but mass murder? Just to achieve a competitive advantage? Seems unlikely to me."

Stallings's face darkened, his comical expression evaporating in an instant. "Yes, well, that's neither here nor there."

Tracie doubted Aaron Stallings had ever uttered a single word in his entire life without working toward some ulterior motive. What that motive might be in this case, though, she had no idea. "So, what does all of this have to do with me?"

"I was just getting to that. The police have already confirmed that the head table was targeted in the Washington Arms function room. Three small blocks of C4, attached to the underside of the table and wired to a small radio receiver, detonated remotely via transmitter."

"Wow. Somebody was angry."

"That's right. If anyone had bothered to check the underside of the table, the whole disaster could have been avoided, but it was a private corporate function and no bomb threats had been received prior. It wouldn't have occurred to anyone to sweep the room for explosives."

"All the National Circuit bigwigs would have been seated at the head table, obviously, so the entire company must have been decimated," Tracie said thoughtfully. Suddenly the idea of corporate espionage began to make a little more sense. "Add in the death of the CEO in his room, and all of the key employees must have been taken out in one fell swoop."

"Not quite all."

Tracie shook her head and waited. It was obvious Stallings wanted her to prod him for information and she refused to give him the satisfaction. Anything she could do to tweak the boss was fair game as far as she was concerned, after all he had done to her.

After a moment, he seemed to realize she wasn't going to take the bait and he continued. "One of the men who had been seated at the head table managed to escape the blast through sheer luck. When the CEO, a guy by the name of Allan Nesbitt, hadn't shown up by the beginning of the event, the head of Research and Development went to Nesbitt's hotel suite to find out why. He had just discovered the dead body when the explosion occurred."

Tracie knitted her eyebrows together in concentration. "Assuming Nesbitt's death and the explosion in the function room are related, wouldn't the killers have expected someone to come looking for Nesbitt?"

"Maybe. Maybe not. The CEO was only a couple of minutes late when the explosion occurred. Perhaps someone's timing got messed up. In any event, that's irrelevant to your assignment."

"Which is?"

"The R&D guy's name is Edison Kiley. He's an old geezer who's been with NCC since the company was founded back in the 1940s. I need you to go out to his home and bring him here."

"Why in the world would I do that? It sounds like he could probably benefit from protection until the authorities sort through this mess, but shouldn't the police be the ones to provide it? What's the CIA's interest in a geriatric scientist?"

"Maybe you've forgotten how this is supposed to work. I don't explain myself to you. I tell you what I want done and then you go and do it. Was I not clear about that when I went against my better judgment and rehired you?"

Tracie breathed deeply before replying. "You were very clear. But a little background would help. I can't imagine an old man agreeing to go anywhere with me unless I can make a pretty convincing argument."

Stallings stared at her for a moment. "Fair enough," he finally said. "That's a valid point. But you might have less trouble than you think convincing him to come to Langley."

"Why's that?"

"Because he used to work for us."

5

The morning had started out overcast, with threatening clouds looming over the DC area, and as the day progressed conditions only went downhill. By the time Tracie left her apartment to make the short drive to Edison Kiley's home in rural Williamsburg, the heavens had opened and rain was falling in sheets.

The conditions seemed appropriate to her mood. *Perfect,* she thought as her wipers struggled to clear the windshield. *This is how far my career has fallen. A year ago I was working under-cover in Moscow and East Germany and now I'm playing cab driver for an eighty-year-old corporate researcher.*

She sighed deeply and tried to change her attitude. Maybe this assignment was a letdown, but at least she still had a job. And if she ever hoped to earn an opportunity to get back into the field for real instead of just being some well-paid errand girl—as unlikely as she knew that possibility to be—she would have to suck it up and be the best damned errand girl that asshole Stallings had ever seen.

She eased off her speed and began looking for the turn that should lead to Kiley's home. He lived in Virginia, less than thirty minutes from DC, but if this part of the drive was any indication, he may as well have been a thousand miles out in the country. This area seemed to be as isolated as any Tracie had seen in the congested northeastern United States.

Her wipers sloshed the rain around and through squinting eyes she spotted a green road sign up ahead and slowed the car. She hadn't bothered to write down the name of the road Kiley lived on because it was so unusual there was no way she could forget it: Woodchuck Hill. She had been surprised when she heard it, but now, based on the rural isolation in which she found herself, it seemed oddly appropriate.

Three quarters of a mile along Woodchuck Hill—which didn't seem to be a hill at all, but felt flat as a board, albeit a heavily forested board—she still hadn't seen any sign of a house. No driveways, no mailboxes, no nicely manicured front yards, nothing. Edison Kiley might be an old guy, but he certainly seemed to value his privacy.

Another half-mile passed and Tracie began to doubt the information she had been given. It wasn't just that she couldn't find Kiley's house, there didn't seem to be *anyone* living out here. She resolved to drive another mile and if there were still no signs of life, she would have to get in touch with Stallings and have him double-check the address.

She rounded a sweeping curve to the right and there it was: a metal mailbox painted to resemble the American flag with the name "Kiley" stenciled on the side. The mailbox had been placed next to a long, paved driveway that terminated at the side of a small ranch home set far back from the road. *At least, I think it's a ranch house,* Tracie thought. *It's hard to see anything through this apocalyptic storm.*

She cruised slowly up the scientist's driveway and then splashed to a stop behind a late-model, well-used Plymouth. She sat for a moment, gazing intently at Kiley's home. Something seemed off about this. It didn't seem like the kind of place the head of research and development for a company like National Circuit should live in. Tracie had pictured something more…ostentatious. More like Stallings's home.

She shrugged and prepared to climb out of her car. What did she know about corporate structuring, anyway? Maybe the guy made a lot less money than she had imagined.

She opened the door and stepped into the deluge, and that was when the house exploded.

A tightly spaced series of muffled *cracks* split the night, one right after the other, *bang-bang-bang-bang,* and the little ranch house collapsed in upon itself with the sound of an extended car accident. Glass smashed and support beams disintegrated and the low-pitched roar of destruction lasted maybe five seconds but felt much longer.

Slivers of broken glass and wood peppered the area like tiny missiles. She dived full-length through the still-open car door, smashing her head against the top of the doorframe and then grunting in pain as she landed squarely on top of the Toyota's floor-mounted gearshift. A heavy clattering of debris fell on and around the vehicle, overwhelming the sound of the rainfall drumming on the roof.

For a moment.

And then it was over. The silence was overwhelming after the obscene sound of destruction that had preceded it.

Tracie shoved herself backward out of the car, landing on her feet in the rain. She felt a small lump growing into a bigger one on her head. Ran her hand over the bruise and then ignored it. Turned toward Edison Kiley's home, now nothing more than a pile of construction debris whose outline resembled that of a house in only the vaguest fashion.

Even with the darkness nearly complete, Tracie could see the damage was significant. Walls canted inward at unlikely angles, bricks from Kiley's fireplace lay scattered in his side yard, two-by-six studs supporting the exterior walls had been broken in half, the lower portions protruding from the rubble, their ragged edges thrust uncertainly toward the sky.

She was too late. Only by seconds, but that was irrelevant. Whoever had decimated the rest of National Circuit's upper management structure had returned quickly to finish the job when they realized someone had survived.

Tracie began to circle the house in a counterclockwise direction. It was hard to imagine anyone surviving the blast, especially an octogenarian who lived alone, but she couldn't simply abandon Edison Kiley until she knew for certain he was dead.

The rain continued to fall, picking up in intensity, the sound loud against the stillness of the desolate area. She listened for sirens and heard none. The closest neighbor was probably miles away, and based on the lack of traffic she had observed on Woodchuck

Hill, it might be hours before any motorists drove by who might see the destruction and alert the authorities.

She reached the side of the house and picked her way through the debris, examining the wreckage as she moved. At the southeastern corner she turned left and continued along the rear of the home. Kiley's backyard included a flagstone patio, and at the far end of the patio was a small utility shed that appeared relatively intact.

She tried to recall the series of explosions, not quite simultaneous but very closely spaced. She was almost positive there had been four separate blasts. Judging from what she could see of the wreckage, she guessed the bombers had attached one device to each exterior wall, probably at the corners and just above the concrete foundation. They had used C4 in the Washington Arms attack; it seemed likely they had utilized the same material here.

She reached Kiley's back door—the only way she could tell where the entrance had once been was by the concrete steps leading to a small landing, which now gave onto nothing but a pile of rubble—and shook her head. There didn't seem to be any way inside the house, and she could see and smell the beginnings of a fire.

A gas line had ruptured, or fuel oil was leaking from a storage tank.

Something.

The possibility of a second explosion or series of explosions loomed. In the unlikely event Kiley was still alive, he wouldn't be for much longer.

Tracie turned and took a step, the sound of the rain splattering off the wreckage.

Heard a muffled sound, almost like a weak cry for help. *That's ridiculous. You're hearing things.*

She stopped anyway and stood perfectly still.

Waited.

She was just about to continue on when she heard it again, this time a little more clearly. It was definitely someone calling for help.

"Where are you?" she said as loudly as she dared. There was at least a small possibility whoever detonated the explosives had stuck around to watch the show. It would make more sense for the attackers to get away as quickly as possible, to put as much distance between themselves and their deadly handiwork as they could. But one thing Tracie had learned was that there were no guarantees; human beings were the most unpredictable animals on the planet.

"Back door," came the reply. The response to her question was almost instantaneous. The voice wavered, obviously belonging to someone well past the prime of life, but it was clear and relatively strong, considering the circumstances.

He's alive!

Tracie hurried back to the stairway to nowhere and leapt to the landing. "I'm here," she said, and began tossing yanking ruined boards and assorted demolished junk out of the wreckage and tossing it aside.

And there he was.

Right in front of her.

She could literally reach out and touch him, and she was shocked to see that he seemed to be standing upright.

"Come on," she said urgently, taking his hand. "A fire's starting and it's only a matter of time before there's another explosion."

"I can't move. My foot is trapped."

"How did you make it this far?"

"I was sitting at the doorway watching the rainfall when the explosion occurred."

Tracie realized Kiley wasn't standing at all; he had been trapped in a seated position in what looked like a high wooden barstool. His position directly under the doorframe must have sheltered him from the worst of the falling debris. Still, the fact he hadn't been beheaded or sliced to ribbons was a minor miracle.

She dropped to her knees and began clawing at the junk. She ripped studs and chunks of drywall out of the way, tearing her hands up in the process and barely noticing. After a moment she could see the problem. A section of two-by-four, at least six feet in length and sliced neatly in half, had fallen onto Kiley's left foot and then been jammed into place be heavy piles of wreckage on both sides.

She pulled desperately at the pile and winced as a fingernail caught on something and tore off. Her hands felt slick with rainwater and blood from a dozen nicks and gashes, and it was hard to get a grip on anything.

Kiley reached down awkwardly and tried to help. "Thank you," he said.

"Don't thank me until I get you out of here."

"No, I'm thanking you now, just in case you *don't* get me out of here. And about this explosion you think might happen: if it's a real threat, just leave me and go. I don't want to be responsible for someone else being killed."

"That's not happening," she said, beginning to pant from exertion. "I'm not leaving without you." She noticed a gap, maybe three inches wide, under a massive pile of rubble, and wedged her left hand as far under it as possible. An exposed nail or something sharp stabbed into her fingertip and she gasped.

"Guess that's far enough," she muttered and began pulling upward against the pile, straining hard.

It was too heavy.

"Dammit." She was still holding Kiley's hand, and she released her grip gently and said, "I'm not going anywhere, don't worry."

She bent down until her face was almost level with the concrete landing and squinted, studying the wreckage. It looked as though there might almost be enough room for her right hand to slither under the pile as well.

"Might as well take a chance," she muttered. "Columbus did."

"Yeah," Kiley answered immediately. "And look what happened to him. He's dead."

Tracie was concentrating hard and it took a moment for the old man's comment to sink in. When it did, she snorted, despite the gravity of the situation. This old guy was as cool as a cucumber, every bit as levelheaded as any operative she had ever worked with.

She shoved her right hand into the gap, doing her best not to get jabbed by whatever she had struck a moment ago with her other hand. Then she began crawling forward on her knees until she was on all fours, her two elbows flat on what was left of Kiley's floor, and her knees on the outside landing.

She kept moving, struggling up to her feet until she was bent over at the waist, hands buried two-thirds of the way up her forearms under a massive amount of mostly unidentifiable wreckage.

Now she thought there was a chance she might have the leverage she needed.

There were still no sirens wailing in the distance. All Tracie could hear was the moaning of the wind in the trees and the steady hiss of rainfall. "If you're a religious man," she muttered through clenched teeth, "this might be a good time for a prayer, because I'm about out of ideas."

"I haven't been a religious man for decades, but the concept is getting more appealing by the second."

Tracie smiled tightly and said, "Here goes nothing." She lifted with her arms and strained with her legs, and for a long moment she made no headway at all.

And then the pile shifted. Not much, not enough for Kiley to slip his foot out from under the two-by-four, but a little. She could sense the change in balance more than feel it.

She redoubled her efforts, and now sweat began mixing with the rainwater streaming down her face. She strained, pushing hard with her legs to supplement her upper body and arms, and without warning the pile gave way with a loud *crack!*

Tracie lost her balance, nearly pitching forward into Kiley and knocking them both back into the rubble. She dropped to one knee and her shoulder smashed into a chunk of siding, and then she regained her balance. She wrapped her fingers around the two-by-four and pulled, and it lifted off Kiley's foot and he was free.

She tossed the piece of wood away and it landed with a clatter. Then she climbed to her feet one more time and wrapped one arm around the older man's back. "Don't put any weight on your injured foot. Lean on me and let's get you the hell out of here."

They struggled forward, Kiley surprising her by making better progress than she expected him to. She helped him down the stairs and then turned in the direction from which she'd come. "Help will be here soon," she said, wondering whether that was true.

Then things went from bad to worse. A bullet ricocheted off something metallic with a loud, unmistakable *ping*. A second shot followed almost immediately, this one embedding itself into the wreckage behind them.

It had missed by inches.

They were in big trouble.

6

She shoved Kiley to the side and he went down behind the utility shed like a sack of potatoes. She expected him to scream or shout or at least let out a curse or two, but to her surprise—and relief—he remained completely silent.

She dropped to a crouch and duckwalked behind the shed, stopping next to Kiley, then reached down to release her Glock from its ankle holster. Her hands were as wet and bloody as before and it took two tries to yank open the leather strap and get a grip on the weapon. Then it was in her hand and she realized she had no idea what to do next.

Probably the only reason she and Kiley weren't dead already was that their attacker had not anticipated a nighttime gunfight, and so had failed to bring night vision equipment along on his deadly mission. In the darkness, Tracie and Kiley had been more or less invisible against the darkened background of the ruined house. Once they separated from the wreckage their outlines had become identifiable.

But the longer they stayed here, the more likely their imminent death became. The bomber had stuck around much longer than was prudent, probably because he had spotted Tracie approaching the house just before the detonation. It was clear he had no intention of leaving until he finished what he had started.

"We need to get to my car," Kiley whispered as another gunshot sounded. Tracie couldn't tell where the bullet struck, and she wondered whether their attacker knew they had taken shelter behind

41

the shed. If he hadn't figured it out yet, he would soon.

Even worse, Tracie had no idea where the shots were coming from, or even how many attackers were out there. She guessed there was only one, but wasn't willing to bet their lives on it.

"No good," she said. "The first thing they would have done is disable both our vehicles, and that's assuming either one was drivable in the first place after that explosion."

She lifted her weapon and pointed it straight up, squeezing off a shot, wanting to let their enemy know he wasn't the only one with a weapon. "That should discourage him from being in any hurry to approach us, but it won't hold him off for long. He knows roughly were we are, and we have no idea—yet—where he is. If we stay here we're going to die. We'll have to make a run for the forest and try to lose him in the undergrowth."

"Run? I haven't run anywhere in thirty years, and that was when I had two usable feet."

She reached for Kiley's hand. Found it and squeezed tightly. "Then we'll make a hobble for the forest."

"My barn!" he said suddenly.

"You have a barn?"

"Yes, it's a couple of hundred yards straight back behind the house."

Tracie leaned around the side of the shed and squeezed off another round, thinking hard. "Does it have a phone?"

"Are you kidding? It's a barn. No phone. Nothing like that."

"Then that's no good, either. Even if we make it, we'll be no better off there than we are here. Eventually it'll occur to the guy to set fire to the thing and wait for us to come out. We'll be sitting ducks."

"But it has something we can use. Something even better than a phone."

"What would be better than a phone?"

"How does a car sound?"

"You have a second car in your barn?"

"Damn right." He hesitated for a moment and then said, "Unless the guy disabled that one as well."

Tracie felt a glimmer of hope. "I don't think so. Even if he knows you have a car in there, it wouldn't have occurred to him to take it out. He's under as much stress as we are, and remember, he was planning a quick in-and-out: blow up your house, watch the fireworks, drive away. He didn't expect me to come along and muck up his plans. I'll bet a second car is the farthest thing from his mind right now."

"Then let's get going, if you think that's our best chance."

She fired another shot, conscious of the fact that her spare magazine was inside her Toyota but not wanting to give their attacker the opportunity to simply waltz up and put a bullet in each of their heads.

"Can you move?" she whispered.

"I thought you'd never ask. Let's get the hell out of here while we're still breathing."

They struggled to their feet and Tracie said, "Stay as low as you can. I think our best bet is to circle around and approach the barn from the side, just in case I'm wrong about this guy not considering the possibility that we'll go there. I'd hate to walk straight into his arms. We're going to move as quietly as we can and hope he doesn't see us, but if we run into trouble, I'll hold him off, and you're going to have to try to make it to the barn by yourself, do you understand?"

Tracie climbed to her feet and then helped Kiley up. He stood next to her and placed his injured foot on the ground gingerly. Put a little weight on it and gasped in pain. "I understand, but I sure hope that doesn't happen. It's not much of a plan."

"Agreed, but it's better than waiting here for our boy to drop another bomb on our heads."

"Good point."

"Now, let's keep quiet and concentrate on staying alive."

* * *

They stuck to what was left of the house as long as they could, counting on the hulking wreckage to keep their bodies as camouflaged as possible. The wind-whipped rain felt like needles pelting Tracie's face, and her clothes had long since become saturated and heavy with rainwater.

But the upside of the weather conditions was that the howling wind and driving rain more than covered any noise they may have been making as they moved. Kiley was managing to put at least a little weight on his injured foot, and they made decent progress, although they were still moving much too slowly for her liking.

The clearing in which Kiley's home had been built wasn't much bigger than the structure itself, so they were forced to cross only fifteen or twenty feet of open space before disappearing into the cover of the forest. They pushed through the underbrush until about eight feet of it separated them from their attacker. Then they turned south. Their progress slowed ever further as they were forced to contend with trees, brush, and the uneven forest floor.

But they were still alive. And unless their attacker had seen them slip into the heavily forested area, their chances of getting shot—for now, at least—had just lowered considerably.

So far, so good. Ten minutes ago, Tracie wouldn't have put much better than even odds on them making it this far.

The rain continued to fall, and Tracie felt herself begin to shiver. The night was warm, tropical almost, yet it was nearly impossible to retain body heat while trudging through a downpour with thoroughly sodden clothing, even though the process of working through the tangled mess of the forest was physically taxing.

Tracie thought about Edison Kiley's age, and the fact he was already injured, and hoped the exertion wouldn't be too much for him. How much could one eighty-year-old man take?

She reached back for his hand and gave it a reassuring squeeze. Decided to risk a few words of encouragement. It would be the first time either one of them had spoken since breaking cover. She wasn't too concerned about speaking; the shooter would have had to be right next to them to hear anything over the roar of the storm.

"How are you doing? Would you like to rest for a couple of minutes?"

"Nah," came the reply. The old man was breathing heavily and limping badly but he was keeping up with her, and they continued to make steady progress southward.

Tracie thought the shooting had stopped, although she couldn't be sure with the wind whipping and the trees rustling and moaning. Had their attacker managed to check out the area behind the shed yet? Had their disappearance been discovered?

If it hadn't been, she knew it wouldn't be much longer before it was. She knew it was imperative they put some distance between themselves and the shooter, and the longer it took to do so, the less likely they were to survive. The sense of safety and security from their current position was deceptive, because it wouldn't matter unless they got to shelter soon.

And the shooter would know that.

And there was only one place where they could go.

"How much farther?" Tracie whispered.

For a moment, Kiley didn't answer and she thought maybe he hadn't heard her. Then he cleared his throat and she realized he was considering the question.

"We should be about there. Maybe we could begin moving toward the clearing again?"

It wasn't something Tracie wanted to do, but putting it off wasn't going to help them. So she reached for his hand again and they started off, angling their course slightly.

Moments later, they had reached the edge of the undergrowth and Tracie peered through. A massive dark blob, outlined against the slightly lighter background of the forest on the other side of the clearing, told her Kiley's estimate had been right on. The barn was directly in front of them.

Tracie leaned over and placed her lips against the old man's ear. "Okay, here's what we're going to do," she said as softly as she could manage while still making sure he could hear her over the shrieking of the storm. "I'm going to go first. If the shooter's ready for us and he sees me, I'll draw his fire. If that happens, you melt back into the forest and start hiking for civilization. But if I can make it to the side of the barn without drawing anyone's attention, you walk across the clearing and I'll cover you. If any shooting starts, I should be able to locate the shooter pretty easily and I'll take him out. Stay as low as you can, and once you start moving, don't stop for anything. Do you understand?"

She felt him nod his head. Left unsaid was her certainty that an injured eighty-year-old wasn't going to get far if he had to try hiking through the forest in a storm like this, especially while being chased by a man with a gun. A scientist didn't get to be head of R&D for a company like National Circuit without having plenty of smarts, and Tracie knew Kiley was as well aware of that fact as she was.

He didn't say a word, though. He nodded again and this time, he reached out and gave her hand a squeeze. He bent to her ear and said, "I've got it. Good luck. I'd say your name but it occurs to me I have no idea who you are."

"We'll do formal introductions later. For now, I've got places to go." Then she slipped through the thin screen of forestation, wind-driven rain pelting her face. She bent as low as she could manage and took off running, sprinting in a direct line toward the side of the barn.

She ran with her Glock at the ready, holding it in a two-handed grip, sweeping the weapon from side to side, leading it with her eyes. She'd had plenty of experience in cat-and-mouse hunts, but normally *she* was the one playing the role of the cat. Being the mouse was an unexpected—and unpleasant—feeling.

Between the rain and the near-total darkness, seeing anything clearly was impossible, and making out more than the vague outlines of shapes was almost as difficult. Windblown trees became strangers turning to point weapons at her, and twice she almost squeezed off a shot before realizing nobody was there.

In ten seconds she had reached the barn, with its massive, high walls, and some of the severity of the storm instantly disappeared. She realized it was unlikely Kiley would be able to see her well enough to know exactly when she had made it, so she turned in his direction and peered into the darkness. She couldn't see anything and realized he may have already broken cover.

She dropped into a shooter's crouch, leaning against the wall for support. Tried to slow her breathing in case she had to squeeze off a shot.

She concentrated hard but still could see nothing. Wondered how long it would take Kiley to traverse the open area. Wondered whether he could even make it.

Given the conditions, it seemed unlikely the shooter would see either of them unless he happened to run into them. Maybe she should retrace her steps and try to find and help the old man.

She took a step away from the barn.

Took another.

Cursed to herself and stared into the blackness, willing herself to see. Failing.

She took a third step and then, out of the corner of her eye, saw a muzzle flash at the same time she heard the sharp report of a gunshot. Its *crack* split the night and then was carried away on the howling wind.

And then Kiley was there. He was limping badly, moving slowly, but still on his feet. He stumbled into her and they nearly fell in a heap. Tracie backpedaled, her feet slipping on the wet field grass, trying desperately not to fall. She planted her feet and regained her balance and grabbed Kiley by the elbow, pulling him as quickly as possible against the shelter of the barn.

"Are you okay?" she asked.

"Aside from my foot feeling like it's been caught in a meat grinder and my body feeling like I've just run the Boston Marathon, sure. Never better."

Tracie realized he hadn't seen the flash and had no idea he'd just been shot at. "The guy knows we're here. We've got maybe thirty seconds before he finds us. We have to go, *now.*"

"What are you talking about? He knows we're here? How?"

She grabbed him by the elbow and got in his face. "Focus, Edison, or we're going to die. We need to get inside this building, *now*. Where's the door?"

"Well, the big main door is behind us, facing the house, but there's a normal-sized access door in the rear of the barn as well."

"We're not going toward the house, that's where the shot came from, so take us to the back door."

Kiley hesitated just a moment and then headed off, keeping his body pressed as closely as possible to the barn. *Quick learner,* Tracie thought, and then followed behind, moving sideways, covering the area behind them with her weapon. Kiley was really struggling, and she began to get a sick feeling that their attacker would be on them before they could get inside.

They reached the corner without incident, and Kiley fumbled around in his pocket. He pulled out a small set of keys and selected one. Tried to slide it into a lock built into the doorknob, but the combination of darkness, rain and his badly shaking hands stymied him.

He stabbed at the lock once, twice, and finally slid the key home on the third attempt. He twisted the knob and the door opened noiselessly inward. They stepped inside and Tracie closed the door behind them as quietly as she could. There was no way their attacker would hear it unless she slammed it as hard as she could, but she wasn't taking any chances.

By now she was shivering badly and knew Kiley must be as well, but there was no time to savor the sudden relief from the wind and the downpour. "Where's the car?" she said.

"Up near the front door."

"Take us there."

Kiley grabbed her hand and led her forward. She wanted to ask about electricity—it would be much faster going if they could turn on a set of lights—but asking the question would be pointless because blazing electric lights would almost certainly get them killed.

Despite his injury and the total lack of illumination, Kiley moved with the easy familiarity of a man who had been working inside his barn for years, probably decades. He wound them around unseen obstacles, only once stumbling into something, and in less than a minute he stopped limping forward and said, "Here we are. Now what?"

"Now we ride the hell out of here. Hopefully we can catch this guy by surprise and be long gone before he can recover."

7

"There's a problem," Kiley said. "It didn't occur to me until now, but I only have one key for this car and it's inside the house, probably buried under a ton of rubble."

"Dammit. We'll have to smash out a window and climb through."

"No, that's not what I mean. The car's unlocked. We can get in, but we have no way to start the engine."

"I'll get the engine running, don't worry about that."

She reached a hand out and her knuckles rapped against heavy sheet metal with a *clunk*. Felt around for a handle and found nothing. "Where's the door?" she whispered.

"The interior light is going to go on the minute we open the door. Aren't you concerned about tipping the shooter off to our location?"

"Of course I'm concerned about it. But there's no other way. I have to see to be able to hot-wire the ignition and besides, your attacker would have to be an idiot not to have figured out where we are after seeing you approach the barn from the woods. And we know he saw you, because he shot at you. We need speed now, not stealth."

Glass shattered from somewhere behind them in the dark, putting an exclamation point on her statement. "Here he comes," Tracie said. "Open that door now if you want to live."

A second later a light flashed on and Kiley climbed into a meticulously maintained Chevrolet Impala, vintage early-to-mid

1960s. The finish gleamed in the weak light and the interior was spotless, with red and white leather seats, a leather-wrapped steering wheel and not a speck of dust on the dashboard or a grain of sand on the carpeted floor.

Tracie slipped into the driver's side, shoving Kiley across the bench seat in front of her. She folded her small body into the foot well and began frantically examining the tangle of wires.

The sounds of the storm were much louder now that a window had been broken out, but from over the shrieks and moans of wind-whipped rain came the unmistakable *pop* of a gunshot and the almost-instantaneous *ping* of a slug ricocheting off the Impala's body.

Tracie ducked instinctively, despite being under the dashboard. She hissed at Kiley, "Get horizontal! Lie down in the seat behind the protection of the metal!"

The old man reacted quickly and flattened himself on the seat just as a second shot blasted into the car. This one imbedded itself into the driver's side door, missing Tracie by inches.

She had always prided herself on her ability to focus, and now she needed every ounce of concentration she could muster. She wanted to return fire but knew the key to surviving beyond the next few seconds would be getting Kiley's car started so they could escape.

A third shot rang out, slamming into the door next to the last one. Finally, Tracie located the ignition wire and pulled it away from its terminal. She yanked the starter wire loose and jammed the two bare ends together.

The Impala rumbled to life, the engine coughing and sputtering for a second before smoothing into a silky purr. Another slug ripped into the door and Tracie cursed. She slammed her hand down on the accelerator pedal and the car shot forward. Something metallic screeched along its side.

Tracie shifted her hand to the brake pedal and shoved it to the floor. The tires skidded along the uneven barn floor and the Impala shuddered to a stop, rocking violently on its springs.

"Get up, quick!" She pushed Kiley upright and lifted herself into the driver's seat. Fumbled for the headlight knob. Found it and pulled, and immediately the barn's interior was flooded with light. Fifteen feet in front of the car was the main entrance, two massive hinged doors that opened by swinging outward from the middle.

The doors were currently closed, of course, presumably secured from the outside with a padlock. Tracie hit the gas hard, praying the doors weren't as solid and heavy as they looked.

They were.

The Impala hit the closed doors at maybe ten miles per hour, not having had enough of a head start to build up much speed. The impact was enormous, though, and both occupants were flung forward despite having braced themselves as best they could.

Tracie hit the steering wheel hard, the blow knocking the wind out of her lungs. Kiley's head struck the windshield and he moaned, the sound clear even over the roar of the big engine and the noise of the storm.

She kept the accelerator pedal jammed to the floor.

Sheet metal crumpled and one headlight went out, and the big car bucked and writhed like an injured animal. For one horrible second Tracie feared they would lose the battle with the heavy wooden doors, and then they blasted through and into the rain.

The engine sputtered and complained, but the car shot forward. She could barely see the rutted track through the heavy rainfall as the car's one working headlight struggled to illuminate the scene. The tires spun, spewing mud and field grass out behind the Impala in a red-tinted rooster tail made visible by the rear running lights. In the back of her mind, Tracie hoped the mud had covered their attacker.

She eased off the gas slightly, now willing to sacrifice a little speed for increased control. The last thing they needed was to slide off the rough track and into a tree. The forest crowded against the left side of the car and she thought about moving slightly right but elected to stay in the established wheel-ruts.

They struggled forward, fishtailing in the rain-saturated field, even at their relatively slow speed. Beside her, Kiley was saying something, but Tracie couldn't make out his words above the guttural rumble of the big V-8 engine and the still-pounding storm.

The wreckage of Edison Kiley's home was clearly visible now. It would have been clearly visible even without the one headlight.

The fire that had just been starting when Tracie struggled to release Kiley was now burning freely, the flames reaching into the rainy sky like a massive bonfire.

Then they were past. Tracie continued along the trail, and halfway between the burning house and still-deserted road it veered right and merged with the long driveway. Once all four tires were on the paved portion, she hit the gas and the engine stopped sputtering and released a throaty roar.

The car leaped forward and in seconds Tracie hit the brakes and yanked the wheel left. Halfway through the turn she punched the gas again and the big Impala fishtailed one last time before gaining traction on the wet road and screeching away from the scene of the attempted murder.

She watched the rear view mirror intently, concerned about being followed, but the blazing wreckage that was once Edison Kiley's home grew smaller and smaller and eventually disappeared as they rounded the sweeping turn. The yellow-orange glow was replaced by rain-lashed darkness, complete and unrelenting.

8

Tracie gingerly turned the knob to Aaron Stallings's home office. Her hands looked as though she had jammed them inside a blender and punched "puree." Knicks, cuts and scratches adorned practically every square inch of skin on both hands, and the finger with the half-missing nail was swollen, ugly and purple. Whatever she had impaled her other finger on while working to free Edison Kiley had left a bloody mess in its wake, and dark bruises had formed overnight around her knuckles and the backs of her hands.

She arranged her face into an implacable mask, determined not to show weakness to her boss. She refused to give him the satisfaction of knowing she was in pain, even though it would have to be obvious the minute he got a look at her hands.

She entered briskly, all business, and was surprised to see not one chair placed in front of Stallings's desk, but two. The second chair was thickly stuffed, considerably more comfortable than the one provided for Tracie.

And it was already occupied.

By Edison Kiley.

After escaping the scene of the attempted murder last night, Tracie had brought the scientist straight to Langley, where she checked in, as she had been instructed to do, with night duty security personnel.

After a short delay, two case officers had appeared, pushing a wheelchair in front of them as they walked. They opened the Impala's door and helped Kiley into the chair. If they noticed the heavy damage the car had sustained, they kept it to themselves. Then they turned and began wheeling him to the on-site infirmary.

The officers ignored Tracie, saying nothing to her, acting as if Kiley had driven himself to the facility, even though they were likely well aware of Tracie's status—*or maybe lack of status,* she thought wryly—as an ex-operative.

The damage to the car didn't seem to have extended to the engine, as it idled smoothly at the gate during the exchange. Tracie was not invited onto agency property, nor was she offered a parking spot. The case officers didn't ask whether she required medical attention, and they didn't offer her so much as a blanket, although she shivered uncontrollably the entire time they were assisting Kiley.

The last she saw of the old man was the back of his head as the agents escorted him away from the Impala. At the time, she had assumed she would never see him again.

But she had been wrong. Here it was, less than twelve hours later, and the man she had saved was here. He turned his head and smiled warmly at her. "I'd get up," he said with a smile, "but..." He gestured at his left foot, wrapped in a swath of bright white bandages and elevated on a padded divan.

It was the first time she had gotten more than a fleeting look at him in the light, and although there was no denying the man's age in his wrinkled appearance, he looked fit and healthy, with the obvious exception of his foot injury.

"Don't even think about getting up," she said, returning his smile. She moved to his chair and extended a hand, but he was having none of it.

"Get down here," he ordered, and as Tracie leaned over, he wrapped two bony arms around her shoulders in a hug and kissed her lightly on the cheek. "Thank you," he said. "I can never repay you for what you did last night, so I won't insult you by trying. Just know you have my gratitude, and if there's ever anything you need that I can help with, any time, night or day, all you have to do is ask."

This was uncharted ground for Tracie Tanner. Secrecy formed the basis for everything in the world of covert operations; it was the key to survival. Praise was rare. Information was parceled out with a miser's touch and guarded jealously. With the exception of contacts she had made in her past life working in and around the Soviet Union and East Germany, Tracie was unused even to *seeing* the people she had helped, much less hugging them and receiving their thanks.

"Uhh, no problem, Mr. Kiley," she said uncomfortably. He released his grip on her and she straightened.

"Please," he said. "I think we've become sufficiently acquainted that you can call me Edison. And I know better than to ask you your name," he added with an impish smile.

Tracie didn't have a clue how to respond, so she said nothing and returned his smile as she sat in the hard-backed wooden chair next to her new best friend.

Stallings had remained tight-lipped during the exchange, and now he cleared his throat. "I've got a couple of things to add regarding last night's...debacle."

Tracie met his gaze steadily. She doubted the CIA director would act out his usual repertoire with Edison Kiley present—pounding his fist on his desk, roaring angrily, and generally acting like an unreasonable lout—but she wouldn't have bet money on it, either. It seemed she was about to find out.

"While I will admit," Stallings said, "that you delivered Mr. Kiley to the company in one piece, more or less"—he glanced pointedly in the direction of Kiley's injured foot—"I had envisioned something a little less dramatic than a gun battle and a house burned down to its foundation."

"So had I," Tracie answered coolly. "And as for a gun battle, it was a little one-sided. I only discharged my weapon a couple of times, and that was solely to remind our attacker that he wasn't the only one with a weapon."

"Be that as it may, you didn't do yourself any favors by leaving your personal vehicle at the scene. While we've ensured that it's not traceable back to you, I think you'll agree it's a complication we don't need."

"I do agree."

"Fortunately," he continued, as though she had never spoken, "*we're* a little more on the ball than you are. A company wrecker was dispatched to Dr. Kiley's home within two minutes of your arrival at Langley last night, and the car was towed away before the first of the authorities showed up. The area surrounding the home is so remote that the first fire/rescue vehicle didn't show up for nearly another two hours."

Tracie was well used to Stallings trying to bait her. She knew she should keep her mouth shut but just couldn't manage it. "Yeah, well, given the fact that there was an armed killer standing in the dark somewhere between Dr. Kiley—"

"Edison," he said. It was the first time he had spoken since Stallings started talking.

"I'm sorry," she said, smiling at Kiley, then turned her attention back to her boss, sitting behind his desk like a massive gargoyle.

"Given the fact that there was an armed killer standing in the dark somewhere between Edison and my car, it seemed as though it might be prudent to make our escape via some other method. Or do you disagree?"

Stallings glowered at her. Had the old man not been present, Tracie was certain this would have been a fist-pounding moment.

Instead, the spymaster shook his head and continued. "We've been keeping a close eye on the police investigation, and it's safe to say they are completely stymied. They're operating on the assumption that the damage to Dr. Kiley's barn came from a vehicle smashing through the closed door, which is obvious, of course. The tire tracks in the mud leave a trail even Stevie Wonder couldn't miss," he said, again casting a disapproving glance in Tracie's direction.

"However," he continued after an uncomfortable silence, "they don't know whether the vehicle was being driven by Dr. Kiley, or by whoever set his house ablaze, or by someone else entirely. For that matter, they don't know whether Dr. Kiley is even alive. They suspect he is not, given the nature of the attack and the age of the victim."

"How long are you planning to keep Dr. Ki—uh, Edison— under wraps? He's the link between two bombings and the death of NCC's CEO, not to mention a half-dozen other corporate executives. I'm sure he's already spent plenty of time with the police—"

"I have," Kiley said.

"But they're going to want to speak with him again," Tracie finished. "They certainly need to know he's alive, if only for his family's peace of mind, don't you think?"

"I have no surviving family," Kiley said. "Ruth and I were both only children, and we were never able to have kids of our own. When she passed away six years ago, I became the only remaining Kiley."

"I'm sorry for your loss," Tracie said.

Then she turned back to Stallings. "But still, what's the point in keeping him under wraps? The police will need to question him, and since my car was removed from the scene and he doesn't know who I am, there's no way anything can come back on me. You obviously believe Edison can be trusted, otherwise you wouldn't have brought him here. You told me he's worked with us before, so he knows how to keep his mouth shut." She spread her hands. "I don't understand. What gives?"

Aaron Stallings was staring her down, his face turning interesting shades of red and purple as she talked. "Are you finished?" he said. "Would it be alright if I spoke now?"

The urge to give a flippant answer was almost overwhelming, but based on her volatile history with Stallings, Tracie knew that would be a mistake. So she choked back the response that had almost leapt out of her mouth and waited for the CIA director to continue.

After a moment, he got his temper more or less under control and he spoke. "Yes, he knows how to keep his mouth shut, and yes, I trust him. Edison Kiley was working with the agency before you were even a twinkle in your old man's eye. I personally worked with him on a number of operations nearly a quarter-century ago."

Tracie blinked in surprise. Aaron Stallings was the rare presidential cabinet-level member whose appointment was more than simply the standard payoff to political hacks and party loyalists who had contributed to a president's election. He had risen through the ranks of the CIA over the course of nearly four decades of service. It was said he had dirt on just about every major player in Washington, and undoubtedly knew more secrets than anyone else alive.

Tracie had known all this about her boss, of course, and yet over the entire period of her employment at the agency, Aaron Stallings had held just one job: CIA director. It was hard for her to imagine the man ever doing anything except sitting behind his big desk, manipulating agents and politicians like puppets on a string.

"You two worked together?" she finally said.

"Dr. Kiley did some electronics work for us, very advanced, high-tech stuff at the time, although back then nobody called it that. So, I hope that answers your questions about what he is doing here."

Tracie considered Stallings's words. "You're no sentimentalist," she said, gazing at her boss thoughtfully. "I'm sure you're glad Edison is okay, but he's not here because you feel the need to keep him safe. The police could—and I'm sure would—assign protection to him until this mess gets straightened out, and he would be in no danger."

Stallings was watching her closely, and she thought the corners of his mouth might have twitched in as close an approximation of a smile as she was likely to see from the man.

"And if that's the case," she continued, "then you think all of this—the murder of Allan Nesbitt, the bombing at the Washington Arms Hotel, and last night's torching of Edison's home—is related to something that happened while Edison was working for the company."

She shook her head, unsatisfied with the logic. "But that doesn't make sense. You said it was decades ago that Dr.—that Edison—worked for the CIA. And besides, you said you thought the attack at the Washington Arms was a case of industrial espionage."

"I said industrial espionage was one possibility. But I never really thought that was the case."

"Which was why you sent me to retrieve Edison in the first place. I get it. But obviously last night's attempt on his life cements your theory about this being CIA-related."

Stallings nodded. "If it was a case of industrial espionage, there would be no reason for the attackers to take the additional risk of going after one scientist, not after they've already decimated the entire management structure of National Circuit Corporation. It will take months, probably years, before the company is back on its feet. Mission accomplished."

"And yet they took that risk. Obviously you called me here because I'm involved somehow."

"You're going to be."

"Care to explain how?"

Stallings leaned back in his chair and laced his fingers together behind his big head. "What do you know about the Bay of Pigs?"

9

Tracie shrugged. "Probably not as much as I should," she admitted. "I know what I learned in school, that a U.S.-led paramilitary force, comprised mostly of exiled Cuban citizens, attempted an invasion of Cuba in the early 1960s with the goal of overthrowing Fidel Castro and the country's Communist leadership. The incursion originated at the Bay of Pigs."

She paused, gathering her thoughts. "I know that the attempt failed. If I remember correctly, everything fell apart within just a few days. There were charges made that the U.S. government abandoned the Cuban exiles, or at least failed to give them the support they needed. I know that some in the Cuban expatriate community still blame our government for mishandling the invasion. That's really all I know, and I'm not absolutely certain that's even all accurate."

Kiley was nodding next to her as she spoke, keeping quiet but listening closely. Stallings said, "That's a fairly accurate description of what occurred, at least from a layman's point of view."

Tracie crossed her legs and leaned forward, elbows on her knees, chin resting in her cupped hands. She was concentrating so hard that she barely noticed the pain in her sliced and bruised palms. "Are you saying these attacks on NCC and Dr. Kiley are related to something that happened a *quarter of a century* ago?"

"Actually, it happened more than a quarter-century ago. The botched invasion at the Bay of Pigs occurred in April 1961, so it's been twenty-six years. The paramilitary forces were trained and led by the CIA, and the failure of the mission was a major setback for the agency, as well as for President Kennedy."

"But what's the connection between the Bay of Pigs invasion and National Circuit Corporation? Why would Castro exact revenge on an electronics manufacturer, of all things? And why would he even bother, given all the time that's passed?"

"Are you going to continue rattling questions off, or would you like me to answer some of them?"

"I'd love to hear what you have to say, including the answer to one more question: what does all of this have to do with me?"

Stallings said, "I'll answer your questions in order. First, do you have any idea what NCC does?"

"Not really," Tracie admitted. "I know they make electronic components. Beyond that, I couldn't really say."

"NCC owns the patent on electronic circuitry for the GPS receivers that have been in use by the United States military for decades. I assume you're familiar with GPS?"

"Sure. I've used a couple of different versions of it in the field in the past." *When I was allowed to work in the field,* she thought, but left the statement unspoken.

"Well," Stallings continued, "One of the projects Dr. Kiley worked on for the agency back in the late 1950s and early 1960s was an early version of GPS. It was a dinosaur compared to today's technology, limited by both the relatively small number of satellites available for position triangulation, and by ongoing problems with radio signal reception. But the technology was gradually improving, and one of the first 'in-the-field' trials of GPS under combat conditions occurred—"

"During the Bay of Pigs invasion," Tracie said.

"That's right. Over the last three decades, of course, different governments have developed their own versions of satellite-based navigation and location systems, most notably the Soviet Union. But at the time, back in 1961, it was revolutionary. Very few governments even knew we had the technology, much less that we were in a position to begin using it.

"That's a quick and dirty answer to your first question, about NCC's involvement with the Bay of Pigs. Allan Nesbitt's father, James, the founder and original CEO of the company, was fully on board and, in fact, loaned Dr. Kiley to us for the duration of that phase of the project."

Tracie sat silently, nodding as she considered the potential effect this previously unheard-of technology would have had on a military operation undertaken by a relatively small number of men in unfamiliar territory. It would have been an incredible boon.

Stallings continued. "I believe the answers to your second and third questions are interrelated. Our working theory is that Castro's motivation for the attacks wasn't based on the nature of NCC's business, but instead was of a more personal nature. A matter of honor. Vengeance. James Nesbitt was a strong supporter of the Cuban expatriate community, the vast majority of whom have taken up residence in South Florida, and he worked tirelessly right up until the day he died to see a democratically elected government replace the Communist dictatorship Castro installed after the revolution.

"This would explain the murder of Allan Nesbitt in his hotel room, separate from the mass murder of the rest of NCC's leadership in the banquet room. The Cubans wanted to single Nesbitt out, to emphasize the personal nature of the attack. Then they simply eradicated the rest of the company's leadership in one fell swoop."

Tracie closed her eyes, considering the logic of the argument. She supposed it was technically possible that the theory was correct. And Kiley, who had been heavily involved in the project so long ago, wasn't arguing with Stallings's conclusions. But the steps necessary to reach those conclusions required leaps of faith that still seemed too great. Twenty-six years was a long time.

Finally she spoke. "But why now? And why seek vengeance on the company that manufactured GPS technology, of all things? Why not wipe out the companies that manufactured the *guns* the expatriates used, or the *boats* they rode on to reach Cuba, or the *bombers* that provided air support, or any of a hundred other factors that would be critical to a successful invasion attempt?"

"First of all," Stallings said, "who's to say the carnage will end here? Maybe the attack on NCC was a warmup, a practice run for attacks yet to come. Maybe some of those other companies are *also* slated for attack. It would make sense: the bombers start off against a relatively small player. They refine their technique, learn from their mistakes, and then move on to bigger and more visible targets."

Tracie remained silent, but something still didn't smell right.

Stallings took a deep breath and then continued. "And as far as the timing is concerned, it actually makes quite a bit of sense. The Soviet Union is crumbling. The formerly ironclad control they've had on regimes like Fidel Castro's is slipping. The Russians have enough trouble maintaining effective leadership at home, much less in tiny, far-flung countries like Cuba. It's entirely possible Castro had planned on extracting revenge within a year or two of the failed invasion, but that the Russians simply would not allow it. Now, with the Soviet empire falling apart, Castro has been emboldened enough to strike against us on his own."

Tracie was still unconvinced, but she knew better than to argue with Aaron Stallings. She wasn't afraid of him, despite his best efforts at intimidation. But one thing she had learned early on in their working relationship was that she needed to pick her battles carefully. Nothing Stallings had said thus far affected her in any way, so nothing he had said thus far was worth challenging him on.

His next words made her reconsider.

"This is where you come in. The United States government cannot and will not tolerate the brazen, murderous attack on one of its critical defense contractors.

"Our response must be swift and unequivocal. While the State Department has already launched a diplomatic effort designed to get to the root of the problem, I believe—and the president believes—that it is important we strike back hard against the Castro government."

"Excuse me sir, but is there any solid proof Castro is even involved? Everything I've heard so far just seems…flimsy. While I don't deny the theory could be one hundred percent correct, it also seems there may be dozens, even hundreds, of alternative scenarios that could be equally valid. Why would we risk starting a war based on conjecture?"

Stallings's face began to redden, a sight Tracie was all too familiar with. The longtime CIA director ruled his agency with an iron fist; he was a dictator in charge of one of the world's most secretive organizations. He was not a man who appreciated—or usually even tolerated—dissent. He was clearly building toward an explosion, and Tracie steeled herself for the verbal abuse that was sure to come.

Before Stallings could open his mouth, though, Edison Kiley spoke up. His voice was thoughtful and controlled, a clear counterpoint to the thunderous diatribe she had expected to hear from Aaron Stallings. "It's not just conjecture," Kiley said. "There's more."

"What other evidence do you have?" Tracie spoke quickly, before Stallings could interrupt.

"Over the past several months, I've received a series of letters that can only be described as…disturbing."

"What kind of letters? Threats?"

"Oh, yes," Kiley said. "Never anything specific, at least not as far as the nature of the threats was concerned, but I received probably a half-dozen of these letters over the past six months, and all of them referenced the Bay of Pigs and my personal involvement in the disaster, as well as National Circuit Corporation's involvement."

Tracie sat back, stunned. This changed everything. She felt a flash of annoyance at Stallings for being so circumspect in his analysis, when he could simply have started off with the most compelling evidence in his possession and convinced her of his position much more easily. But that was how he operated, and he wasn't about to change his methods to suit the desires of a covert operative working on such a secret clearance only Stallings and the president were even aware of it.

And she often wondered how much President Reagan really knew about the arrangement.

"It wasn't just me," Kiley continued. "I know for a fact that Allan received a number of similar letters, as did several other top management people at NCC."

"Nesbitt didn't take them seriously?"

Kiley waved a hand disgustedly, like he was shooing away a bothersome fly. "The only things Allan Nesbitt took seriously were his drugs and alcohol. And I suppose—given the manner in which he died—his prostitutes, although it would be a stretch to think I was at all familiar with that part of his private life."

"Still, Tracie said, "it seems that even the most cavalier of people would be shaken up by having their lives threatened."

"As I said," Kiley answered, "the nature of the threats was very nonspecific. My letters contained statements like, 'The time has come for you to pay for your treachery at the Bay of Pigs,' or 'Your failure in Cuba in 1961 must be addressed,' that sort of thing."

"Were Nesbitt's letters similar to yours?"

"As far as I know, yes," Kiley said. "Although, to be honest, we never actually sat down and compared them side by side. Nor did I compare my letters with those received by other NCC people. Truthfully, I did my best to avoid Allan and most of the rest of the management team. I wanted to concentrate on my work, not on office politics or administrative matters or anything else.

"But, assuming the letters *were* similar to mine, it's not hard to imagine Allan simply ignoring the threats. It is not particularly unusual for upper management people at defense-related compa- nies to receive death threats and other nasty correspondence from disgruntled citizens. And given the fact that the letters consis- tently referenced an event that occurred before Allan even entered college, it would have made perfect sense for him to disregard the potential danger. And, as I said earlier, he wasn't the most... involved...of executives."

By now, Stallings's anger seemed to have subsided, or at least he no longer appeared to be teetering on the verge of a meltdown. He said, "Convinced?"

Tracie shrugged. It was now certainly much more difficult to discount Stallings's theory, and he *did* have the benefit of decades of CIA experience behind his analysis.

Still, something continued to nag at her. The idea of anyone, even Fidel Castro, being so hell bent on revenge that he would orchestrate the murders of more than a half-dozen people related in only the most superficial way to a decades-old military con- flict—a conflict Castro *won*—struck her as a real stretch.

And yet it was hard to discount the evidence.

"Do you have copies of these threatening letters?"

Kiley began to answer but before he could, Stallings interrupted. "I have copies of everything you'll need to review before you begin your assignment. There's an entire package of material.

"But if I'm right about this attack being only the beginning, with a series of similar attacks on others defense contractors to follow, it goes without saying that time is of the essence. I want you to root out these terrorists and eradicate them. Bring them to justice if you can, but that is *not* the top priority."

"No?"

"No. The top priority is to take them out of the game. By any means necessary."

10

Tracie stared at the sheets of plain white stationery scattered across Aaron Stallings's desk like giant snowflakes. The CIA director had pulled them out of a drawer and dropped them onto the polished surface just before pushing himself up from his chair and leaving his office. Edison Kiley had offered to stay and examine the letters with her, but she wanted an opportunity to study them free from distraction.

"I'll let you know when I have questions, thank you," she said. She felt a little guilty watching the elderly man struggle to his feet and then leave the room on his crutches, but if she was going to get a handle on this killer or killers, it was critical she turn her full attention to the documents.

Kiley had been right when he said he had received "probably a half-dozen" of the threatening letters over the last six months. There were exactly six, assuming he had turned all of them over to Stallings.

He was correct also regarding their lack of specificity. It made sense, of course, that the attackers would not reveal their plans to one of their prospective victims, but they weren't shy about making clear that Kiley was to suffer for his role in the 1961 Bay of Pigs invasion. Every single letter referenced the disastrous mission.

They were all slightly different, but all basically the same. Short, terse, and meant to frighten. The letters were unsigned, of course.

And that was it.

Except for a mark at the bottom.

The mark was located in the same location on each letter, in the approximate spot where a signature would be placed in normal correspondence. It was relatively small, circular in shape but with an opening at the bottom and a short horizontal line protruding outward from each side of the opening. Inside the open circle was an odd design that vaguely resembled a child's stick figure drawing of a family of three.

The letters had already been checked for fingerprints, she was sure of that. It was the first thing law enforcement would have done, and Stallings would have ensured the process was repeated at Langley. There were no envelopes included with the letters placed on Stallings's desk, but Tracie felt certain they would have been thoroughly examined for fingerprints and trace evidence as well.

She took one last look at each letter. Turned each one over and examined the backs. All were plain, white and empty.

It was time to have a chat with Edison Kiley.

* * *

Tracie didn't waste any time getting to the point. No sooner had Kiley struggled into Stallings's office and gotten seated than she tossed the first question at him. She was a little surprised that the CIA chief hadn't accompanied the old scientist back into his office, but Kiley told her it looked like Stallings was busy with an important phone call.

Kiley lifted his injured foot onto the padded divan and leaned his crutches against the desk.

Tracie said, "This young woman you saw in the hotel hallway as you were getting off the elevator—you're sure she exited Nesbitt's room?"

Kiley took a deep breath and looked up at her. He was clearly exhausted and had to be suffering from the knowledge that his home was gone, as was nearly everything he had owned, all destroyed in the massive fire following the bombing of his house. Still, his expression was resolute and his voice strong.

"I'm sure. I never took my eyes off her from the moment I

stepped off the elevator until the moment she disappeared behind the fire door at the rear stairs. I had nearly arrived at Allan's door by that time. There is no doubt. She came out of his room."

"Could you describe her for me?"

"I've been through all of this with the police, multiple times," he said tiredly.

"I know," Tracie answered as gently as she could. "But if you've worked with the agency in the past, you probably realize our coordination with the DC police—and even with the FBI, for that matter—will be minimal. Getting copies of police reports, etc., is time-consuming and problematic, given the…limited…nature of the CIA's mission domestically. And although I have every confidence Director Stallings could expedite the process, you heard him yourself when he directed me to begin working on this assignment immediately. So if you don't mind going over a few things again with me, that would be very helpful."

"Of course," Kiley said. He smiled gamely and straightened in his chair. "I apologize. It's just been a long couple of days. Anyway, keeping in mind that I never got a close-up look at her, and also that my eyes at eighty aren't what they once were, here is what I observed: the woman was young. If I had to guess, I would say she was your age, or within a couple of years either way. She had dark hair and a dark complexion."

"She was a black woman?"

"No, no, she wasn't black. She looked as though she might be Hispanic, or even just a young white woman with a very deep tan. The hallway was relatively dark and, as I said, I never got very close to her, so I really can't be much more specific than that, I'm afraid."

"I understand. What about her height and weight? Any identifying characteristics?"

"She was slim, like you, and beautiful, also like you, if you'll excuse me for being so forward. Hers was a different type of beauty, though. She looked somehow…hard. She was dressed like a prostitute—very provocatively, with a leather vest and leather short-shorts over black lace stockings and boots—and the look was not at all hard to believe. It didn't seem out of place on her at all.

"But it was more than that," he continued, gazing over Tracie's shoulder at nothing in particular as he relived the moment and tried to recall every detail. "The young woman radiated a sense of danger. I felt it the moment I laid eyes on her. My first thought was that she was going sprint down the hallway and shoot me between the eyes, or stab me in the heart. And this was before I had any idea that something had happened to Allan. As far as I knew at that point, he was just late for the NCC banquet."

Tracie was quiet for a moment as she absorbed Kiley's statement. It was entirely possible—likely, even—that the sense of danger the elderly scientist claimed to have felt after exiting the elevator was something his subconscious had inserted into his memory after the fact. Although there was not yet any proof the mystery woman had killed Nesbitt, simple logic said her appearance and his death immediately subsequent to that appearance had to be related.

Still, she believed his words. Or rather, she believed *he* believed his words. His unease was clear when he spoke about the prostitute. His posture stiffened, his voice trembled, his hands shook. All these manifestations were so slight that he probably didn't even notice them, but she did. In the field, the difference between life and death often depended upon her ability to read people.

Edison Kiley was telling the truth.

"What about identifying marks?" she prodded. "Any visible scars, tattoos, skin blemishes?"

Kiley shook his head. "I simply can't answer that question. There was nothing that stood out to me, but again, due to the distance between the two of us, and the dim lighting in the hallway, I can't tell you for certain that she *didn't* have any identifying characteristics. All I know is that I didn't see any."

"I understand," Tracie said, nodding. "What about—"

The door to Aaron Stallings's study opened with a *bang* as the CIA director strode into the room. He must have turned the knob and then kicked the door open. He was reading something written on a piece of paper as he walked, and he started talking without lifting his head or apologizing for the interruption.

"These autopsy results are unofficial and only preliminary," he said. "The official autopsy won't be released to law enforcement for quite some time yet. But I have sources in the DC Medical Examiner's office, and I was able to get some early findings on cause of death for Allan Nesbitt."

Tracie was by now well used to Aaron Stallings's annoying habit of stringing her along, of forcing her to dig for information instead of just giving it to her. It was something new for Edison Kiley, though. He remained silent, but raised his eyebrows and spread his hands as if to say, "Well?"

Stallings reached the middle of the room and stopped walking. He raised his eyes from the paper for the first time and looked at them both. "Allan Nesbitt was poisoned."

"With what?" Tracie said.

"He had been ingesting cocaine just before his death. The amount of the drug in his system was staggering, according to the autopsy. But that wasn't what killed him. He was killed by strychnine. It had apparently been mixed with the coke. The autopsy revealed enough strychnine in his system to drop a circus elephant."

Tracie ran a hand through her hair, tucking it behind her ear as she considered this development. She turned to Kiley. "Didn't you say Nesbitt was a serious drug user?"

"He didn't share that part of his private life—or any other part, for that matter—with me, but I heard enough rumors from people in a position to know to answer with a reasonable amount of certainty. Yes."

"So, wouldn't he have been able to detect that something wasn't right with the cocaine?"

Stallings shrugged. "Who knows? He had a lot of champagne in his bloodstream as well. Maybe his first few hits of coke weren't altered, or maybe he was so drunk by the time he started into the drugs that he just didn't notice. But it's reasonable to assume he didn't mix the rat poison in with the coke himself. There are easier and far less painful ways to commit suicide than by ingesting strychnine."

He raised his eyebrows and shook the paper at Tracie for emphasis. "Allan Nesbitt was murdered, just as certainly as the rest of the NCC management team was murdered. It's time to stop sitting around and get to work."

Stallings turned to Kiley. "Edison, I'll have to ask you to move to the den. I need a word with my agent alone. Once we're done here, I'll have someone bring you back to your quarters at Langley to pick up your personal belongings."

"That won't take long," Kiley said ruefully. "I lost everything."

"I'm sorry," Stallings said perfunctorily. Empathy was not his dominant personality trait. "Once you've had an opportunity to get your things together, an agent will transport you to the appropriate DC police precinct. All the authorities need to know about the last eighteen hours is that you were detained by the CIA on a matter of national security. I'll give you a number they can call to verify the truth of the statement."

Kiley nodded unhappily.

"The police will, of course, question you as to your whereabouts since the attack on you last night. They'll also want to know what was discussed here. It goes without saying that everything we talked about is classified, as is the assistance you received from our operative last night at your home. All of that is on a need-to-know basis only."

"And law enforcement has no need to know," Kiley said wryly.

Stallings either missed the sarcasm or chose to ignore it. "That's right," he said. "The police will provide you with protection, and we'll be in touch if we need to follow up on anything we discussed."

Kiley struggled to his feet and reached for his crutches. He looked old and defeated and Tracie felt a stab of sympathy for him.

"Don't worry about that," Kiley said wearily. "I'll be fine."

11

"That poor man," Tracie said as the door closed behind the departing Edison Kiley.

"Focus, Tanner," Stallings said. "You have a lot of work to do and not a lot of evidence to go on. Plus, you're starting out behind the power curve. The police and the FBI both have nearly a twenty-four hour head start on you."

She felt an instant flash of annoyance. "And here I thought we were all on the same team." She knew her comment would get under Stallings's skin, and she couldn't resist taking the opportunity to tweak her boss.

"Get real," he said. "The DC police want to arrest these terrorists, and so does the FBI. Your assignment is simply to neutralize the threat. By any means necessary. An arrest would be ideal, but your assignment, first and foremost, is to make this threat go away."

"I understand that," she said. *And I also understand that if I'm caught or killed, it will be like I never existed.* She didn't bother speaking the words. What would be the point?

Stallings eased into his desk chair to the accompaniment of a *whoosh* of air escaping the overmatched leather cushions. "I said you don't have a lot of evidence to go on, but I do have a starting point for you. It's clear, based on the letters Dr. Kiley received, that the motivation for this attack was the failed Bay of Pigs invasion. Someone in Cuba, likely inside the Castro government, has gone to a lot of trouble to take revenge on the management team at NCC for their part in that invasion."

He handed her a packet. "Inside this envelope are copies of the letters Kiley received, the letters you just studied, as well as the name of a contact in South Florida. This contact is a man we've used in the past who is as familiar as anyone you'll find inside this country with the...unofficial...workings of the Castro government. Find him and talk to him. With any luck, he will have heard or seen something that can serve as a starting point for your investigation."

Tracie opened the envelope and thumbed through the documents until she found the one she was looking for. "Juan Gonzalez?" She looked up at Stallings and shrugged. "Who is he?"

"Juan Gonzalez is a Cuban expatriate who has been active in the anti-Castro movement in south Florida stretching all the way back to the Bay of Pigs fiasco. As I said, he is as familiar with the unofficial workings of the Castro government as anyone you'll find, probably including any official sources in the State Department."

"By 'unofficial workings,' I assume you mean..."

"That's right. Terrorism."

"You're sending me, alone, to meet with a known terrorist."

"You know how this game works, Tanner. You should, you've played it long enough in and around the Soviet Union. We deal with unsavory characters all the time. That's our job. It's how we develop sources and mine information, the kind of information that the straight-arrows who follow all the rules don't have access to."

"I understand how the system works, Director. I was simply asking for clarification."

"That's not how it sounded. If you don't feel you're up to the mission, let me know and I'll find someone else to do it."

Tracie chuckled without a trace of humor. As dangerous as many of her assignments around the globe had been, at least they had been in keeping with the CIA's charter: intelligence-gathering outside the borders of the United States. If she were apprehended in the company of a known terrorist inside the U.S., Stallings would cut her loose without a second thought and she would be alone, facing prison time or worse. Charges of treason would not be out of the question, depending on how bad this guy Gonzalez really was.

So Stallings was full of shit when he intimated that this mission was in any way similar to anything she had done overseas. Tracie knew it, and furthermore, she knew that *he* knew it.

Unfortunately, none of that mattered. If she wanted to remain in the agency's employ, she would set off immediately for South Florida to meet with this Juan Gonzalez.

She ignored Stallings's sarcasm and said, "How much coordination do you expect on this assignment?"

"I don't expect to have to hold your hand, if that's what you're asking. My expectation is that you will do your job: find out who is murdering high-level executives and single-handedly destroying American corporations that have a history of working with the defense community, and put a stop to it. By—"

"I know," Tracie said. "By any means necessary."

She looked again inside the packet of information, flipping through the documents. "I see a name written in Spanish next to Juan Gonzalez's name. Is that the street he lives on?"

Stallings snorted. "Come on, Tanner, you know better. It doesn't work that way. The address is of a bar in Miami's Little Havana neighborhood. There's no guarantee you'll find Gonzalez there, of course, but his organization has a history of using that establishment as a sort of unofficial base of operations. If he's not in the wind, that's as good a place as any to start looking for him."

12

The name of the bar was *Noches Habana,* and despite Tracie having the address, it wasn't easy to find.

She wasted nearly an hour driving around Miami, even after stopping several times to get directions. The first couple she asked, a youngish man and woman dressed oddly, in shorts and flip-flops with mismatched shirts and multicolored neckties, stared at her blankly before wandering off without answering. The second and third responded, although neither had ever heard of the tavern and both claimed to have lived in the area for years.

Finally, she hit pay dirt when she asked an older, Hispanic-looking man. The man stepped out of a corner store wearing a sharply creased white suit over a snow-white dress shirt and white tie, and he looked her up and down for what felt like a full minute, eyes narrowed, before answering. "What business do you have at *Noches Habana,* little girl?"

Tracie returned his gaze evenly. "I'm thirsty."

"There are plenty of other *tabernas* in the city you would be more…comfortable…in, I assure you. Now go on your way, little girl." The man spun on his heel and began striding briskly toward his car.

"Do you know where it is or don't you?" She put steel in her voice and the man stopped short.

He hesitated, and then turned slowly to face her. "You don't want to go to *Noches Habana,* believe me." His voice was soft, his tone neutral, but the menace in his words was clear.

"Thanks for your concern, but why don't you let me be the one to decide that?"

The man looked as though he'd just bitten into a lemon, and Tracie had the absurd thought that he looked exactly like Aaron Stallings, despite the fact he looked nothing like Aaron Stallings. *I seem to have this effect on a lot of people,* she thought.

A long moment passed, and Tracie was certain the man was going to tell her to pound sand. Or whatever the Spanish equivalent might be. Then he smiled acidly. "It's all the same to me, *puta.* You want to take your life in your hands, you go right ahead."

She smiled and waited for him to continue.

"Go to First Street," he said, inclining his head to the left. "Turn West on First and drive into the heart of Little Havana. Turn left on Twelfth Avenue and drive until you see a Catholic church on the corner of Twelfth Avenue and Sixth Street. *Noches Habana* will be about a half block south of the church."

"See? Now was that so hard?"

"You're welcome, puta. But it's not too late to turn around and go back where you came from. Go to one of the bars all of the other tourists visit."

"I'll take it under advisement. And thanks."

Tracie spun on her heel and walked to her rental car, conscious of the man's eyes burning a hole in her back. She started the car and eased down on the gas and accelerated away. The man in white never moved.

As she drove, she watched the man shrink in the rearview mirror. He wore a pensive expression, and he tracked her progress until eventually he disappeared behind a gaggle of pedestrians on the busy sidewalk.

* * *

There was no parking available for *Noches Habana;* or if there was, Tracie couldn't find it. The bar was located exactly where her reluctant tour guide had told her it would be. She slowed as she drove past and then continued along Twelfth Avenue, eventually pulling a U-turn and passing the tavern again from the other direction.

Santa Barbara Old Catholic Church seemed aptly named. It was tiny by church standards, especially by Catholic Church standards, and had been constructed of red brick, with black wrought iron bars protecting the one tiny window she could see, and a wrought iron railing lining the concrete steps leading to the front door.

On one side of the steps was a tiny courtyard, and on the other, a small driveway. At the street the driveway appeared wide enough to accept two cars, but then it narrowed steadily until it looked as though even a single small vehicle would scrape the side of the church if it tried to drive all the way to the end.

And that was the extent of the on-site parking for Santa Barbara Old Catholic Church. Apparently, Little Havana's Catholics all walked to church on Sundays.

Impatient, Tracie yanked the wheel to the right and nosed into Santa Barbara's miniscule lot. She hoped she wouldn't get towed, but decided that if anyone might be inclined to put up with an illegally parked car for an hour or so, it would be the priest in charge of this little church.

She killed the engine and climbed out. Locked the door and pocketed the key. A steady stream of people passed by on the sidewalk just a few feet away. While most of them gazed at her curiously, nobody challenged her or questioned why she had just parked in the church lot.

She fell into the flow of foot traffic, moving at a brisk pace toward *Noches Habana*. As she approached, she crossed Twelfth Avenue and walked past the entrance, examining the bar from the other side of the street and trying to get a feel for the place.

The way Mr. White Suit had made it seem, *Noches Habana* would be filled with cutthroats and backstabbers, the Miami equivalent of *Rick's Café Americain* from the old Humphrey Bogart film, Casablanca. The place she observed as she walked past looked like any one of a thousand similar bars she might have encountered in any American city.

Out of date, slowly going to seed, but with a distinctly Spanish flair, *Noches Habana* featured a neon sign hanging in its dirty front window advertising Bucanero, presumably a Cuban beer. The bar's interior was so weakly lit that Tracie had no way of knowing as she gazed through the plate glass how many people might be inside the place, much less what those people might be up to.

She strolled along the sidewalk for another fifty feet. It was obvious she had learned all she was going to learn from outside the place and while the prospect of entering unprepared for what she might find inside was daunting, it seemed there was no way to avoid doing exactly that.

She took a deep breath and strode briskly back to *Noches Habana*. At the bar's entrance, she didn't hesitate. She pulled open the door and walked inside.

Salsa music was playing softly from speakers hidden somewhere in the ceiling. A few men sat at tables scattered randomly around the bar's interior, and a couple more men were perched on stools at the bar.

Tracie's first thought was, *desultory*. All the patrons seemed to be drinking, but no one looked all that enthusiastic about it. A few conversations were taking place, but the men who were speaking were doing so in hushed tones. The atmosphere was expectant, as if everyone in the place was just passing the time, waiting for… something.

She wasn't sure what she had expected to find inside *Noches Habana*, but this wasn't it. She had been prepared for noise and activity, and had instead gotten what looked like a funeral mass at Santa Barbara Old Catholic Church up the street.

And there was something else.

As far as she could tell, Tracie was the only female in the place.

Every head turned in her direction, and all eyes tracked her as she crossed the room. The bartender was a middle-aged man who seemed every bit as unenthusiastic as his customers, and he took his sweet time ambling over.

Tracie waited patiently. Finally the man wiped his hands on a dirty apron and said, "You are lost, miss? You require directions?"

The hostility in the man's heavily Spanish-accented English was clear. She noticed also that not one of the drinkers inside *Noches Habana* seemed to have returned his attention to his drink, or to his conversation, or to anything besides the new female arrival.

"No, I don't require directions, thank you. I'm exactly where I want to be." She kept her tone as coldly neutral as the bartender's.

"Then what is your business here?"

"Maybe I'm thirsty."

"In that case I suggest you find a tavern where you will be welcome."

"Are you saying I'm not welcome here?"

The bartender regarded her distrustfully. "What is your business at *Noches Habana?* Look around you, niña. You do not fit in here."

"I'm looking for Juan Gonzalez." She kept her eyes locked onto his, aware that she was still the focus of every man's attention inside the bar.

"Never heard of him." The bartender's eyes glittered dangerously, and it occurred to Tracie she had no way of knowing how many of the men behind her were armed, or what sort of weaponry might be stashed behind the bar. Undoubtedly there was something.

In for a penny, in for a pound, she thought. "I don't believe you. Would you like to know what I *do* believe?"

The man stared her down without speaking.

"I believe that you *do* know Señor Gonzalez. I believe also that Señor Gonzalez is here. Tell Señor Gonzalez that Aaron Stallings sends his regards." She spoke loudly enough to be heard by at least a few of the customers scattered around the room. All other conversation seemed to have died away. Even the salsa music playing softly in the background seemed to have lowered in volume.

The bartender stared stonily back at her. He seemed off-balance, surprised by her last comment. After what felt like at least a minute, he turned and stalked along behind the bar toward a doorway. The man looked back at her once, then he shoved his way through the swinging Old West-style doors and disappeared.

Tracie pivoted and leaned back against the bar but stayed on her feet. She offered the staring customers a smile and waited to see what would happen next.

13

She didn't have to wait long to find out. Less than a minute later, the bartender reappeared, moving with a purpose in his stride that had been missing before. He wiped his hands on his apron as he walked in what she assumed must be a nervous habit, since it seemed unlikely he had been washing dishes during his short stint in the back room.

"Follow me," he said gruffly, then turned and retraced his steps.

Tracie kept her face impassive, pushing through the swinging doors as the man waited for her to pass and then followed her through. She wondered whether Aaron Stallings would ever reveal her last known location to anyone if she disappeared, and then realized she was being ridiculous.

Of course he wouldn't.

The entryway led to a combination kitchen/storage area. A massive sink separated a counter from an ancient stainless steel stove. Cases of beer, Cuban brands that presumably had been smuggled out of Castro's country, were stacked along one wall next to an array of untapped kegs.

Not a soul was back here besides Tracie and the bartender, who shoved her straight through the storage area to a second door, this one latched and much heavier than the first. It was painted to look like wood, but was clearly heavy steel, probably reinforced. Someone had taken great pains and gone to considerable expense to protect whatever—or whoever—was on the other side of that door.

The bartender finally did what Tracie had been waiting for him to do since she mentioned Stallings. He pushed her face-first against the closed door and kicked her feet apart.

The bartender's frisking technique was sloppy, and even from this seemingly vulnerable position, it would have been a simple thing for Tracie to disable him, but she allowed herself to be manhandled. The only alternative would be to resist, and that would likely mean fighting her way out of here, which she wasn't prepared to do.

Yet.

That might come later, but first, she had business to attend to. The man frisked her with an enthusiasm he had not previously displayed about anything. His hands lingered longer than they needed to on certain parts of her anatomy, and she put up with that as well. It wasn't the first time she had been sexually assaulted while being frisked, and realistically, given her line of work, probably wouldn't be the last.

Despite his amateurish technique, the bartender did manage to relieve her of the 9mm Glock in the holster at the small of her back, as well as the backup pistol in the ankle holster on her right leg and the combat knife in its sheath on her left leg.

He placed the weapons on the stainless steel table and slid them to the other end. Though he remained silent, he seemed to regard her with a newfound respect. When the weapons were well out of her reach, he turned to the heavy steel door and rapped on it twice, hard. He waited a second and then rapped again.

A muffled voice answered from the other side, and the bartender turned the knob and opened the door. He ushered Tracie inside a large, lavishly appointed office with a scowl and a wave of his hand. Then he stepped back, closed the door and was gone.

Across the office, seated behind a desk so large even Aaron Stallings would be envious, was a clearly furious man. The man regarded Tracie through angry eyes, and after a moment, said, "I should cut you now and be done with it." He spit the words out like bullets.

Tracie smiled easily. Her heart was pounding but she knew she had to appear completely relaxed. Unworried. She had been in similar situations enough to know that the key to staying alive was getting on top of the situation and keeping her target off-balance. "Señor Gonzalez, I presume?"

"Who the *hell* do you think you are, pulling such a reckless stunt out there? Are you trying to get me killed?"

She shrugged. "I tried to get your man to bring me to you, but I was making no headway. I had no choice but to invoke the name of our…mutual friend."

"Let me tell you something, young lady. If the wrong people even *suspect* a connection between me and the director of the CIA, I will be dead within twenty-four hours."

Tracie shrugged again. It was time to take control of this meeting, while Gonzalez was still angry and off-balance. "I had to see you, so I did what I needed to do to make that happen. If our situations were reversed, you would have done the same."

Gonzalez glowered at her from behind the desk but didn't argue.

Tracie nodded at a chair placed next to the desk. "May I sit?"

"No. Not until I know why you are here."

"Fair enough. I was told by sources in a position to know that you have as much understanding of the inner workings of the Castro government as anybody in this country, including anyone in the State Department or in any other official capacity."

Gonzalez said nothing. He simply lifted his right hand and rotated it in a "keep talking" gesture.

At least I've gotten his attention. "Perhaps you've heard about the murders of the top executives at National Circuit Corporation? It's been all over the news, even here in South Florida."

"Perhaps. What does that have to do with me?"

"We have reason to believe someone inside Fidel Castro's government was responsible for those murders."

Gonzalez wrinkled his forehead. He seemed to have forgotten about being angry, at least for the moment. "Who is the 'we' you are referring to?" he asked.

It was Tracie's turn to keep her mouth shut. She stared at Gonzalez, giving away nothing. He was obviously not a stupid man; therefore he had already put two and two together when she mentioned Director Stallings's name. He was playing mind games, trying to get Tracie to admit a connection she would never—she *could* never—acknowledge.

An uncomfortable moment passed, and then Gonzalez continued as if he had never asked his previous question. "What makes you believe Castro would attack a technology company? For that matter, what makes you believe he possesses the capability of attacking the corporate structure of a relatively small business located right here in the United States? In Washington, DC, no less?"

"I can't answer the first part of your question other than to say the working theory is that Castro, or someone in his immediate inner circle, wishes to extract vengeance against NCC for what they believe is a past...indiscretion...on the part of the company.

"As for your second question, it would certainly be possible for a representative or representatives of a small island nation located just off the U.S. mainland to come ashore undetected, to accomplish their mission successfully, and then to leave the country and be back in Cuba in a matter of hours. In fact, not only would it be possible, it would be fairly easy to pull off, if the individuals were sufficiently motivated and willing to risk the obvious danger."

Gonzalez considered Tracie's words and then shrugged noncommittally. "Perhaps," he said. And then, "Again, I ask you, why are you here? What does any of this have to do with me?"

"Señor Gonzalez, you've cooperated with my government in the past. If you do so again, it will not escape the attention of certain highly influential people in Washington. There is little risk to you, since all I want is information. Give me that information, and I will be out of your hair quickly and you'll likely never see me again.

"However, if you elect to shut me out," she continued ominously, "those same influential people I just mentioned are perfectly capable of making your life a living hell." She spread her hands and smiled, the picture of reason and common sense. "Presumably you don't wish your life to become a living hell?"

Gonzalez smiled tightly, his bloodless lips stretched tightly over his teeth. "What do you require of me?"

This time, Tracie sat without asking. She reached into the back pocket of her jeans and pulled out a small, folded piece of paper. She unfolded the paper and placed it on the desktop, smoothing it with her hand. Then she turned it to face Gonzalez. "Do you recognize this?"

The CIA collaborator chewed on his lip as he examined the paper, eyes narrowed. On it was just one item: a copy of the mysterious open circle with the odd stick-figure design inside that had adorned each of the threatening letters Edison Kiley had received.

"Where did you get this?" Gonzalez asked.

"I can't tell you that."

"Was this design accompanied by anything else or did it appear by itself?"

"I can't tell you that, either."

Gonzalez sighed noisily and cleared his throat. "You're not giving me anything to work with. How can I help you if you won't share any information?"

"That's the way it has to be," Tracie said. "I can't tell you any more than I already have. Now, do you recognize this design or am I wasting my time?"

The man leaned back in his chair, regarding Tracie through hooded eyes. "All right," he said. "I am somewhat familiar with this unusual-looking design."

"And?"

"You must understand something. Cuba under Fidel Castro is no different than any country under any government, at least in one respect. People are always vying for power. Now, in Cuba's case, the ultimate power resides in Castro's hands and always will, at least until he is overthrown or dies. But that doesn't mean there isn't plenty of other power and influence to be had."

"Okay. What does that have to do with this symbol?"

"Following the revolution, in the early days of Castro's Communist dictatorship, private property was being seized, and incredible wealth being amassed, by those individuals in the power structure savvy enough and quick-witted enough to do what had to be done.

"Doing what had to be done," Gonzalez continued, "often meant assembling paramilitary organizations entirely separate from those of the official Castro military. Many of the same men populated both organizations, but they were necessarily separate from, and independent of, one another. Do you understand?"

What Gonzalez described was strikingly similar to what Tracie had seen firsthand in the Soviet Union. She narrowed her eyes, concentrating. "So, you're saying these symbols"—she nodded at the paper on Gonzalez's desk—"represent one of those private paramilitary organizations being run by someone in Castro's government?"

"Contrary to what you have been told," Gonzalez said, "my familiarity with the workings of Castro's Cuba is not complete. But I do have contacts in place in the country, and while I cannot tell you with total certainty that is what these markings represent, I do believe that to be the case."

"Who runs this particular organization?"

"Unless I am mistaken, it belongs to General Antonio Polanco."

"Who's he?"

"Minister of the Revolutionary Armed Forces."

"I assume he's a powerful guy?"

Gonzalez leaned back in his chair and laughed. The sound was long and loud and, as far as Tracie could tell, completely genuine. "Yes, you might say he is 'a powerful guy.' He is probably the second-most powerful man in Cuba, behind only Castro himself."

Tracie nodded.

Waited for Gonzalez to finish laughing.

Said, "Okay. How do I get at him?"

Juan Gonzalez looked at Tracie incredulously. "Get at him?" he repeated. "You don't 'get at' General Antonio Polanco."

"You can get at anyone," Tracie said calmly. "You don't 'get at' the president of the United States, either, and yet four presidents have been assassinated while in office and two more have been injured and nearly killed in assassination attempts. You don't 'get at' the entire management structure of a significant U.S. defense contractor, and yet National Circuit Corporation has been decimated.

"You can get at anyone," Tracie repeated, "provided you're motivated enough. I'm motivated enough."

Gonzalez shook his head. "Young lady, you are crazy."

Tracie shrugged. "Look at it this way. If representatives of this General Polanco were able to enter the United States undetected, murder a CEO and plant explosive devices to take down more than a half-dozen people, and then vanish into thin air, presumably disappearing back to Cuba, why would you think it's impossible to manage it the other way?"

"You are serious."

"Damn right I'm serious, and with the proper assistance it shouldn't even be all that difficult. As the foremost expert in Communist Cuba's affairs, you're going to give me that assistance. I know you are an expatriate of Cuba, I know you look forward to the day you can return to your homeland. Think of this as a way to bring that day a little closer, to strike a blow against the government you want so badly to be rid of."

Gonzalez was quiet for a long time. Tracie hoped she hadn't pushed him too hard, but she really had no choice. Contrary to everything she had just said, she knew that getting access to the second most-powerful man in Cuba would be nearly impossible without the kind of help he could presumably provide.

She waited quietly, letting Gonzalez think through all they had discussed, doing her best to keep her expression impassive. It wasn't easy. If he refused her request, she could play hardball, but beyond threatening him with the name and influence of Aaron Stallings again, the arm-twisting tools available to her were basically nonexistent.

"What kind of help do you require?" Gonzalez asked the question quietly, much of his previous bluster gone.

Tracie told him.

14

Tracie crouched as far down in the bow of the rubber craft as she could manage. Near-constant exposure to sea spray had left her cold and shivering, even in the tropical air off the Florida coast and despite being bundled up in the much-too-big rain slicker Gonzalez had provided. The other occupant of the little boat seemed impervious to the conditions and stared stolidly ahead, ignoring her.

The majority of the one hundred sixty-five mile trip from Homestead, Florida had taken place in a speedboat that offered only slightly better protection from the elements. But Tracie had to admit it was fast.

After setting out from a private dock, Gonzalez's sleek, blue-and-white twin-engine Scarab had turned immediately southwest and hugged the shoreline, staying just far enough off the coast to be invisible to anyone not scanning the ocean through binoculars. The pilot navigated along the Florida Keys until reaching Marathon, then set a course almost due south and headed into the open sea.

Less than two hours later the speedboat began to slow. Tracie started trying to loosen up while the second member of Gonzalez's taciturn crew worked at inflating a small rubber landing boat. The man would ferry Tracie in the rubber boat the rest of the way to the shoreline east of Havana.

When the rubber boat was ready, the Scarab's pilot dropped anchor and they began riding the gentle swells, the lights of Cuba's largest city dimly visible in the distance. The sun had set during their three-hour boat ride, and now stars glittered in the clear sky, impossibly bright and seemingly close enough to touch.

The man who had inflated the rubber craft dropped it into the water next to the speedboat and nodded to Tracie. She grabbed her backpack, checked her shoulder rig for roughly the hundredth time—the Glock was still exactly where it had been every other time she checked, nestled cozily against her left breast—and then clambered over the side of the speedboat.

She dropped heavily into the rubber boat, which felt insubstantial after the relative solidity of the Scarab. A moment later, Gonzalez's man dropped in beside her and fired up the small motor located at the rear of the craft.

Then they were off.

The Scarab's pilot would remain here, while the man guiding the rubber boat would ferry Tracie to a small inlet near the Havana suburb of Santa Cruz del Norte. According to Gonzalez, the inlet was sheltered and private, far too inaccessible for Cubans to bother with in an island nation with miles and miles of beaches. It was certain to be deserted.

The man in the rubber boat had been instructed to remain on the beach and wait for Tracie to return. At that time, he would ferry them back to the speedboat, which would then reverse course and return to Homestead.

"You will have until three a.m. to complete your insane mission," Gonzalez had said. "There will be no negotiation on this point. If you have not returned to the inlet by that time, my men will leave you. *Three a.m.*," he repeated for emphasis. "Not one minute later. I will not risk my men being seen anywhere near Cuba at sunrise."

The rubber boat moved slowly, its progress hampered by its tiny electric motor, which offered the advantage of near-total silence but at the cost of very little power. Tracie hoped no sharp-eyed Cubans were scanning the Atlantic at this time of night, because if the rubber boat were to be spotted, there would be no way to outrun even the most anemic patrol vessel. She doubted they could outdistance a rowboat.

She felt herself becoming queasy. The speedboat's progress had been so fast—more than seventy miles per hour for most of the trip—that the ocean swells hadn't been noticeable beyond a constant heavy chop. But now, puttering along at a snail's pace, the waves felt as high as a skyscraper.

She forced herself to ignore the sick feeling in her stomach. Hopefully it would disappear shortly after her feet were back on solid ground.

Behind her, the man guiding the boat tapped her on the shoulder and grunted something unintelligible. He hadn't spoken a word since they departed Homestead and she wondered what he wanted now. Then he gestured with his hand and Tracie saw it: the Cuban shoreline was approaching faster than she would have anticipated.

The little rubber boat glided smoothly toward a small strip of bleached-white sand. The beach was miniscule, surrounded by thick foliage and mature palm trees. Tracie wondered how often Gonzalez's men landed their little boat here and what sort of mischief they inflicted on Castro's government when they did. The location was hard to find, yet the silent man behind her had guided the little boat to the inlet with no hesitation whatsoever.

This was obviously not his first incursion into Castro's Cuba.

The boat bumped up onto the beach and the man killed the electric motor. He sat motionless while Tracie shrugged her back-pack onto her shoulder and stepped for the first time onto the shores of Communist Cuba.

* * *

With less than twenty-four hours of preparation time, Tracie wasn't about to kid herself that she was ready for this mission. Self-delusion was the sort of thing that would get her killed.

And while covert ops required the ability to adjust to changing circumstances and to make things up on the fly when situations started spiraling out of control, as situations inevitably did, there were still tangible benefits to be gained through preparation. Those benefits were lacking in this hastily devised mission.

She walked away from the rubber boat, on which Gonzalez's

man sat as unmoving as a gargoyle, and plunged into cover of the tropical vegetation. Once certain she was out of view of the man, she stripped off her rain gear, folded it neatly, and weighed it down with a rock at the base of a palm tree.

With any luck she'd be able to locate it upon her return—assuming, of course, she was still alive after the next few hours—but if not, it wouldn't be the biggest tragedy in the world. The prospect of spending three-plus hours getting soaked to the skin in a boat rocketing along at seventy miles per hour didn't seem so bad if it meant she was finished with this dubious little mission inside this dubious little country.

She covered the rain gear and then straightened, checking her waterproof watch. It was ten-fifteen p.m., which meant she had four hours and forty-five minutes to complete her mission and get back here before Silent Cal in the rubber boat fired up his electric motor and putted back to his equally tight-lipped buddy on the Scarab.

Hopefully it would be enough time, but she couldn't afford to drag her ass. She began walking as she mentally reviewed one of two maps Gonzalez had provided and which she had committed to memory. This one gave an overview of the Santa Cruz del Norte area and would be essential to her locating the home of her target, General Antonio Polanco.

If Gonzalez's information was accurate—always a questionable assumption when working with a new or unproven informant—Tracie needed to hike west, toward the town.

This area was sparsely populated, which was presumably why Polanco had chosen it as the location upon which to build his palatial estate. Private, but still close enough to Havana to make the commute an easy one should Castro summon him.

She worked her way toward the road, which Gonzalez had labeled "Villa Blanca," and which more or less followed the waterline. When she reached it, Tracie double-timed along the verge, keeping a close eye out both in front of and behind her for the headlights of oncoming cars, planning to melt back into the foliage when she saw them.

Traffic was minimal, though, and she made excellent time. The crumbling pavement was badly in need of repairs, but it still made a much better hiking surface than the sandy terrain, most of which was overgrown with vegetation.

Tracie pushed hard, conscious of her limited time on the island, and fifteen minutes later acquired a visual on her target's home. Gonzalez's crudely drawn map had been right on the money, but there would have been little chance of her mistaking the general's residence for any other—the houses she had seen during her hike were little more than shacks in comparison to this massive, ostentatious mansion.

Still, Tracie breathed a little easier. She would be relying on Gonzalez's second map to get around inside Polanco's home, and it came as a welcome relief to learn that the displaced Cuban's intel was solid.

So far.

Tracie approached, easing forward under cover of the vegetation. She swatted mosquitos as quietly as she could and wiped sweat from her eyes as she surveilled General Polanco's home. She set her backpack on the ground and unzipped it quietly, then lifted out a pair of binoculars. Slowed her breathing and trained the glasses on the house.

The mansion was a thing of beauty, flowing and graceful, and to Tracie's untrained eye looked like something that had been designed with an architect's touch. Even in the States the house would have been something special, but here in Cuba, decimated as the country had been by more than a quarter-century of Communist rule, the structure stood out like a jewel among lumps of coal.

A red brick walkway ran from an oversized dock that jutted into the Atlantic Ocean—there was no boat tied to the dock, Tracie noted—all the way along an immaculately maintained lawn sloping gently up to the house. The walkway ended at a patio, also constructed of red brick pavers.

Jutting off the rear of the house onto the patio was a screened-in addition, what would be called a three-season room in the northeastern U.S. where Tracie had grown up. Venetian blinds hung from the ceiling on all three exterior walls, giving Polanco the option of lowering them when he wanted to shut out the tropical Atlantic sunshine. At the moment, all of the blinds had been raised, allowing Tracie a full view of the room's interior.

A man sat inside it, smoking a cigar and sipping what looked like a glass of wine. He puffed contentedly and stared out at the empty Atlantic. A single low-wattage yellow-tinted bulb hung from a lamp in the corner, providing soft illumination that was probably easy on the man's eyes but that made it difficult for Tracie to distinguish details, even with the binocs. Bamboo furniture dotted the interior.

Tracie focused the glasses on the man and studied him closely. He wore loose-fitting camouflage trousers and black t-shirt, with partially laced combat boots on his feet. A bushy moustache that had once been black but was now as salt-and-pepper as his hair sprouted under his nose.

It was General Polanco. He matched perfectly the description—not to mention the photograph—provided by Gonzalez. The snapshot was out of date, having been taken years ago, but this was definitely the same man. He was in his late fifties, but looked at least ten years younger, strong and fit and confident.

Tracie's pulse quickened as she breathed a sigh of relief. There had been no guarantees the general would be home, and she hadn't relished the prospect of leaving the island with her mission unaccomplished and then trying to persuade Gonzalez to transport her back here again in a few days.

She slowly scanned the rest of the house—at least the portion she could see—with the glasses. Most of the windows were dark, and the ones that weren't glowed with the same low-wattage illumination. The lack of strong interior lighting struck Tracie as a good indication the homeowner was alone.

That was by no means certain, though. Tracie had learned from Gonzalez that Polanco was unmarried and lived by himself. She had also learned, however, that the general had an insatiable appetite for young women, sometimes entertaining three or even four pros in the same night. He was also rumored to enjoy underage girls, a fact that, if true, disgusted Tracie.

Well, she thought, *he won't be entertaining anyone after tonight: old, young or otherwise. He'll either be dead or on his way to a U.S. prison.*

Although conscious of the time passing and well aware that her three a.m. deadline to get off the island was approaching rapidly, Tracie was determined not to rush things. Her lack of opportunity to plan ahead for this mission didn't need to translate into reck-lessness now, and she stayed in her surveillance position for nearly half an hour.

During that time, no cars came or went, either on the general's property or along Villa Blanca. The same lack of activity was true inside the house. No lights went on or off, no shadows passed behind closed shades, and no activity disturbed the nighttime stillness.

Polanco sat nearly motionless, sipping wine and puffing cigar after cigar with the look of a man content with his circumstances in life.

That would soon change.

Eventually, the general crushed his tiny remaining cigar stub in a small ashtray, drained his wine glass and rose. He turned and entered his home and closed the door behind him. A moment later the light went off behind the door.

It appeared the general was going to bed.

It was time to act.

15

Breaking into the house via the three-season room presented obvious challenges and risks. Tracie would be fully exposed as she crossed the general's lawn, and also during the short time it would take to slice through one of the screens encircling the room.

She wasn't particularly concerned about being seen by a passerby. There had been little vehicular traffic and no pedestrian traffic along Villa Blanca during her surveillance, plus the front of the massive mansion would shield her from view of the road.

Gonzalez had said nothing about video surveillance, and Tracie had seen no evidence of cameras anywhere on the property.

But the three screen-covered walls meant there would be nowhere to hide should the general—or a guest, if it turned out Polanco wasn't alone—decided to take a little stroll or get up for a midnight snack.

On the other hand, the hour was late enough that the general was likely doing exactly what it appeared he was doing—going to bed. He *had* turned and presumably locked the door as he entered his home. And he *had* extinguished the interior light. And she *had* observed the slight but very definite wobble of a man who had had too much to drink.

All of it added up to manageable risk. Even now, Polanco was probably snoring away in his bed.

Tracie had spent several minutes of her surveillance scrutinizing the interior door as much as possible with the binoculars, and as far as she could tell it offered very little in the way of real security.

A locking brass knob seemed to be the only barrier to entry. And if that were the case, it should take Tracie less than a minute to pick the lock and access the home.

Her next move now set, she prepared to break cover. But there was still one wildcard that was cause for concern: a large, indistinct object she could see at the far end of the property. The object was covered in shadows, and even with the glasses, Tracie couldn't determine to her satisfaction what it was.

That was a problem.

The object didn't seem to be the right shape for a guardhouse, and it would be in a poor location strategically if it was. Gonzalez hadn't mentioned anything about private security in his briefing, but how trustworthy was he, really? She wasn't about to take anything he had said, or any information he provided, for granted.

She had to check it out herself.

She reversed course, backtracking along the side of Villa Blanca until out of sight of anyone inside Polanco's house. Then she crossed the empty road and disappeared into the brush and vegetation on the other side.

From there, she turned and paralleled the road until reaching a point west of the mansion and, again, out of sight. She crossed the road again—it remained empty—and made her way slowly and as quietly as she could manage, back in the direction of the house.

When the side of the mansion became visible through the scrub brush, Tracie turned north and moved toward the water. The thing that had been a vague, indistinct object from her surveillance point on the other side of the house suddenly appeared directly in front of her, and her eyes widened in surprise.

It was a helicopter.

General Antonio Polanco owned his own helicopter.

The craft was sitting in the middle of a small helipad, secured by four cables connected to iron bolts sunk into the pavement. An orange windsock hung limply a few dozen feet away, and in the starlit darkness Tracie could clearly see white markings painted on the pad.

Apparently the prospect of driving the short distance from Santa Cruz del Norte to meet with Fidel Castro in Havana was too daunting for Polanco. She wondered whether the general flew the chopper himself or whether he had his own personal pilot.

More importantly, what were the chances that if he *did* have his own pilot, the man lived here on the estate?

This development had the potential to change everything, and Tracie melted back into the trees to consider altering her plan. Ultimately, even if a pilot lived somewhere in or around the rambling home, her mission remained the same. She might have to add one step: immobilize the pilot before capturing or eliminating Polanco.

It was a hurdle, but not an insurmountable one.

Upon reflection, Tracie concluded nothing had changed.

She slipped her combat knife out of its sheath and held it loosely in her left hand, then pulled the Glock 9mm out of her shoulder rig and held the weapon in her right. Then she eased out of the scrub brush and walked boldly toward the three-season room.

There was no way to advance under cover, thus no reason to attempt stealth. If she was wrong about the general being asleep in his bed and he happened to look out a window, he would see her crossing his lawn. And if that happened, she knew she would find out about it quickly enough.

Seconds later she arrived at the screened-in room. No shouts of alarm went up inside the darkened house; no gunshots rang out in the night. She worked quickly and sliced a north to south gash in one of the screens along its aluminum frame, widening the slit just enough at the top and the bottom to permit access.

Then she placed the knife back in its sheath and slipped through the opening.

She was in.

She moved to the rear door and examined it closely. Tracie still wasn't one hundred percent certain the general's mansion had no electronic alarm system, and she wasn't anxious to find out the hard way she way that had missed something. She peered through the glass in the door, looking for telltale wiring or the magnetic connections that might trip an alarm the moment she opened the door.

Nothing. It was difficult to be certain, since the general had turned off the interior light, but it appeared as though the man's confidence—maybe even arrogance—had convinced him that no one in Cuba would be foolish enough to attempt a break-in at the home of one of the two or three most powerful men in the country.

Tracie guessed that his confidence was probably well founded. She didn't know what the punishment would be for any peasant foolish enough to get caught attempting what she was about to do, but she assumed it would be something extremely unpleasant. And that would be nothing compared to what *she* would face, were she to be apprehended.

She turned her attention to the lock built into the knob, feeling exposed and vulnerable. The lock's design was nothing complicated and it would offer virtually no resistance to a skillful and determined lock-picker, both of which Tracie Tanner was.

She placed her backpack on the floor and unzipped it slowly, doing her best to muffle the zipper's noise. Then she pulled her lock-picking tools from the pack and straightened, turning toward the knob.

And was shocked to see the door swing open.

16

Tracie dropped her tools and brought her gun to bear, swinging it up and dropping into a crouch.

But she was directly in front of the door, within arm's reach of a surprised General Polanco, and the older man moved faster than Tracie would have expected. His left hand snapped out in a reflexive slapping motion and he swatted at the gun, connecting and knocking it out of her hand and across the brick floor.

The weapon clattered away and Tracie unleashed a sidekick at the general's knee. She overcompensated for her crouch and her foot grazed the joint rather than connecting solidly.

Still, the general's leg buckled and he gasped in pain, falling sideways into the doorframe but recovering immediately and launching himself at Tracie. His bulky body smashed into her slim one and they tumbled to the floor, rolling once as each desperately worked to get leverage on the other.

Tracie knew she had to subdue the general fast. The longer the fight went on, the more likely Polanco would be able to use his superior size and strength to his advantage. She allowed herself to be rolled onto her back, and the general reached up with one ham-handed fist to punch her in the face.

Tracie waited a split-second for his fist to pound down at her. When it did, she twisted her head to the side and lifted hard with her legs and Polanco tumbled forward, trying desperately to stop the downaward motion on his punch, which was now aimed at the brick floor.

While he was preoccupied attempting to prevent a broken hand, Tracie reached up and laced her fingers together behind his head. Then she yanked hard, using his own momentum against him, and his forehead smashed into the bricks.

He groaned and rolled onto his side. Tracie scrambled to grab her gun, which had bounced almost all the way to one of the screens. She picked it up and whirled to see Polanco still prone on the floor, his hands clasped to his head in an effort to halt the flow of blood.

"Don't move," Tracie said quietly, her pulse pounding but her hands steady and her voice calm.

"What is the meaning of this?" the general said in heavily accented English.

"We need to talk."

"No, we do not need to talk. You need to turn around and leave my property this instant, or you will rot in a jail cell for the rest of your life. Assuming you even survive."

"Shut up and sit down," Tracie said. She inclined her head in the direction of the table where he had been sitting earlier and then backed away. There were some questions she wanted answered before she dragged him back to face justice in the U.S.

The general rose slowly to a standing position and regarded her carefully. His head was bleeding but not severely, and Tracie reached into her backpack and tossed him a towel. He plucked it out of the air and placed it against his bleeding forehead.

Polanco's initial shock at being confronted by an intruder with a gun had receded, replaced by a calculating shrewdness. Although much older than Tracie, the general was also much bigger and in outstanding physical condition. She could see him considering the odds of success should he make another play for her gun.

"Don't even think about it," she said. "Take a seat or die. You won't get lucky a second time."

Polanco's already angry expression darkened, but he seemed to recognize now was not the time to resist. He walked across the room, moving slowly but with a swagger that seemed strangely out of sync with his situation. Then he eased his bulk into a chair and gazed up at her expectantly.

"Now what?" he said.

"Now you explain to me why you had your people murder more than a half-dozen innocent Americans in Washington last week."

Polanco leaned back in his chair. The furious look on his face had disappeared, replaced at least for the moment with one of confusion.

Over the course of her career in the field, Tracie Tanner had become adept at reading people's expressions—that ability was often the only thing standing between life and death—and her immediate impression was that the Cuban general truly had no idea what she was talking about.

"You are an American," the general said slowly. "What the *hell* are you doing in Cuba?"

"That's not how this works," Tracie said, her voice steely. "I'm holding the gun, therefore I'll ask the questions and you will answer them."

"But you have not asked a question that I *can* answer. You are raving about murders in Washington, and I can assure you, little niña, that I have not ever been to Washington. Nor would I want to be," he added sharply, "until I can raise the Cuban flag over your capitol."

"I'm not talking about you personally. I'm talking about your people."

"My people? And what people would that be?"

"The people who do your bidding. The people who have helped you steal private property and amass wealth far beyond what you would be capable of earning on your own. The people that helped you afford...this." She waved her gun around, indicating the palatial estate.

Polanco erupted in laughter. "You think," he said after a moment, "that I have the kind of influence that would allow 'my people,' as you call them, to infiltrate your capitol city? And not just to infiltrate it, but to murder a half-dozen people in it? And then get away? You are obviously insane. How did you get into this country, anyway?"

"Let me refocus you," Tracie said. "This is my gun. I will use it to ventilate your skull unless you answer these questions to my satisfaction. And you're running out of time, because I'm running out of patience. Do you understand, General?"

"Ask a reasonable question and I will answer it. So far you have made no sense."

"Okay," Tracie agreed. "Let's try doing this a different way." She bent toward her backpack.

Polanco's left hand dropped slowly into his lap.

Tracie froze and said, "Put your hand back on top of the table. Do it now." She had no doubt the general was armed to the teeth inside his home, and his actions here indicated he must have, at the very least, a knife if not a gun hidden somewhere on his person.

The general glowered at her but did as he was told.

"The next move you make that concerns me," she said, "even a little bit, will be your last. Don't make the mistake of thinking I won't shoot you where you sit."

The ghost of a smirk flashed across the general's face and then disappeared, replaced with the innocent expression of a student trying to convince his teacher he hadn't been cheating on his math test.

Tracie kept the gun pointed at the general as she reached into her backpack and pulled out the same folded sheet of paper she had shown to Gonzalez back in Miami, the paper containing the unusual circular symbol with the odd stick-figure design inside that had taken the place of a signature in the threatening letters received by Edison Kiley. She placed it face-up on the table in front of General Polanco, keeping her gun hand well out of reach.

"Look at it," she said, and he did. She watched closely to gauge his reaction. His eyes widened and he wasn't able to stop himself from doing a little double take. It was nothing major, just a little shake of the head. Very minor. If she hadn't been zeroed in on him she might have missed it.

But she didn't miss it, and she said, "Okay, General, tell me that's not the symbol your followers use when they loot and pillage Cuba and now, commit murder in the United States. And then explain yourself before I haul your ass back to the United States to stand trial."

Polanco huffed softly and then looked up at Tracie. "All right, I will."

"Don't try to bullshit me, General. I saw your reaction when you looked at that paper. You tried to hide it but you couldn't. You recognized that symbol."

"You are right," he said, "I did react. But not for the reason you think. What you have shown me is not the symbol of these supposed 'followers' of mine that you have convinced yourself are so all-powerful they can sneak into your country and murder people, and then sneak out again."

Tracie stared down the general as he continued. "That is the symbol of an enemy of the State of Cuba, an *American* enemy that has done in my country exactly what you accuse me of doing in yours."

Now it was Tracie's turn to be confused. "What are you talking about?" she asked.

"The person or persons who claim ownership of that symbol have managed to enter my country several different times somehow—we do not know how—and wreak destruction on an innocent nation, blowing up buildings and in the process killing innocent people."

"Bullshit," Tracie said, but in the back of her mind she thought of Gonzalez's henchman piloting the rubber landing craft into the tiny, secluded inlet just a couple of miles away in complete darkness, with the skill and confidence of a man who had made the trip many times before.

"It is not 'bullshit,'" Polanco said calmly. "It is the truth."

"I don't believe you."

"You don't have to believe me. I can prove it to you."

17

General Antonio Polanco owned a vintage Lincoln Continental Mark II that would be the envy of any classic automobile enthusiast in the States. Its all-white finish gleamed in the stark light of Polanco's garage, as pristine as new-fallen snow, complemented by fat whitewall tires straight out of 1950s Americana.

Tracie's eyes widened at the sight of the car, which had not a speck of dust or road grime on it, and which looked as though it had just rolled off the showroom floor. Despite the gravity of the situation, Polanco smiled at her reaction. "This is a 1956 model," he said proudly, "one of only three thousand that were manufactured. Most have been lost to history in the more than three decades since rolling off the assembly line in Detroit, but not this one."

"Yeah?" Tracie said gruffly. "Who'd you steal it from?"

Polanco waved a hand as he opened the driver's door. "This beautiful relic of a bygone age belongs to the *people* now. Its previous owner was the proprietor of a Havana casino in the pre-revolution days, a man who refused to surrender his unlawfully secured property to its rightful and proper owners. Suffice it to say, he no longer had need for a car—or any mode of transportation, for that matter—following its seizure."

"Unlawfully secured," Tracie said scornfully. "That's a good one." She slid into the passenger seat and waited as Polanco fired up the engine. It turned over immediately and purred like a kitten, and the general backed the car out of the garage. He turned around in his circular driveway, rolled down to Villa Blanca, and then accelerated smoothly toward Havana.

Tracie hoped she wasn't being set up. Polanco wasn't going to be able to hurt her directly; she had disarmed him before taking one step beyond the man's screened-in three-season room. And her caution had served her well: Polanco had had a knife *and* a pistol in his possession.

He was now weapon-free, and although he was much bigger than Tracie, she felt confident that even without the gun in her hand, she could hold her own against the older man in a physical confrontation. He was injured and unarmed, and although she had allowed him to clean and bandage his wound, the gash was ugly and had to be bothering him.

But the fact was that if he chose to stop the car and begin screaming for help once they arrived in any well-populated area, there was little chance she would ever leave Cuba alive. By the time she could react it would likely be too late.

She thought the chances of Polanco screaming for help were slim, though. The general's anger and tension seemed to have melted away upon seeing the strange little symbol on Tracie's piece of paper, until now he was acting almost sociable. He very clearly believed he could prove the symbol did not belong to him or to anyone associated with him, and while Tracie couldn't imagine how he might manage that, her gut told her to play along and see what happened.

Her vague sense of unease about Gonzalez and his men played a major role in her decision. The feeling that she had been played for a fool back in Miami was getting stronger, and she was inclined to think Polanco was telling the truth, at least insofar as the symbol was concerned.

But while the general had become calmer over the last few minutes, she had not, and she continued to train her gun directly on him as he drove. "You know what's going to happen if you take one turn I don't like, or if you make any threatening moves, correct, General?"

He turned and smiled across the front seat at her. "Don't worry, little niña, I have no reason to attempt to harm you now. Soon you'll see that whoever sold you the pack of lies serving as your motivation is your real enemy. It is not me, it is not Secretary Castro, and it is certainly not the peace-loving people of Cuba."

* * *

The time was now past one a.m., and while Tracie knew a United States city like Miami would still be active at this time of night, the tiny island nation of Cuba seemed to have burrowed into a cocoon.

Even as they approached the outskirts of Havana in General Polanco's prized classic car, she had to strain to see electric light burning anywhere. Tiny homes, no more than shacks, really, constructed along Villa Blanca gave way to neighborhoods of houses clustered together, all uniformly dark and silent.

The occasional remnant of Cuba's bustling past could still be seen as they drove, but for the most part the evidence of Havana's sharp decline under nearly three full decades of Communist rule was everywhere. Decaying infrastructure, shuttered businesses and ancient automobiles—when automobiles could be found at all—testified to the consequences of the Castro government's iron grip.

They drove for a time in silence, the general perfectly at ease, acting almost as though being hijacked at gunpoint from his own home in the middle of the night was just another day at the office.

They entered the Havana city limits and Tracie's pulse quickened. "Where's this proof you claim to have?" she said tersely. The farther they got from the relative privacy of Polanco's mansion, the more concerned and tense she became.

"Almost there, little niña," the general said, rubbing the bandage on his forehead gently, almost absently.

He wasn't kidding. Two more turns, a right followed by a quick left, brought a down-in-the-dumps plaza into view. Most of the buildings were old, predating Castro's revolution. Some of them had clearly been standing for a century or more. The few examples of newer construction were utilitarian Soviet-style concrete cubes with all the charm and sophistication of a sledgehammer blow to the head.

But regardless of age, none of the buildings were ornate enough to serve as Fidel Castro's offices, Tracie was certain of that. This entire plaza was the province of much lower-lever bureaucrats, the kind of place where faceless apparatchiks trudged to work every day, cogs in the Communist governmental machine.

Polanco began slowing the car. The area appeared to be deserted except for one man, who lounged on the concrete steps of one of the buildings. The man sipped from a bottle ineffectively concealed in a brown paper bag, watching the progress of the Lincoln with the disinterested gaze of an alcoholic preoccupied with drinking himself into oblivion.

One of the buildings in particular drew Tracie's attention almost immediately, and it appeared to be where Polanco was even now aiming his car. It was among the older ones in the plaza and was in far worse condition than any of the others. And that was saying something.

The front of the building was two-thirds gone. It had obviously been bombed. The charred, blackened remains of a devastating explosion were clearly visible despite the lack of streetlights. Polanco stopped the car and aimed the headlights at the building and Tracie could see directly inside, through a gaping maw where the front exterior wall—and presumably the front door—had once been.

Interior support beams hung haphazardly, broken into pieces by the force of the blast. A staircase rose out of the rubble but went nowhere, the upper two-thirds having tumbled to the first floor and broken apart. Every window was gone. The explosion had been devastating.

But as badly damaged as the building was—and it was obviously unusable—none of the wreckage was what caught and held Tracie's attention. All she could do was stare in stunned surprise at the small portion of the front wall that had been left undamaged. On it, someone had painted a symbol, in bold white strokes.

It was the circular shape with the unusual open bottom, complete with the almost childlike rendition of three stick-figure people inside. It was the very symbol Tracie had shown Polanco inside his mansion less than thirty minutes earlier.

18

"What are you trying to pull here?" Tracie demanded, even as she knew what this discovery meant.

"Trying to pull?" Polanco answered. "I am not trying to pull anything. I said I could prove to you that this symbol does not belong to me or to any of my so-called 'followers,' and that is exactly what I have done. The symbol was placed here by the terrorists who destroyed this building. Clearly, I had no idea you would break into my home and threaten me with deadly violence, just as I had no idea you would show me your version of this symbol."

"This doesn't prove anything," Tracie said, although her heart was telling her otherwise. "Who's to say your people weren't responsible for bombing this building?"

Polanco put his head back and laughed. "What possible motive would I have for destroying the property of the Cuban people?"

Tracie shrugged. "A political rival works here. The husband of a lover works here. There could be any of a dozen reasons."

"You are stretching, little niña, and I think you know it. I have no political rivals, at least not inside my country. I have the ear of the most powerful man in Cuba, I have wealth and status, and it is to my advantage to build my country up, not to destroy it.

"And as far as me leveling an entire building because of a romantic rivalry, well, that theory is simply ludicrous. I have no romantic rivals any more than I have political ones, little niña. But if I did, I would simply arrest them and have them shot. I have the authority to do exactly that any time I wish, and I wouldn't lose even one minute's sleep at night afterward. I have executed many men over a lifetime of service to the state, it would not be a problem for me."

Tracie stared at the general, who was gazing back at her steadily. Even in the darkness of the Mark II's interior, she could see his eyes glittering cold and hard. This was a man not unaccustomed to violence, and she believed him when he discussed his personal familiarity with executions.

Polanco continued. "We have had a rash of similar bombings over the past couple of years. They always occur at night, and the targets are always the same—the people's office buildings. We believe these unprovoked acts of aggression are being perpetrated by a group or groups inside *your country*—" he stabbed a stubby finger in Tracie's direction, his voice tight with self-righteous anger—"by terrorists dedicated to overturning Cuba's legitimate government, the true government of the people."

Tracie was quiet, thinking, and Polanco said, "We are even fairly certain we know the name of the terrorist group."

"Is that so?"

"Sí, that is so. We believe the terror group is called 'Omega 7.' They have been responsible for a rash of bombings inside your own country against supporters of the people's government in Cuba. We feel certain there is an offshoot of Omega 7 that has found a way to enter this country and harass, intimidate, and murder peace-loving Cuban citizens."

A light bulb went on inside Tracie's head. She had known from the moment she first laid eyes on the strange circular symbol with the open bottom that she had seen it somewhere before, she just hadn't been able to put her finger on exactly where. Now she knew. It was the Greek letter Omega.

Tracie forced herself to disguise the shock she was feeling and said, "There have been other bombings?"

"Yes," he said simply. "I told you that already."

"Was this symbol present at any of the others?"

"Yes."

"At how many of the others?"

"All of them," he said.

Tracie fell silent as her mind churned through the possibilities this information represented. It was of course possible Polanco was lying through his teeth, that either he or his people had in fact been responsible for this bombing, for reasons unknown to her. But she doubted it. His anger was too real, too unrehearsed, too... *raw*...for a man putting on a front.

Again she thought back to the ease with which Juan Gonzalez's Atlantic Ocean chauffeurs had found and navigated into the tiny inlet from which she had come ashore. She recalled the flicker she thought she had seen in Gonzalez's eyes when he had first laid eyes on Tracie's rendition of the symbol. The Omega symbol.

Had the flicker of recognition represented something other than what she had been assuming? Had it represented his recognition of his own organization's symbol?

If General Polanco was telling the truth—and Tracie had to admit she was starting to think he was—then it probably had. That symbol might well belong to *Gonzalez* or, at the very least, to some of his people.

And if that was the case, it changed everything.

Polanco seemed to interpret her silence as disbelief of his statement. "Would you like to see more of the destruction, little niña? I can drive around Havana all night."

Tracie considered the general's words. On balance, she believed them. There *were* no rabid paramilitary followers of General Antonio Polanco. Or if they existed, they weren't the group who had snuck into the United States and murdered the entire management structure of one relatively small company with ties to the defense community.

There was no reason to see more of the devastation Polanco claimed had occurred throughout Cuba's capitol city.

And there was another factor to consider. She was running out of time. She checked her watch and saw that it was already nearly one-thirty a.m. Gonzalez's men had warned her that they would leave Cuba no later than three o'clock, whether she had returned or not.

It was time to get moving.

She had to get back to the States and regroup.

She opened her mouth to tell Polanco to fire up his classic car and then she froze, watching in shock as a vehicle marked "Policia" eased into the plaza and stopped. Its headlamps bathed the Mark II in weak yellow illumination.

Polanco turned to Tracie and smiled, completely at ease. "This is a problem, sí?"

The adrenaline kicked in and she considered potential escape scenarios as the police cruiser sat unmoving across the plaza. Polanco was a powerful man in his country. His car was unique, and must be instantly recognizable to the authorities. Same with his fondness for local prostitutes. Perhaps the officer would simply turn around and drive away.

But somehow she knew he wasn't going to simply turn around and drive away, and she was right. After another thirty seconds or so, during which time Tracie held her breath and felt her mouth going dry, the officer inside the vehicle flipped on a bubble light mounted atop the small car that made the cruiser look like something out of an old 1940s Hollywood movie.

Hookers, she thought again. *They'll know he loves hookers.*

She slid across the passenger seat and leaned into the big bear of a man, jamming her Glock into his ribs, hard. "I'm a prostitute and we're out for a moonlight drive," she said quietly, her voice hard and cold. "Get rid of this man right now or you're going to die in this fancy car of yours. They can bury you in it as far as I'm concerned."

Polanco tensed but didn't have time to answer as the police car pulled up next to the Mark II. The cruiser had a hand-controlled spotlight mounted on the door, and the officer trained it straight at the Lincoln's driver's side window.

The interior of the general's car was lit up like midday, and Tracie hoped the officer couldn't see her outfit past Polanco's bulk. She wasn't dressed much like a hooker and was still grimy and dirty from her fight with the general over her gun. There was nothing she could do about any of that now; she was committed.

"Get that damned light out of my eyes!" Polanco demanded gruffly in Spanish, and the officer immediately extinguished it.

That's a good start, Tracie thought, hoping the general wouldn't try to alert the officer to his predicament. Thanks to her background in linguistics, she could easily follow everything that was being said, but Polanco would have no way of knowing that she could understand him.

"General," the officer said warily. The young man obviously recognized Polanco and was just as obviously intimidated by him.

"What is it?" Polanco said gruffly. He didn't react at all as Tracie jammed her gun even harder into his side.

"Uh…is everything…all right?"

"Yes, yes, everything is fine," Polanco said. "I am simply enjoying this beautiful evening with my…date." The general had thrown his right arm over Tracie's shoulder and now she felt his hand pull away as he indicated her to the officer. He let his hand drop and she felt it linger on her breast. She cleared her throat quietly and the hand disappeared.

The young policeman bent down and peered more closely through Polanco's half-open window. Tracie nuzzled her face into the general's neck, pretending to kiss him but trying not to gag from the smell of cigars and stale sweat. She prayed the officer didn't lean far enough into the car to see her gun.

The cop focused on the bandage wrapped around Polanco's head and said, "What happened to you?"

"Rough sex." Tracie could hear the note of amusement in the general's voice, despite the tension of the moment. *He's enjoying this*, she thought, almost shaking her head at the thought but stopping herself in time.

"Sex."

"That's right."

"And then you came…*here*…with your date?"

An awkward silence followed, broken when an exasperated Polanco finally said, "Yes, Officer, I came here. Is there some kind of problem I should know about?"

"Uh…no, sir."

"What was your name again?"

"Uh…Cortez, sir."

"Yes, Officer Cortez. I brought my date here. Is that all right with you, Officer Cortez?"

"Of course, sir, of course. I, uh, I just wanted to make sure… uh…"

"That will be all, Officer Cortez. Thank you for your sharp eyes and your fine police work. I will be sure to phone your precinct captain tomorrow and tell him what an outstanding job you are doing keeping our city safe."

"Thank you, General Polanco, thank you very much." Tracie could hear the pleasure in the receding voice as Officer Cortez climbed into his cruiser and slammed the door. A moment later the blue bubble light on top of the car stopped spinning, and a moment after that, the policeman was gone and they were once again alone but for the vagrant drinking on the steps of the building across the plaza.

Tracie pushed herself away from General Polanco and slid across the car to the passenger side, her heart hammering in her chest. The older man glared at her. "I got rid of him. What happens now, you are going to shoot me anyway?"

"I'm not going to shoot you unless you give me a reason to," she said. "Just start up this rust bucket and get back to your house."

19

Tracie wrapped the duct tape around and around Polanco's wrists and ankles, taking her time and packing it down hard as she went, immobilizing him in the heaviest-looking chair she could find. It was important to ensure the general would be fully incapacitated for at least the amount of time it would take her to get off the island and safely away.

Polanco huffed in anger. "This is ridiculous," he said. "Do you have any idea how long I am going to be stuck in this chair?"

Tracie scoffed. "It won't be long. The minute you don't show up for a meeting and then don't answer your phone, you know as well as I do that enough people will swarm this house to take over a small country. Oh, wait," she added sardonically, "you already did that."

She finished packing down the tape and then tested her work by yanking on the general's hands and feet, one at a time. He shook his head and sighed deeply but said nothing else.

Finally satisfied that he wouldn't be going anywhere on his own, Tracie turned to leave. Polanco probably had a housekeeper or gardener or personal assistant—perhaps all three and maybe more—who would be arriving at his house first thing in the morning, so she guessed he would spend—at most—five to six hours immobilized before being released.

And given the fate Tracie had been planning for him just a couple of hours ago, he was getting off easy.

She finished by wrapping a strip of tape around Polanco's head and slapping it over his mouth, hard. "Your mansion is so far from the road that I doubt anyone would hear you screaming, but there's no reason to take chances, is there?"

She stepped back and pretended to wait for a response. "Nothing to say?"

Polanco glared at her over the duct tape gag and she said, "I didn't appreciate you feeling me up back in Havana. This is for every girl you've taken advantage of, whether she's a pro or not." She placed her gun back in its shoulder rig and then wound up and slugged the general in the jaw.

His head snapped back and his eyes glazed over but he didn't lose consciousness. The anger in his eyes had turned to fury, but Tracie ignored it. She hefted her backpack. "Thanks for an interesting evening," she said. "You really know how to show a girl a good time."

Then she slipped out the back door and through the slit in Polanco's screen. She disappeared into the cover of the vegetation and began hiking back toward the secluded little cove and her escape to the U.S.

*   *   *

Gonzalez's man was gone.

So was the rubber boat.

Tracie checked her watch for the third time and it read exactly what it had read each of the previous two: two thirty-five a.m.

She tried to tell herself she was surprised, but couldn't quite manage it. She had had a bad feeling about the direction this mission was taking almost from the moment she left *Noches Habana,* and seeing the unusual symbol splashed across the remains of the bombed-out office building in Havana had only increased her concern.

Gonzalez had promised that his men would wait for her until three am. He vowed they would not stay one minute later, but he'd been very clear that as long as she arrived back in the cove by three, she would be fine.

She had been set up.

And she had fallen for it hook, line and sinker.

Undoubtedly the man piloting the rubber boat had waited just long enough for her to clomp off through the underbrush and get out of earshot before firing up the electric motor and rendezvousing with the guy who had stayed offshore in the Scarab.

By now the two men would be back in Miami, fast asleep in their beds, probably. And Gonzalez—who had either committed the murders at NCC himself or knew who had—was busy congratulating himself on his cleverness in solving the little problem Tracie represented.

She forced herself to focus. Right now she had bigger problems to worry about than Juan Gonzalez.

She was alone in a Communist country, unarmed except for two semiautomatic pistols and a combat knife.

And nobody knew she was here.

20

Tracie moved as fast as she could, slashing through the underbrush along Villa Blanca. If she were to have any chance of escaping Cuba, speed would be essential. Once day broke, it would likely be too late: she would be stuck here with no supplies and no possibility of help.

After recovering from the shock of discovering she was trapped inside Cuba, Tracie had forced herself to slow her racing pulse and think. She had been in bad situations before and knew that succumbing to panic was the quickest and surest route to an early grave.

A few minutes of careful consideration allowed her to formulate the outlines of a plan. It was a desperate plan, one likely doomed to failure, but it was better than standing around waiting for Castro's soldiers to discover her and put a bullet in her head.

And at least she would be *doing* something. If everything fell into place, there was still the possibility she could survive this fiasco.

At least that was what she told herself.

Once committed to her long-shot plan, Tracie reversed course and returned the way she had come. A few minutes later she reached jungle-like vegetation at the edge of General Antonio Polanco's property.

Despite the fact that every passing minute brought daybreak closer, she forced herself to slow down and once again observe the home from a distance. It was highly unlikely anyone would have arrived and freed the general in the short time she had been gone, but walking into a trap wouldn't do anything to help her situation.

Nothing seemed to have changed as she scanned the mansion with the binocs. The property was as still and silent as she had left it, and if Polanco had been discovered, the exact opposite would have been the case. The place would be swarming with police and military.

She zipped the glasses back into her pack and slung it over her shoulder. Then she set out across the open expanse of felt-green lawn, moving directly to the slit she had cut into Polanco's screened-in room earlier. Now that she had decided upon a course of action, she wasted no time, slipping through the general's back door and into his home.

He was right where she had left him, bound and gagged, and he glared at her with a hatred that was palpable.

She smiled sweetly. "Hi Honey, I'm home. Did you miss me?"

Polanco responded with words that were, of course, unintelligible thanks to the duct tape gag, but whose meaning was, nonetheless, crystal clear. He didn't seem to have missed her at all.

"You know," Tracie said, squatting down next to the general and slicing through the tape on his ankles with her combat knife, "I can't help but feel we got off to a rocky start. I think we should give this relationship another try and see if we can make it work."

He glared at her, but some of his fury seemed to have leached away into confusion. It was clear he never expected to see her again, certainly not less than an hour after she had departed, and had no clue where this sudden reappearance might lead.

She freed his ankles and got back to her feet. Stepped back and gazed down at him thoughtfully. "If I release your hands, are you going to remember that I still have a gun and you don't?" To emphasize her point, she lifted the weapon and displayed it just inches from his face.

His eyes narrowed and his glare returned and Tracie said, "I asked you a question and I want an answer. Now. Nod or shake your head." Her voice was cold and quiet.

Polanco stared for a moment longer and then nodded his head abruptly, once, with a violence that more than adequately summed up his mood.

"Fine," Tracie said. "I'll release you. But if you so much as breathe in a way I find threatening, I'll splatter your brains all over this beautiful Oriental rug."

She leaned over and ripped the tape off Polanco's mouth. A sharp intake of breath was the only indication it had been painful. His gaze never wavered, nor did the hatred burning in his eyes. Then she sliced through the wrist bindings and stepped back quickly, leveling her gun at the general.

"Now what?" he muttered, rubbing the circulation back into his arms. "I thought I was finally rid of you."

"Now you're going to help me get back to the United States."

"Why don't you go back the way you came?"

"Why don't you shut your mouth and let me ask the questions?"

The general shook his head in disgust and said, "Would you explain to me why in the world would I help you get back to the U.S.? Why would I help you in any way?"

"Because I still hold the balance of power, remember? I'm telling you, Antonio, you really need to try to keep up. This relationship will never work if you can't."

Polanco muttered something under his breath.

"Excuse me?"

"I said, just what the *hell* do you expect me to do?"

She ignored his question and said, "Do you know how to fly that chopper tied down in your backyard?"

"Of course." The reply was curt, but Tracie could sense the pride in the general's voice. "It can get me from here to the Presidential Palace—or to any location in Cuba—in a very short time. I can—"

Polanco stopped short and stared at Tracie in disbelief.

"Wait a minute," he said. "You do not think I'm going to—"

"Fly me back to Miami? Of course not."

Polanco seemed to relax a bit.

"It won't be necessary to take me all the way to Miami. You can drop me off at Homestead. I can find my way from there, I'm sure."

21

Polanco muttered steadily under his breath as he moved around the chopper, disconnecting lines and prepping the craft for departure with an easy familiarity that soothed Tracie's raw nerves, at least slightly. It was obvious he hadn't been lying when he said he knew how to fly the bird.

Either that or he was full of shit and one of the best liars she had ever seen.

She followed the angry general as he performed his preflight duties, staying well beyond arm's reach but close enough so he wouldn't be tempted to forget her previous threat about putting a bullet in his head.

The chopper was secured to the concrete landing pad by four guide wires, each clipped to a bolt sunk into one corner of the pad and then connected to the landing skids, one at the front of each skid and one at the rear.

"What's the range of this thing?" Tracie asked doubtfully. She had ridden in helicopters before and had never liked it. Airplanes were one thing; they were big and solid and felt like they could at least take on foul weather or high winds and have a chance of surviving. But helicopters struck her as tiny and insubstantial, as if the barest puff of a breeze would carry them away.

Or worse, break them apart and send the occupants tumbling thousands of feet to a gruesome death.

Polanco muttered an answer and Tracie said, "Speak up!"

"I said the range is more than sufficient to get to South Florida.

And, since you'll never let me leave the United States, there is no reason to be concerned about getting back to Cuba, now, is there?"

"Why would you think I'm not going to let you out of the States?"

Polanco had been bent over, studying something on the body of the chopper. He stretched up to his full height and gazed down at Tracie through scornful eyes. "It will be a huge boost to the career of the CIA agent who delivers General Antonio Polanco to the United States government. Do not try to convince me that such a boost does not appeal to you."

"What makes you think I'm CIA?"

"Please," Polanco said. "Do not insult me. I have spent a lifetime fighting for my country and against Americans just like you, people committed to bringing down my government. I know CIA when I see it."

Tracie shrugged. "Think what you want," she said. "But don't pretend to know what does or doesn't appeal to me. It just so happens that I believe you when you say neither you nor your people are responsible for the NCC murders. If I *didn't* believe you, you would be correct in assuming you'd never get out of the U.S. alive.

"But as things stand now," she continued, spreading her hands in a conciliatory gesture, "if you get me to Florida and back onto United States soil, I have no reason to interfere with you lifting back off and returning to Cuba."

Polanco stood motionless, his eyes narrowed to slits. It was obvious he wanted to believe her, but the idea that a representative of the United States government would allow a Big Fish from an enemy to escape once they had that Big Fish in their clutches was so foreign to him that he couldn't quite bring himself to accept it.

Tracie gestured with her gun at the helicopter. "Move it along," she said. "Because if you *don't* get me to the States, all bets are off and you'll end up buried at sea with two 9mm slugs in your head. Your buddy Castro will never know what happened to you."

Polanco grunted angrily and returned to his preflight preparations. After a moment he turned to her and said gruffly, "Sí."

She shook her head in confusion. "Yes? Yes what?"

"Sí, this Bell JetRanger carries enough fuel for a round trip to South Florida and back. Barely."

"Speaking of which," Trace said, scratching her head. "I don't see any way of refueling. How are you going to gas this thing up?"

"I refuel at San Antonio de los Baños Airfield when necessary. It is a just short flight from here, and I filled up before returning home after my last trip. The tank is almost completely full."

She couldn't imagine Polanco would have anything to gain by lying, so she took him at his word. He finished his preflight inspection—no easy task in the darkness, even under the ambient light of the moon and stars—and quickly unsnapped the four cables keeping the chopper moored to the pad.

Then he opened a surprisingly flimsy-looking door and gestured her inside. Tracie had the absurd vision of a chivalrous high school boy opening the car door for his prom date. This was no date, though, and of all the potential descriptions she could think of for General Antonio Polanco, "chivalrous" would be nowhere on the list.

She gestured with her gun. "You first," she said.

The general shrugged and turned toward the helicopter and Tracie said, "General!" Her voice was harsh and it stopped the Cuban in his tracks. "I'm sure you have a weapon or two stashed in there somewhere. Keep your hands where I can see them. If you make a single move I don't like, you'll be dead before you hear the gunshot, do you understand?"

Polanco turned. His voice was quiet but cold when he spoke. "If you kill me, you will never get off this island."

"And you'll still be dead," Tracie said without hesitation.

It looked as though the general was poised to say more, but he bit the words off and turned back toward the JetRanger. He clambered into the cabin, his big body seeming to fold in upon itself as he squeezed through the doorway. He made sure to keep his hands in plain sight, though, and the moment he forced his bulk inside, Tracie followed, gun trained steadily on the big man's body.

Inside, the Bell helicopter seemed even smaller than it had looked from the outside. Polanco had settled into the pilot's seat and was already busying himself reading gauges, flipping switches and turning knobs as Tracie closed and latched the door behind her.

A bench seat that looked like it belonged in the back of a station wagon took up virtually the entire interior of the chopper behind the pilot's chair. It was big enough to hold two adults comfortably. Maybe three if they weren't the size of Polanco or didn't mind being stuffed inside the helicopter like sardines.

Tracie considered climbing into the back but knew that to keep an eye on Polanco, she needed to be seated next to him. The general seemed to have picked up his preflight pace considerably, and was prepping for departure with an urgency that had been missing until now.

She eased into her seat and reached for her safety harness as the Jet Ranger's engine fired up with a high-pitched whine. The rotors began spinning, slowly at first and then with increasing speed. And then they were airborne, the JetRanger gaining altitude at a breathtaking rate, much faster than Tracie had expected.

She gasped and slapped the seatbelt's buckle at its receptacle. Missed.

Then the little chopper began shifting, turning onto its side as it hovered perhaps one hundred feet directly above the back yard landing pad. Polanco maneuvered the collective expertly and Tracie felt her weight shifting and she knew he was doing it intentionally, trying to dump her out of her seat and jar her gun loose.

The pitch-black Atlantic rotated through forty-five degrees out the windscreen, seeming to turn sideways, and she knew she had one more shot at getting her safety harness buckled before she tumbled into the door, the flimsy piece of sheet metal on hinges that would be the only thing standing between her and a terrifying fall to her death.

She stabbed the buckle at the receptacle again, now barely able to control her rising panic.

It locked into place with a satisfying metallic *click*.

And then she was hanging sideways, the harness holding her in her seat.

She twisted toward the general and raised her Glock, now aiming not at center mass but at Polanco's head. "Straighten this thing out, *now,* or you'll die where you sit!" she screamed.

The helicopter seemed to hesitate for just a moment, as if Polanco couldn't decide whether she meant what she said, and then they were once again hovering in an upright position above the general's property.

"Move," Tracie said. "Now. Get going toward the Florida coast." She could barely contain her anger and her fear and her racing pulse, and she was half-tempted to put a bullet in Polanco's head as payback for his frightening stunt, consequences be damned.

He said nothing, just maneuvered the controls with lips compressed into a tight slash. The chopper accelerated relatively smoothly—at least, smoothly compared to the violent pitches and rolls Polanco had just put the little craft through—and then they were churning forward, the dim lights of Cuba receding steadily into the distance. Soon the lights disappeared and the helicopter was alone, suspended over the massive black expanse of the Atlantic Ocean.

22

The sky was lightening noticeably when the South Florida coast began to come into view. High, thin clouds streaked with pink and purple stretched out over the endless Atlantic, and the impending sunrise made Tracie even more anxious to get on the ground.

The chopper moved forward, their progress feeling agonizingly slow despite the fact Polanco told her they were traveling at nearly one hundred fifty miles per hour.

She thought about air traffic control and the limits of ATC radar coverage, wondered what controllers might think seeing one lone target approaching the U.S. coastline from the south. The chopper was very low, skimming over the wave tops, presumably staying under the radar, but who knew?

This was exactly the tactic drug-runners used when bringing shipments to the mainland, and she guessed radar coverage was on Polanco's mind as well. And while the prospect of being greeted by law enforcement or even military fighter jet interceptors held a certain reassuring appeal, Tracie knew that if that happened, the resulting attention, and the pointed questions about why she was in the company of a top Cuban Communist general—questions she could not possibly answer to the satisfaction of the authorities—would blow her mission completely out of the water, and likely end her career.

She glanced across the small cabin at the general and wondered what was going through his mind. As risky as this daybreak incursion into the United States was for her, it was much more so for him. Unlike earlier, when Polanco had been almost jovial, conversation had been sporadic over the nearly ninety-minute flight; it seemed the potential of capture by his enemy was limiting his interest in small talk.

Her eyes were beginning to droop as exhaustion, along with the effects of stress and adrenaline, began to take their toll. The helicopter buzzed along, the sound of the rotors combining with the motion of the aircraft to remind her how tired she was, and how much she needed sleep.

When Polanco spoke, Tracie's eyes popped open and she realized she had been about to doze off. *Thank God the general picked the right time to open his mouth,* she thought, her heart now pounding madly. *Two more minutes and he could have unsnapped the safety harness, opened the door and rolled me into the ocean before I had a clue what was happening.*

She cleared her throat in an attempt to steady her nerves. And her voice. "I'm sorry, I missed that. What did you say?"

"I said how are we going to do this? What is your plan?"

"Come on, General, get real, there's no plan. I'm making this up as I go, remember?"

Polanco grunted. Tracie didn't catch what he said, but she didn't really need to. It was obvious the general expected to be caught at any moment, and probably tried and executed before noon.

Good.

Fear could be a good motivator and it was important that Polanco stay focused, at least until Tracie was on the ground and free. After that he was on his own, and while she had no particular interest in seeing the general captured, it wouldn't break her heart, either, especially after the stunt he pulled right after they had gotten airborne.

His question was a legitimate one, though, and Tracie spent a few minutes pondering it. She realized she had no idea where they were. They had been skirting the Florida Keys for quite some time, but the Keys stretched for dozens upon dozens of miles, thrusting into the Atlantic like a bony, misshapen finger.

Finally she spoke. "It's not like we have many options," she said. "We'll stay far enough offshore that anyone who spots us will hopefully not be able to read your tail number and realize it isn't U.S. registration. Then, when I see what looks like a secluded section of beach, we'll head straight for it. You'll put this thing on the ground, I'll hop out and you can be back in the air and headed for Havana in a matter of seconds."

He didn't answer and Tracie was glad. She wasn't interested in his opinion.

As crowded as she imagined the Florida Keys being, Tracie had begun to doubt her "plan" even as she spoke the words. But she was surprised to discover that much of the coastline they were passing seemed to be deserted.

It didn't escape Polanco's attention, either. "You know," he said. "If I am going to have enough fuel to make it back to Cuba, I must turn around soon. This round-trip flight is close to the very limits of the helicopter's range and I have little desire to drop into the sea five kilometers from home."

Tracie was quiet for a moment. She checked her watch. It was almost six a.m. Now was the time to make a run for the beach if they were going to; any delay and the likelihood of running into early-rising beachcombers rose dramatically.

She lifted her binocs to her eyes using her left hand only. In her right she was careful to keep her weapon trained squarely on the pilot. Polanco had proven himself to be a quick thinker and a dangerous opponent, and she had no doubt he would take advantage of any opening if he saw one.

Off in the distance the shoreline continued to slide past along the left side of the JetRanger. While it was difficult to see clearly—using just one hand to steady the glasses was a challenge, given the steady vibration of the chopper and their one-hundred-fifty mile per hour speed—Tracie became convinced that the stretch of beach due west of them was as good a potential landing spot as they were likely to find: the shoreline was secluded and shielded by a thick palm grove, but a decent-sized town was visible in the distance just a couple of miles away. Whether that town was Marathon or Islamorada or Key Largo she had no idea, but it looked large enough to support at least one car rental agency, which was what she would need.

The clock was ticking.

"Okay," she said, lowering the glasses and nodding in the

direction of the shoreline. "Let's do it."

Polanco didn't bother answering. He turned the bird and advanced toward the beach at full power. As the shoreline rushed up to meet them, Tracie could see they had chosen a decent spot to put down. The immediate area looked deserted.

For now.

The JetRanger crossed over the strip of beach and continued on. Tracie was about to ask Polanco what the hell he thought he was doing, but then it became clear. He brought their forward motion to a stop, then hovered for a moment and eased onto a grassy clearing between the beach and the trees. The landing was as smooth and uneventful as any she had ever experienced in a fixed-wing airplane.

The skids had no sooner touched the ground than Polanco turned in his seat. He fixed her with a glare and said, "I did what you asked, now get out."

"Gladly," Tracie shot back. She had dropped her binoculars into her backpack as they approached the shoreline, and now she grabbed the pack and unlatched the door. She swung it open and dropped to the ground, conscious of the lethal rotors slicing the air just above her head.

She ducked low and moved toward the trees, anxious to get out of here but well aware of how dangerous Polanco was. She hadn't forgotten her earlier concern about the general having weapons stashed somewhere on board his chopper, and to protect against that possibility, she moved sideways away from the JetRanger, keeping her gun aimed in the general direction of the pilot.

By landing on the grass, the general had minimized the amount of sand being kicked up by the rotors, but he had not entirely eliminated it. Flying grains pelted her face and bit into exposed skin like a thousand stinging bees. Tracie shielded her eyes as best she could and abandoned the notion of training her gun on the chopper. The moment she was out of range of the deadly rotor blades, she sprinted for the cover of a palm grove in the distance.

Behind her the JetRanger's engine whined and its blades began biting the air again in earnest. The chopper rose into the sky in a cloud of choking sand, and as she reached the trees, she turned to watch its progress. Polanco had already pivoted the aircraft on its axis and was even now adding power, putting distance between himself and the enemy state as quickly as he could.

Tracie watched the helicopter grow smaller and smaller in the early-morning sky, until eventually it disappeared and she was alone.

23

Juan Gonzalez glanced up from behind his desk with a scowl as Maria Carranco entered the office and closed the door softly behind her.

It hadn't been easy locating this particular member of Omega 7. Although she was technically a member of his own household, living in her own wing in his sprawling mansion, she was also an unstable loner who sometimes disappeared for weeks at a time into her retreat in the Everglades. Juan had been to the rickety cabin once and vowed never to return.

For all her flaws, though, Maria's dedication to Omega 7 could not be questioned. The organization consisted of a loose amalgamation of members, most Cuban-born expatriates who had been forced out of their country during, or immediately following, the Communist revolution. All were dedicated to the overthrow of the Castro government, but some—like Maria—were willing to go to much greater lengths in working toward that goal than others.

Omega 7 had been classified a terrorist organization by the U.S. Department of Justice and the FBI, the result of a string of pipe bomb attacks—and assorted other disruptive activities—aimed at intimidating backers of the Castro regime here in the states. The goal of the attacks was to convince Castro apologists that supporting the Communist government did not come without risks.

Gonzalez knew the "terrorist" label was bullshit, of course. He and all of Omega 7 were fighting a war to regain a country that had been stolen out from under them by an illegitimate regime.

They were no more "terrorists" than the Minutemen had been in the U.S.'s own Revolutionary War. Freedom fighters, that's what Omega 7 should be classified as, heroes even, and if the FBI and the Justice Department couldn't see that, then that was their problem, not his.

But the "terrorist" designation did present more than a few difficulties when it came to administering the organization. Maintaining absolute secrecy was essential, as was retaining control—not always an easy task—over the activities of Omega 7. Every action they took must be carefully considered and planned, because every move they made could be the last thing they ever did. The possibility of an FBI raid that would render Omega 7 extinct hung over their heads like the sword of Damocles.

Which was exactly why Juan Gonzalez was so angry with Maria Carranco. The young woman was technically a U.S. citizen, born here in Miami mere months after her father's death during the doomed Bay of Pigs invasion in 1961. She carried a white-hot resentment, just as most victims of the Castro revolution did.

But hers went far beyond the typical hatred of Castro that burned inside so many dispossessed Cubans, including Juan Gonzalez. Maria blamed the United States for the death of the father she had never met, believing the U.S. government had misled the Cuban freedom fighters during that disastrous invasion twenty-six years ago. She felt—as did many Cubans—that the rebels had been promised more support than the U.S. government was willing to deliver, and that the United States had abandoned the men when the fighting became too intense and the tide of battle began to turn against them.

Juan agreed with Maria's assessment for the most part, and himself held no great love for the U.S. But while the passage of time had dulled his anger, it had done nothing of the sort inside Maria. In fact, just the opposite seemed to be true. As the beautiful young woman grew up without a father, immersed in the Cuban expatriate culture and surrounded by stories of the American treachery at the Bay of Pigs, her fury seemed to grow stronger by the day.

As a young teen, Maria Carranco had been welcomed into Omega 7 and had begun working toward the liberation of Cuba.

Her early assignments were simple ones—money transfers, courier jobs—but before long her zeal and dedication to the cause had led to more significant assignments.

By the time she turned eighteen, Maria had become one of the most valued members of Omega 7, with the ability to use her dazzling beauty to insinuate herself into places no one else in the organization could.

And there was more.

Her orientation with the group had included training in weapons use, guerilla tactics and bomb making, and instructors had been delighted to discover the young woman possessed a natural aptitude with explosive devices. Their construction and deployment seemed to come as innately to her as her incredible beauty. Assignments taking advantage of that aptitude soon followed: pipe-bomb attack after pipe-bomb attack on wealthy Castro supporters.

It wasn't until a couple of years ago that Maria came to Juan with an audacious plan: to sneak into Cuba under cover of darkness and attack the Castro government on its own territory, using Gonzalez's speedboat and one or two of his men for transport.

Although proud of his prodigy and impressed with her dedication to the cause, Gonzalez was reluctant initially to approve the seemingly suicidal mission. Given the plan's potential for disrupting the Cuban government, however, he eventually signed off on it, praying he hadn't sentenced the young woman to death. Or worse.

But she didn't die. Her first incursion into Cuba was a smashing success. Maria blew up a government building, working entirely on her own, in the dark, in Havana. And to Gonzalez's utter shock, she managed to escape capture and return unharmed to Miami.

Over the intervening months she had returned to the island nation several times, sandwiching the trips in between her other work for Omega 7. Each time, she managed to avoid Cuban naval patrols and inflict damage on the Castro regime before escaping into the night.

At the insistence of Gonzalez and other top members of Omega 7, Maria had been limited to using pipe bombs in her domestic assignments. Utilizing more powerful explosives would result in attention the group didn't need, and the crude bombs were more than powerful enough to do accomplish Omega 7's goals of destruction and intimidation.

But for the Cuban missions, Maria had used C4. Where she obtained the C4 was not a question Juan had been prepared to ask, and it was something Maria wasn't about to volunteer freely. Although unstable, the young woman was incredibly resourceful, able to leverage her extraordinary beauty in countless creative ways. Undoubtedly she had done exactly that in finding a supplier for the explosive.

And there was one more thing about Maria Carranco: she had "signed" her handiwork in Cuba using an unusual symbol, a series of three figures representing herself, her mother and her now-dead father, placed inside the semicircular Omega symbol: Ω. She had shown her "signature" to Juan just once, after her first incursion into Cuba. "I want Castro to know who is destroying his precious Communist government," she had said proudly, her eyes bright with fanaticism.

He had warned Maria to limit her use of it to her Cuban missions. "We do not need to give authorities in the U.S. any unnecessary evidence with which to identify us," he had said.

Maria had agreed, and Juan had forgotten all about the odd little "signature."

Until yesterday, when he had seen it on the sheet of paper the redheaded CIA bitch shoved under his nose.

Maria Carranco was like a daughter to Juan. Her father had been a close friend and confidant, and after Jose Carranco lost his life in the failed assault on his homeland in 1961, Juan had taken it upon himself to care for Maria and her mother.

He was closer to the young woman than to either of his own children, which made what he had to say today that much more difficult.

He steeled his expression and stared the young woman down as she stood inside his office doorway. "You wanted to see me?" she said, her voice sweet and feminine, betraying none of the hardened freedom fighter Juan knew was inside.

"I had an interesting visitor yesterday." He didn't invite Maria to sit down.

"Really? What does this have to do with me?" Her tone was polite, almost disinterested, giving away nothing, and for the thousandth time since she was a young girl, Juan's heart swelled with pride. He wished her father could have seen the accomplished warrior she had turned out to be.

But his pride in her was not limitless, especially not where the future of Omega 7 was concerned. Juan Gonzalez had dedicated his life to the overthrow of Fidel Castro, and he hadn't sacrificed everything in the name of the cause to see all he had worked for vanish in a blast of C4.

"It has much to do with you," he said coldly. "It has *everything* to do with you."

24

Juan opened his top drawer and removed a sheet of paper.

The moment the CIA bitch left his office yesterday, Gonzalez had copied down she image she showed him: the omega symbol with the stick-figure drawing inside. He gazed at the paper for a moment, and then slapped it down on the desk with a loud *thump.* Maria jumped slightly in surprise.

"Does this look familiar to you?" He removed his hand from the paper and directed her attention to the symbol drawn on it.

"You know that it does."

"Would you care to guess where I obtained this?"

Maria shrugged. "I couldn't possibly."

Juan leaned back in his chair, his hands clasped together, fingers steepled. He stared at the young woman he had grown to love.

The silence lingered. Maria stood quietly. Expectantly, but not nervously.

At last he spoke. "Have you visited Washington, DC recently?"

"Why do you ask?"

"You *know* why I am asking."

Maria shrugged. "Yes," she said simply, no trace of apology—or of regret—in her tone.

"Would you mind explaining to me why your focus has become so unclear that you are murdering executives in a small technology company we could not begin to care about?" Juan was doing his best to remain calm, but he could hear his voice tightening with rage. He had had plenty of time to contemplate the ramifications of the redhead's visit yesterday and none of them were good.

"Could not begin to care about?" Maria raised her voice in an angry explosion that caught Juan off guard. "Maybe you have forgotten the people sacrificed by the United States at the Bay of Pigs, but I have not! I *can* not! I never knew my father thanks to that sacrifice!"

"Of course I have not forgotten. Nor will *I* ever forget. But seeking vengeance now, more than a quarter-century after the fact, will do nothing to accomplish our long-term goal of retaking Cuba. And, if you determined it was so necessary to blow up United States citizens *other than* Castro sympathizers, why National Circuit Corporation? What possible relevance could they have to the Bay of Pigs?"

"National Circuit Corporation supplied receivers for the GPS technology that was supposed to give the freedom fighters the edge they would need when the fighting got serious. It was supposed to allow commanders to coordinate troop movements. And if the tide of battle began to turn against our men—people like my father—it was supposed to aid in their retreat and allow them to escape the country safely."

Maria's voice was cold and hard, and she took a deep breath before continuing. "It was *supposed* to do all that. But in reality, it did none of the things the freedom fighters were promised it would do. There were not enough satellites airborne at the time to provide data quickly enough. The data that *was* provided to commanders lagged badly and was unreliable. And people died because of it. Good people like my father, people who should never have been sacrificed.

"That is why I took action against NCC, because the passage of time has done nothing to ease the burden of guilt they, and others like them, share for the atrocity that was the Bay of Pigs invasion. I do not regret for one second taking the action I did. I would do it again."

Juan Gonzalez stared at the young woman who had become like a daughter to him. He had heard the stories of everything that had gone wrong during the invasion, of commanders desperate for updated GPS coordinates, some of which would not come for hours and some of which would never come. Of GPS receivers that failed seemingly for no reason, leaving soldiers trapped with no clue as to the whereabouts of troop support and lifesaving medical assistance.

He had heard all the stories, many times. The failure of the new GPS technology was just one of many issues contributing to the disaster at the Bay of Pigs, and most of those who had participated in the attack and survived agreed that the GPS issue was a relatively minor one. Other failures were much more significant.

Obviously Maria Carranco had heard the stories as well, and obviously she did not concur with the general consensus. Or perhaps she had decided the retribution must start somewhere and was even now planning further attacks against others she had determined to be at fault.

Whatever, a terrible sadness clutched at Juan's heart as he listened to Maria's passionate defense of her actions. He had expected her to deny involvement, to claim her symbol had been misappropriated somehow, or to break down and cry when confronted with the evidence and ask forgiveness for allowing herself to get so far off-track.

None of those things had happened, however, and it was obvious none of those things was *going* to happen. Maria was neither ashamed nor regretful. Instead of offering excuses or begging for forgiveness, she stood calmly in front of his desk and nodded at the sheet of paper resting on its surface. "Who was the visitor that brought you the paper?"

Gonzalez considered how to proceed. His goal in arranging this meeting had been to frighten Maria, to intimidate her into ending her campaign of misplaced violence. It was too late to do anything about her destruction of NCC's corporate structure, but by the same token, Omega 7 was in no immediate danger, either.

By manipulating the beautiful red-haired CIA agent into going to Cuba, Juan had at the very least gained his organization valuable planning time, time he could use to determine how best to shift the agency's focus elsewhere. The agent would never escape Cuba alive, and with no way off the island it would only be a matter of time before she ended up in Fidel Castro's clutches.

Once *that* happened, the CIA—and by extension the rest of the U.S. government—would be far too preoccupied dealing with the public trial and subsequent execution of one of their covert operatives to waste much time worrying about a relatively small anti-Castro group in South Florida.

Juan figured that given the CIA's well-known reluctance to share information, even among other intelligence professionals, it was entirely possible no one left alive would even be aware of the link between Maria's clever little symbol of destruction and the Omega 7 organization. Director Aaron Stallings had sent the redheaded bitch to Miami but that didn't mean he had any actual operational knowledge of the case. The doomed agent had told him Stallings only sent her to speak with him because of his extensive knowledge of the workings of Castro's administration.

So the immediate danger posed by the CIA seemed to be past.

Still, Juan knew he had to be careful how he answered Maria's question. He could not afford to slip up and allow her to guess—or even to suspect—his prior involvement with the CIA. To do so would be to ensure his death, given her instability and her virulent hatred of all things American.

The safest course of action would be to put her and keep her on the defensive. He allowed his voice to become even chillier. "It was a young woman. A beautiful redhead. She was almost as beautiful as you. But she was incredibly dangerous. She was from the Central Intelligence Agency."

"CIA? Why would the CIA come here?"

"Isn't it obvious? They've tracked that little 'signature' you are so proud of back to you."

Maria blinked in surprise. "Tracked it to me? How?"

"How in the hell should I know? But the agent came here looking for *you*."

"Then why…"

"Why are you not in custody or dead?"

Maria nodded. She seemed to have lost her voice.

"Because I sent her running off in the wrong direction. I made her believe your 'signature' was a symbol belonging to someone else."

She shook her head in confusion. "Someone else? Who?"

Juan smiled. He was still angry at his protégé but allowed a bit of warmth to creep back into his tone. "General Antonio Polanco."

Maria's eyes widened as she considered the implications of what Juan had just said. "You don't mean to say she—"

"That's right," Juan interrupted, his grin widening. "She charged off to Cuba to confront the general. To apprehend or kill him. My men transported her in the boat exactly as they do you. The moment she walked away from the shoreline, they left her. I thought you of all people, given your history on the island, would appreciate the irony."

She shook her head in amazement. "But she will never…"

"That's right," Juan agreed. "She will never."

Maria's shoulders slumped in relief and Juan pressed his advantage, his voice growing cold again. "We dodged a bullet over the last two days. We could have lost everything thanks to your rash actions. You must stop your bombing campaign against U.S. defense-related companies immediately, at least until we have succeeded in driving Castro into the sea. Once that happens, feel free to do anything you want to the Americans. But for now we cannot risk a repeat of what happened here yesterday, do you understand, Maria?"

Her face flushed in anger and she clenched her fists. "I cannot agree to that," she hissed. "My father—"

Juan's fury erupted. "Your father would agree with *me!* Your father was a patriot who gave his life to get his country back! Your father would condemn any action that puts our ultimate goal at risk. I *know* how your father thought. I was as close to him as any man alive, and you never even met him!"

"Exactly," Maria said quietly, her voice strong and her eyes clear. "I never even met him."

25

Tracie stretched and yawned, rubbed the sleep out of her eyes and glanced blearily at her watch. Nearly three p.m. She had slept for more than six hours—an eternity for a covert operative in the middle of an assignment—but it didn't feel like it. Her body ached and her eyes wanted nothing more than to close, allowing her to drift off to sleep for *another* six hours.

But it wasn't going to happen. She had work to do. She rolled out of bed and stumbled to the shower, shocking herself awake under an ice-cold spray before adjusting the temperature of the water to a more comfortable level.

After watching Polanco lift off and turn toward Cuba this morning, Tracie had shrugged her backpack over her shoulder and set off in the direction of civilization. Twenty minutes of vigorous walking later she found herself at a franchise motel that looked as though its better days had never existed. The town in the Florida Keys was not Marathon, Islamorada, *or* Key Largo, but rather a small village whose name she forgot the moment she saw it on a chipped and weathered sign.

But it was large enough to support a motel, and that was all she cared about at that particular moment. Dingy stucco exterior walls covered a sagging, low-slung one-story structure badly in need of overhaul, if not demolition. The handful of cars scattered throughout the pockmarked parking lot told Tracie that finding a vacancy would not be a problem.

She entered and booked a room, a little surprised that the guy behind the desk—a middle-aged Hispanic man who looked as tired and rundown as the establishment—didn't even give her a second glance. She was dirty and exhausted, with no luggage and no companion, and the clerk never even batted an eye. In fact, he barely glanced at her, handing a room key across the desk with the bored expression of someone who would rather be somewhere else. Anywhere else.

Good. The last thing Tracie needed was to draw unwanted attention. She accepted the key and stumbled to her room, stripped down to her underwear and tumbled into bed. She fell asleep in minutes.

Now she showered and dressed. She wasn't thrilled to be pulling dirty clothes back on, but at the moment, hygiene was the least of her problems. She would buy a new outfit later while preparing for what would likely be a very busy night.

She hefted her backpack and left her room. Walked to the front desk where she paid the clerk—a different middle-aged Hispanic man who looked just as tired and just as rundown as last night's—and asked for directions to the nearest car rental agency.

The clerk counted her money, the first time a glimmer of interest had appeared in his eyes. "You need to rent a car?"

"That's right."

"How did you get here if you don't have a car?"

"Magic carpet. Now are you going to give me directions or not?"

The clerk made a point of running his eyes up and down her body. Tracie stood quietly, letting him have his moment, and then held his gaze when his eyes finally rose to meet hers. "Turn right out of the lot and there's a rental place about a quarter-mile north of here. It's hard to miss. I'm surprised you didn't fly over it on your magic carpet."

"Thanks," Tracie said, ignoring his comment and turning toward the door. There wasn't time for petty games. She had a lot of work to do.

26

The drive north to Miami took a little over an hour and a half. Although she had slept much of the day away and then wasted more time buying new clothes, Tracie didn't feel as though there was any real reason to hurry, other than her burning desire to reintroduce herself to Juan Gonzalez.

The trip was uneventful, and by seven-thirty Tracie found herself back in front of Santa Barbara Old Catholic Church, a stone's throw from *Noches Habana*. She cruised the neighborhood in her new rental, waiting for a parking spot to open up on the street. It had to be the right location: close enough to afford her a clear view of the bar's front entrance, but far enough away so Gonzalez—or anyone providing security for him—would not take notice of her.

After several minutes spent cruising Little Havana, Tracie watched as a rusted-out Honda Accord with a hideous lime-green paint job and fat whitewall tires pulled away from the curb in the perfect location. The Honda had been parked on a corner next to an alleyway, a couple of dozen feet away from the entrance to a mom and pop convenience store.

She spun the wheel and hit the gas and aced out a man in a massive pickup truck who had been gunning for the same spot. The driver stopped in traffic to glare at her but then drove away when the driver behind him honked at the delay.

Tracie smiled, pleased her patience had paid off. She settled into her seat, prepared for a long—and possibly fruitless—stakeout. Gonzalez might already have gone home, or he might never have been here at all today.

She didn't care. This was Juan Gonzalez's base of operations for Omega 7, she was sure of it. If he didn't show himself tonight he would do so tomorrow, or the next day, or the day after that.

It really didn't matter to Tracie how long it took.

She had a score to settle.

*   *   *

As it turned out, she didn't have to wait until tomorrow or the next day. She only had to wait a few hours.

The stakeout was boring, as stakeouts tended to be, and with nobody to share the duty it was mentally and physical tiring as well. Maintaining focus was critical, since diverting her attention, even for a moment, from *Noches Habana* would mean risking missing Gonzalez if he exited.

Of course, there was always the possibility she would miss him anyway—Tracie assumed the club must have a rear entrance, if only for deliveries and to satisfy fire regulations. But she doubted the big boss would use such an entrance. From her vantage point, she could see there was nothing back there but a narrow, trash-strewn alleyway just wide enough to accommodate a delivery truck.

And Gonzalez would have no reason to feel anything was amiss, which would be the only reason Tracie could think of why he would consider entering or leaving his business through a rear door. There was no way he could know Tracie was back in Miami. Undoubtedly he thought she was stuck in Cuba, either desperately running for her life or, more likely, being interrogated and tortured by Castro's thugs.

She felt her anger and resentment rising and tried to tamp it down. She'd been played for a fool by Juan Gonzalez; that much was true. The evidence was indisputable and obvious.

But that wasn't his fault; it was hers. She had taken unveri-fied intelligence from an unreliable source—Juan Gonzalez—at face value. For that matter, she should have known better than to blindly trust Aaron Stallings's information as well. She had accepted intel from both men without seriously questioning its authenticity, even in the face of her own nagging suspicion that something was off about it.

And it had nearly gotten her killed.

That will not happen again.

*   *   *

The sidewalks remained crowded with pedestrians well into the evening. Almost no one took notice of the young woman sitting alone in her car with the windows down. The sweltering Miami heat began gradually leaching away after sunset but the inside of the car remained uncomfortably warm.

One thing became evident quickly: *Noches Habana* was not a popular destination for Little Havana drinkers. Very few passersby paid any attention to the bar, most not giving it a second glance.

Seems odd, Tracie thought, *given that this is a Friday night.*

But maybe it wasn't so odd, after all. Maybe most of the locals knew what she had guessed shortly after entering the bar yesterday: *Noches Habana* wasn't a business in any traditional sense. It was little more than a front for Juan Gonzalez's Omega 7. The few drinkers she had seen during her visit inside the tavern yesterday were likely all organization members, and any strangers to make the mistake—tonight or any other night—of strolling into the place in search of a cold Cuban beer would be treated as rudely as Tracie had been, encouraged to leave, and then physically forced out if the slightly subtler initial message wasn't received.

After midnight, the crowds in Little Havana began to thin, and by the time one a.m. rolled around, they had dried up considerably. Tracie began to feel more conspicuous as the numbers of pedestrians diminished, but she was determined to continue her surveillance at least until closing time. She was far enough away from the bar that she felt reasonably confident she hadn't yet been made.

No one had exited and locked the doors, so *Noches Habana* was technically still open for business, although she would never have known it from the lack of activity. By one-thirty, Tracie was yawning constantly, and when two a.m. came and went with the lights still on inside *Noches Habana* and the neon sign advertising Bucanero Beer still flickering in the grimy window, she rubbed her eyes and decided that maybe the damned place was never going to close, maybe it was just going to stay open all night in defiance of Miami's liquor laws.

Two-fifteen.

Time to call it quits for the night.

She reached for the ignition to turn the key when two men trudged out of *Noches Habana* and began walking away from Tracie along the sidewalk. One of them she didn't recognize, but the other was the bartender she had tricked yesterday into bringing her to see Gonzalez.

Neither man bothered to stop and lock up the club, which meant there was at least one more person inside. Tracie guessed that person would be Juan Gonzalez. She breathed a sigh of relief that she hadn't yet abandoned her post, and resumed the stakeout. Her previous exhaustion was now just a memory, gone in a rush of adrenaline.

Moments later out came Gonzalez. He was dressed in a three-piece vested blue suit, the creases in his trousers sharp enough to slice paper. He looked like a banker leaving work after a long day at the office, not a Cuban revolutionary whose people Tracie theorized had been responsible for blowing up the entire executive structure of a small American corporation.

Juan Gonzalez turned a key in the lock, jiggled the knob, and then started off along the sidewalk in the same direction his compadres had gone just moments ago.

Tracie tracked his progress closely while gripping the key in the ignition. She had a decision to make: pull out onto the street and risk alerting Gonzalez to her presence—vehicular traffic was extremely light now and there would be no way to tail a pedestrian for more than a few dozen feet in a car without him becoming aware of her—or exit the rental and follow on foot and thus risk losing him if he climbed into a car and drove away.

She made her decision in a split second. The way Gonzalez was dressed, it was hard to imagine him living in this decidedly urban, lower-middle-class section of Miami. He struck her as a South Beach guy and if that was the case, his home would be too far from Little Havana to walk.

Plus, among the cars she had been watching throughout her surveillance was a black Cadillac Eldorado Biarritz convertible parked half a block north of *Noches Habana* that had sat empty and untouched since her arrival. It looked exactly like the kind of car Gonzalez might drive, and she was willing to bet it was his.

She turned the key and waited as the engine sputtered to life. Decided that if he continued past the Caddy and walked another block she would ease onto the street and attempt to follow by moving to the next cross street and turning, driving a block along Eleventh Avenue and then backtracking to Twelfth and—hopefully—reacquiring Gonzalez.

None of it was necessary. The man she suspected as being the leader of Omega 7 walked straight to the convertible. He veered off the sidewalk and passed behind the Caddy before stepping to the driver's side door. Slid a key into the door and dropped into the front seat. Then he started the car and pulled onto the now nearly empty Twelfth Avenue.

Tracie waited until Gonzalez had passed three city blocks. Then she eased away from the sidewalk and followed.

27

Tracie was wrong about Gonzalez. He didn't live in South Beach.

But he didn't live in Little Havana either, and she tailed the Cadillac carefully as it left Miami and headed south on I-95, merging onto the South Dixie Highway and then cruising into Coral Gables. Gonzalez exited the highway just north of the University of Miami and turned southeast toward the ocean.

Tracie was thankful the suspected Omega 7 leader was unaware of her escape from Cuba, because keeping him in sight if he was concerned about being followed would have been a tall order at this time of night and with this amount of traffic.

She was reasonably sure she hadn't been detected, though, because Gonzalez was not behaving like a man trying to lose a tail. He drove straight and true, maintaining a steady speed, not making any abrupt maneuvers nor attempting to backtrack. He was driving exactly like what he undoubtedly was: a tired man with nothing more on his mind than getting home and falling into bed.

The idea held some appeal to Tracie. The initial rush of adrenaline that swept over her when Gonzalez left *Noches Habana* had long since subsided and she found herself yawning and rubbing her eyes as she followed the Cadillac. Not knowing how long it would be before the man decided to stopp wasn't helping, either.

The urban sprawl of Coral Gables began to thin and she was forced to drop back even farther to avoid detection. Losing Gonzalez was becoming a distinct possibility, and she almost missed it when he hit the brakes and turned, seeming to disappear into thin air.

Even from as far behind the Caddy as she was, Tracie knew immediately he hadn't turned onto another road. This section of Coral Gables, a wide, well-maintained stretch of pavement paralleling the shoreline, featured massive mansions set back from the road, accessed by serpentine driveways, most protected from the rest of civilization by fences, walls and gates.

Gonzalez was home. Tracie would have bet money on it.

She slowed and pulled onto the sandy verge. Squinted into the darkness and tried to determine exactly where the car had disappeared. Waited to see if Gonzalez would reverse course and appear again. It didn't seem likely, but there was no reason to risk detection now.

One minute went by, and then two, and Tracie began to feel exposed sitting in an idling car on the side of a deserted road at nearly three a.m. If a police cruiser should come along it would result in a lot of questions she wouldn't—and probably *couldn't*—answer. She killed the headlights and eased down on the gas and the car crept forward until reaching the spot where Gonzalez had turned.

Her guess had been right. It was a driveway. But it was easy to miss unless you were looking for it, and she assumed that was by design. A man in Juan Gonzalez's position undoubtedly had enemies, both inside and outside the United States. He wouldn't want to make it too easy for those enemies to find him.

Like most of the other homes in this area, the massive structure was separated from its neighbors by acres of dense woodland surrounding acres of lush, emerald-green lawn so lovingly maintained it looked exactly like felt covering the world's largest pool table.

But this home was different from all the others. First, the exterior grounds were lit up brighter than Tracie's old high school football field for a Friday night game. Floodlights and spotlights were omnipresent, leaving not a single spot uncovered.

The glare was unrelenting, and her first thought was to wonder how the neighbors felt about it. Then it occurred to her that the Juan Gonzalez she had met, the man who had sent her to Cuba and then abandoned her to a horrific fate without so much as a second thought, wouldn't likely waste much time worrying about the opinions of his neighbors.

The other difference between this home and the surrounding ones was that while Gonzalez had constructed a fence around his property like nearly all of the other homeowners, his looked more like what might encircle a maximum-security prison than a decorative but useful security measure.

Where the other properties featured brick or granite fences designed to appear unobtrusive and to blend into the surroundings as much as possible, Gonzalez's looked stark and intimidating: ten-foot-high reinforced chain link fencing, complete with a remotely operated steel rollaway gate preventing unwanted entry to anyone not in possession of a tank.

Anyone expecting access would have to enter a code on a keypad mounted next to the gate, or pick up a handset mounted next to the keypad and request to be buzzed in from the mansion.

But Tracie wasn't worried about entering access codes, and she wasn't expecting to be buzzed in, either. During her shopping spree earlier this afternoon, she had purchased a number of items with the potential to be useful. One of those items was a sturdy bolt cutter, which she had stashed away in the trunk of the car and which she knew would be more than sufficient to snip through the chain links when she was ready to enter the property.

She checked the road ahead through the windshield and behind through the mirror. It was dark and empty in both directions. She spun the wheel and made the ninety-degree turn onto Gonzalez's property, pulling just far enough ahead to render her car nearly invisible from the road.

Then she shut it down and left it blocking the drive. This would serve a dual purpose: preventing her prey from leaving by car until she decided he could leave, and giving her at least the possibility of making a quick exit should she need to. If all went according to plan, she would not be here very long, hopefully returning before the rental was towed away by Coral Gables police.

And if things *didn't* go according to plan, Tracie had the feeling a car blocking Gonzalez's driveway was going to be the least of her problems.

She picked up her backpack and padded behind the car to the

trunk. Lifted the lid and felt around in the dark until locating the bolt cutters. She eased the trunk lid closed and disappeared into the brush, following the chain-link fence along the edge of the road until reaching the point where it turned ninety degrees and proceeded east, presumably along the edge of Gonzalez's property. As she moved she kept a close eye on the mansion, whose interior seemed mostly dark, in stark contrast to the searing brightness of the exterior grounds.

As she picked her way along the fencing, moving away from the road and toward the shoreline, Tracie contemplated the likelihood that Gonzalez maintained an alarm system or employed armed security. It would seem prudent for a man in his position, and she slowed her already cautious pace to a near crawl, observing as much as she could about the property while she moved forward.

The prospect of breaking into the man's home cold, with no backup and no preparation, was not a comforting one. Soaking in every detail she could manage might spell the difference between surviving the night and ending up chopped into shark bait and tossed into the Atlantic.

Plus, she wanted to allow Gonzalez time to fall asleep. An exhausted man awakened from a deep sleep, disoriented and afraid, would be much easier to control than a fully alert one, and Juan Gonzalez had already proven himself a clever and capable opponent.

By now, she had reached a point she guessed to be roughly half-way between the roadway and the southeastern edge of Gonzalez's property, which terminated at a small sandy beach. Tracie could hear waves crashing in the distance with hypnotic repetition. The palm grove separating Gonzalez's property from his neighbor's was thick and the brush heavy, and she thought this would be as a good a place to breech the fence as she was likely to find.

She slipped her backpack off her shoulder and placed it quietly onto the ground. She worked quickly, slipping a pair of surgical gloves out of the backpack and pulling them on. Any fingerprints she inadvertently left behind would lead nowhere—she was unidentifiable through standard fingerprinting methods by law enforcement or other government agencies—but Tracie didn't believe in taking unnecessary risks. Leaving no fingerprints behind was a far better option than leaving them behind and assuming they could never be traced to her.

Gloves on, she lifted the bolt cutters and snipped through the chain links, moving from the ground up, one after the other, grateful for the roar of the waves, which almost totally overwhelmed the metallic *ting, ting, ting.*

In less than a minute, she had opened up a gash in the fence big enough to slip through. She wiped down the bolt cutters and placed them on the ground, reluctant to leave them behind but mindful of the need for speed and agility. The tool was big and heavy and would only slow her down if she brought it along. Hopefully she wouldn't need it later.

Once inside the fence, she pulled the links back together as carefully as she could. The hole would be obvious to anyone patrolling the fence line, but hidden as the fence was in the middle of the trees, she guessed such a patrol would not take place until daylight, as even the megawatt brilliance of the lighting on Gonzalez's grounds mostly failed to penetrate these woods.

She eased toward the lawn. As she moved, Tracie reviewed the basics of her plan, such as it was. She assumed the bedrooms were on the second floor of the mansion—it was a little disconcerting how much the house resembled General Polanco's—but before moving upstairs she wanted to enter the house on the ground floor and clear every room.

Work methodically.

Eliminate surprises.

By now she had made it nearly all the way through the forested area. She stopped just short of the lawn and focused her attention on the mansion's exterior. Her hope was that she might be able to determine which of the upstairs windows opened into Gonzalez's bedroom. It didn't seem likely she would be able to—the rooms behind the windows were dark and still—but without having any clue as to the home's layout, Tracie was desperate for any information she could gain that would help her avoid entering completely blind.

The home was massive, and the bulk of it was now mostly between Tracie and ocean, dampening the roar of the crashing waves.

That was a good thing.

Because the sound of a twig snapping underneath a combat boot brought her attention immediately back into focus.

She had company.

Tracie stopped, freezing in her tracks, grateful she had thus far elected to remain hidden. The footfalls were measured and steady, the sound of a man on routine patrol unaware that he was not alone. They were not the furtive steps of a man stalking his prey.

Which meant that *Tracie* could become the stalker.

Orienting herself to the sentry's location would not be easy. The ceaseless rumble of Atlantic Ocean breakers, combined with her lack of familiarity with the estate, made tracking him solely by sound nearly impossible.

She crept forward a few feet. The movement added to the risk of being seen but provided her with a clearer view, something she desperately needed.

Her gaze swept right to left and then she saw him. A security guard, dressed entirely in military-style camouflage clothing and combat boots, was indeed making his rounds. His back was to her and he moved slowly, bored and tired.

They had to have passed within a few feet of each other. It was a miracle the guard hadn't seen or heard her, and she cursed herself for allowing him to get so close before realizing he was there. Had things gone a little differently, she would already be captured or dead.

The man continued his patrol and Tracie eased closer to the well-maintained lawn. The guard's patrol route would likely take him to the electric gate near the end of Gonzalez's driveway.

Where Tracie had parked her rental car.

If he were permitted to get close enough to the road to see that car, her plan would be blown sky high. She would still probably be able to escape, but catching Gonzalez with his guard down would become impossible.

There was no time for stealth. No time to consider alternatives to direct action. If Gonzalez looked out his window into the brightly lit front yard, or if a second guard was somewhere in the area, she would be caught, maybe even killed.

But she had no choice. She needed to act now.

She dropped her backpack and broke cover, sprinting parallel to the driveway, angling toward the sentry in an all-or-nothing attempt to cut him off before he rounded the bend in the driveway. She drew her weapon as she ran. Concentrated on moving as quietly as possible for as long as possible. It was critical she get closer to him before he realized he was being ambushed.

Twenty-five feet behind him.

Twenty.

Fifteen.

Then he heard her. He dropped into a defensive crouch as her one hundred five pounds raced along the damp grass.

She was still too far away. She wasn't going to make it.

The guard spun to face the threat and reached for the holster at his right hip. He fumbled for the snap.

Missed.

Fumbled again and this time released his weapon and began to draw down on Tracie.

But she had never stopped running, hadn't even slowed, and now she lowered her shoulder and plowed into the much bigger, stockier man like a runaway freight train.

Her shoulder connected with his gut and she heard the muffled "Uhhh" as the air whooshed out of his lungs. Then they crashed onto the grass, tumbling and sliding, Tracie already scrabbling to regain her feet, her Glock still held firmly in her right hand.

The guard hadn't had time to brace himself, and his gun was jarred out of his grip. It tumbled through the air end over end and plunked to the ground a good ten feet from the struggling adversaries.

Tracie staggered but smashed the butt of her weapon against the side of the man's face. He was struggling to catch his breath, unable to scream for help, and his head snapped to the side.

He offered up a weak roundhouse right in return, the blow glancing harmlessly off Tracie's shoulder.

Then she hit him again and he dropped straight down. He crumpled to the ground and lay still, and Tracie stood over him panting from exertion and shaking from the effects of adrenaline.

She slowed her breathing and held her gun in both hands, scanning three hundred sixty degrees for another guard, or for a dog, or for any sign of further trouble.

Nothing. The property was silent. No alarms sounded, no surprised shouts were raised, no gunshots rang out.

The security guard had been patrolling alone.

Tracie bent over the man carefully, alert for any sign that he might be playing possum. But he was down and out, bleeding from a pair of gashes on the left side of his face.

His pulse was strong, though. He would be fine.

She shifted her attention back toward the front of Gonzalez's house. She was far too exposed here; it was essential she move the unconscious guard immediately.

But he was big. And he was stocky. And he was out like a light. Moving him would be like moving a two hundred-forty pound sack of bricks.

Tracie sighed deeply and grabbed the guard by his combat boots. Then she began dragging him across the grass toward the scrub brush at the edge of the property.

28

The moment they were out of sight of the mansion, Tracie frisked the guard. In addition to his pistol, the man had been armed with a backup revolver in a shoulder holster. She removed it from its holster and placed both weapons on the ground a dozen feet away.

On his left hip was a walkie-talkie, which she removed and placed next to the weapons. Hanging off one of his belt loops on the same hip was a small metal ring with a set of keys. These she took and pocketed.

She unhooked the man's belt and pulled it off the waist of his camouflage trousers. Then she lifted him by the armpits and dragged his body up against the base of a solid-looking palm tree whose trunk was perhaps a foot in diameter. The man was still unconscious, but his eyelids were fluttering and he was beginning to moan softly as she wrapped his arms around the trunk.

There you go, she thought. *Now you're a tree hugger. Literally.* She brought his wrists together and wrapped the belt around them several times, binding them together behind the tree. Then she buckled the belt and gave it a tug, trying to pull it loose.

It was secure. The guard wouldn't be going anywhere when he awoke, which, from the looks of things, would be soon. His eyes were open now, but they remained glazed and unfocused.

Tracie knew he would awaken with a massive headache, but she knew also that a headache would be unlikely to prevent him from screaming for help.

Moving quickly, she unlaced his combat boots. She pulled them off and threw them deeper into the brush. She slipped his socks off his feet—they were soaked with sweat and she grimaced as she worked—and then stuffed them into the unfortunate guard's mouth.

He gagged and coughed and began complaining, and while the exact wording of his complaint was indecipherable, his meaning was crystal clear. Tracie ignored him and pulled her own belt off her jeans. She duplicated the makeshift bindings she had constructed for his wrists, wrapping the belt around his mouth, then wrapping it a second time and buckling it behind his head.

She was forced to pull it tighter than she would have liked in order to buckle the belt on the first hole, and the man's face reddened in panic as the gag was jammed deep into his mouth. He could still breathe, though, and that was all she cared about. She had a few questions to ask her prisoner, and it would be a shame if he suffocated before she could get around to it.

With the guard neutralized, Tracie worked her way through the underbrush to where she had dropped her backpack. It lay on the edge of the lawn, plain as day in the glare of the floodlights, and potentially deadly to Tracie should anyone look out a front window in the Gonzalez mansion. She had to move it immediately.

Once she had grabbed the bag and disappeared back into the woods, she began to breathe a little easier. She hurried to where her immobilized prisoner lay, and as she approached, the man glared at her, his arms wrapped awkwardly around the trunk of the palm tree.

There was no time to waste. Without any idea of the guard's patrol schedule or whether he was working with a partner, it was impossible to know if he might have been expected to check in with someone by now. The worst-case scenario would be that the young man had nearly finished his patrol when Tracie ambushed him, and another guard or guards were even now being dispatched to find out what had happened to him.

Tracie dropped her backpack next to the man. She knelt and placed the barrel of her weapon against the uninjured side of his face. He squeezed his eyes shut, his entire body tensing as he feared he was about to die.

She leaned in close, the act oddly intimate, as if she was about to kiss him. Then she placed her lips against his ear and whispered, "I'm going to remove your gag. If you scream, it will be the last thing you ever do. You'll be dead in less than a second. Nod if you understand."

The man—now that she had had a chance to study him, Tracie thought "boy" might be a better description, because despite his considerable size and bulk, his face had the fuzzy-cheeked look of a teenager—nodded instantly and enthusiastically.

She jammed the gun into his cheek hard and said, "Don't forget what I said," her voice knife-edge sharp.

She double-checked the belt that secured the guard's wrists to the tree, giving it a sharp yank with her left hand while keeping the gun trained on her prisoner with her right.

Still tight.

Satisfied, she reached behind the guard's head, unbuckling and then unwinding the belt. She plucked the socks out of his mouth and dropped them onto the ground.

Then she lifted her weapon and replaced it against the man's cheek. "What's your name?"

"Andres."

"How many other guards are here tonight, Andres?" she whispered.

"None," he said. His English was heavily accented but understandable.

"Bullshit," she hissed, jamming the barrel of the gun against his face, scraping his cheek and pushing hard enough to leave a bruise.

"I swear!" he said, squeezing his eyes closed again. The already nervous man began breathing heavily, sharp gasps causing his entire body to shudder. "We have two-man crews during the day, but at night just one."

"How often do you do foot patrols?"

"Every two hours, give or take."

"Who are you expected to check in with, and when is that supposed to happen?"

The guard swallowed heavily. It was clear he wanted to give Tracie answers that would satisfy her, and just as clear he didn't know what would accomplish that goal here. "Ch-check in? What do you mean?"

"Isn't there someone you report to when you've finished your patrol? What if you encounter a problem? Who do you notify?"

"Señor Gonzalez says that if we run into a problem, we are to handle it ourselves. If we are not able to do so, we are to notify him by walkie-talkie. But that is to be done only as a last resort." The words came tumbling out quickly.

"So no one else is here with you tonight?"

"No. There is no one." The frightened young man shook his head for emphasis, causing the barrel of Tracie's gun to scrape up his cheek even more. "I'm alone until my relief comes at seven."

There was no real reason to believe him, but Tracie did just the same. He was a kid, untrained and terrified. It was obvious Gonzalez maintained security at his home not because he was truly concerned about threats but rather to feed his ego.

Any man seriously worried that he might be a target—especially a man in Gonzalez's position and in possession of his obvious wealth—would never abide this type of shoddy security arrangement. He would pay the going rate for professionals, not hire kids who looked as though they should be asking their date to the movies on a Friday night.

Tracie glanced back toward the mansion. She couldn't see it through the brush, but the glare of the spotlights was visible over the tops of the trees. She turned back toward the security guard. "Does the house have an alarm system?"

He blinked in confusion. "Alarm system? Why would Señor Gonzalez need an alarm system when he has armed security?"

You see how well that worked out for him. Tracie bit back the reply and moved on to her next question. "Who else is inside that house besides Gonzalez?"

"I do not know."

"How can you not know? Were you sleeping on duty, Andres?"

A look of wounded indignation flitted across the guard's face. Under different circumstances it would have been funny. "Of course not. I would never…"

"Then answer the question. Is anyone else in that house with Gonzalez?"

"Probably," he said, "but I cannot say for sure."

Tracie felt a flash of annoyance. This was taking too long.

"What's that supposed to mean?"

"Señor Gonzalez has a girlfriend who usually stays with him. She is probably there now, but I do not know for certain. I have not seen her come or go since the start of my shift. There is another woman who lives here as well, but I have not seen her in days."

"Isn't that the sort of thing you should know? Weren't you briefed on the status of the occupants by the guard you were relieving?"

Andres shook his head miserably. "I forgot to ask," he admitted. Tears began to fill his eyes. "I was not expecting any trouble."

Tracie felt badly for the kid. He had obviously been hired and then given only the most rudimentary training. Had been handed a gun and told to protect the very important Señor Juan Gonzalez and his family. Had been put in a position of risk by a man who didn't give a damn about the fact that not only was he utterly unprepared to face that risk, he wasn't even *aware* of the risk.

She shook her head in disgust at the thought.

Andres misinterpreted her action and his eyes widened. "I swear to you, everything I said is the truth. Please, I do not want to die."

"You're not going to die tonight, Andres," she said, reaching down and picking his socks up off the ground. "You're going to have an uncomfortable, unhappy night, but you're not going to die unless you do something extremely stupid."

"I am not going to do anything stupid," he said. "I promise you."

"Good. But I'm sure you'll understand if I don't just take your word for it, either."

He began shaking his head. "I will not scream, I swear, you do not need to..."

Tracie timed it perfectly, shoving the socks back into the terrified guard's mouth while the words were tumbling out. She pushed them in tightly and although he continued to protest, his voice once again became muffled and unintelligible.

"I'm sorry," she said, surprised by the fact that she actually meant it. "But I can't take the chance that you're lying to me, Andres. For what it's worth, though," she added, "I do believe you."

She grabbed the belt and began winding it around his head

once more. He struggled, fiercely at first, and then seemed to realize the futility of the effort and sagged against the tree. All the fight seemed to go out of him at once.

Tracie secured the belt tightly and then gave the guard a reassuring squeeze on his shoulder.

Then she got her things together and began making her way toward the house.

29

Dealing with the overmatched security guard had taken time Tracie was reluctant to sacrifice and had involved exposing herself to greater risk than she was generally comfortable with while working alone, but overall she was pleased with the result. Rather than going into the house totally blind, she now had at least a small amount of intel with which to work.

Assuming, of course, her new friend Andres was telling the truth.

Given the fact that he was trussed up less than one hundred feet away, unarmed and helpless, and with the understanding she could return at any time and put two bullets in his head, she was confident he had been as straightforward with her as she had any right to expect.

Getting into the home would be a simple matter now that she possessed a key, but she wasn't about to take anything for granted. There was no way to totally eliminate the possibility of walking into a trap, but she could do everything possible to lessen that risk.

Which meant that first she needed to verify the guard's claim that he was working alone. She eased past the northwestern corner of Gonzalez's home, taking her time, keeping the screen of scrub brush between herself and the brightly lit yard. When she reached the southwest corner she stopped and scanned the area behind the home.

Like Polanco's mansion, the beachfront property had been set back from the Atlantic Ocean a sufficient distance to minimize the risk of flooding during hurricane season, but not so far that the occupants didn't receive the benefit of a breathtaking view. Waves crashed onto a small, private beach no more than one hundred feet from the back door at high tide.

The house had been constructed in an enviable location. Despite the heavily populated surrounding area, it had the feel of a secluded estate, with the ocean knocking at the door to the south and a thick growth of trees and brush on the other three sides.

None of this mattered to Tracie Tanner at the moment. She was focused on a small structure at the edge of the property, halfway between the main house and the beach.

It looked like an oversized shed, and probably was. Undoubtedly, this building was where the estate's lawn mowing and landscaping equipment was stored. But it bothered Tracie that she couldn't see a guardhouse. There should be somewhere Andres and his security guard buddies could park their butts while waiting to patrol the property.

She supposed there might be an area of the house dedicated to the security staff—certainly the place was big enough for it—but based on what she had seen of Juan Gonzalez, fraternizing with the hired help didn't seem to be his style.

Either way, she was going to have to clear the building before entering the main house. Approaching the mansion without doing so would mean exposing her back to a potential threat, and prudence—not to mention self-preservation—dictated she ensure it was empty.

She continued along the edge of the underbrush until reaching a point diagonal to the southwest corner of the building. She was very near the water now, and the pounding of the waves onto the shore provided excellent cover for any noise she might make during her approach.

Also, while there would be no way to cross the open portion of yard toward the structure without making herself visible to at least one window, coming at it from the rear should—theoretically, at least—offer the greatest chance of remaining unseen. Any security personnel inside the building *should* have the majority of his attention focused in the opposite direction: toward the house.

She crouched in the underbrush, remaining perfectly still,

watching the outbuilding with the patience of a cat hunting a bird. Like the rest of the estate's exterior, the shed—or whatever it was—was lit up like a Christmas tree. Lights shone through each of its windows, and she watched through them for any sign of activity.

After five minutes with nothing, she decided it was time to move. She rose out of her crouch, gun drawn, and moved to the edge of the underbrush. Broke cover and sprinted toward the building, tensing for a shouted challenge, or worse, a gunshot that would knock her off her feet.

But nothing came, and seconds later she pressed her back against the side wall. The sound of the waves breaking over the sand made it feel like the water was practically lapping at her feet, although it was still a good fifteen to twenty feet away.

She waited for a moment, getting her breathing under control, and then crept along the rear wall to the nearest window.

Paused when she reached the side of it.

And then eased along the frame until she could peer inside.

There were no security guards monitoring closed-circuit footage of the property. No command center with a second sentry, prepared to spring into action and shoot Tracie in the back the moment she approached Gonzalez's home.

It was a simple storage shed, filled not just with gardening and lawn care supplies, but also with various leisure toys and watercraft: a pair of Jet Skis, an inflatable boat that looked as though it might be similar to the one Gonzalez's man had used to bring Tracie ashore outside Havana.

She leaned against the side of the shed, grateful for the knowledge she was truly alone out here and would not have to neutralize a second guard before entering Juan Gonzalez's palatial estate.

But this was no time to relax. She would be walking into an unknown situation with no backup and precious little intel. She breathed deeply and turned toward the mansion.

It was time to get some answers.

30

Tracie had broken into more buildings than she could recall over the course of her career. Armories, government offices, military barracks, private homes. Most had been in and around Russia and various Soviet satellites. None had been as easy to access as this one.

She took her time before entering, examining every window at the rear of the house for anything that might indicate Gonzalez and/or his girlfriend or other resident—who may or may not be inside—were still awake and wandering around the interior.

In contrast to the home's exterior grounds, which had been lit up so brightly it felt like midday, the inside appeared mostly dark. A couple of lamps had been left on in different locations, but her surveillance revealed no signs that anyone was awake.

With nothing left to learn from the outside, Tracie moved through the lights to the back door. Stealth would be impossible, given the lack of cover and the unrelenting brightness, so she didn't bother trying to achieve it. She walked calmly but at a brisk pace, reaching the door in seconds. Then she pulled Andres's key ring from the top of her backpack and inserted the keys, one after the other, into the lock until she found the one that would open the door.

The lock turned with a barely perceptible *click*. Gonzalez would have had to be standing just on the other side of the door to hear it, but Tracie winced anyway, her body tensing. After a moment it became apparent Gonzalez *wasn't* just on the other side of the door and she slipped inside.

The house was dimly lit and deathly silent. She moved through the first floor quickly. Thanks to her impromptu interrogation of Security Guard Andres, Tracie expected to encounter no one on the ground floor and did not. In a matter of minutes she was ready to move upstairs.

*   *   *

Tracie found him in the master bedroom at the end of a long hallway. Gonzalez lay on his back, snoring quietly through his open mouth. A young woman, much younger than Gonzalez, lay on her side next to him, one arm flung over his chest.

Both were sleeping on top of the bedcovers on this warm, humid night. The woman's short nightgown had bunched up around her waist, revealing more of her than Tracie had any desire to see, especially since the girlfriend had chosen not to wear underwear to bed.

Gonzalez's seeming obsession with driving away the darkness was just as apparent in his bedroom as everywhere else on his estate. A pair of nightlights, one on each side of the room, provided a soft illumination that was more than enough to allow Tracie to see clearly.

She slipped her backpack off her shoulder and set it quietly onto the floor.

Padded to the bed.

Leaned down over Gonzalez.

Placed the barrel of her gun inside the sleeping man's mouth.

And then she *shoved* it hard, pushing his head into the pillow.

His eyes flew open and he coughed and gagged and sputtered. A second's worth of sleep-addled confusion showed in his eyes, followed by the shock of sudden recognition.

Tracie's sudden, violent movement with her gun woke the sleeping woman next to Gonzalez and almost instantly she began to scream. The sound was sharp and panicked, a quick yelp that sounded almost like the bark of a small dog, and then she sucked in a breath to scream again, and Tracie leaned down until her face was almost touching Gonzalez's.

"Shut her up," she said, her voice intense. *"Now."*

She leaned back and removed her gun from his mouth and he turned to his girlfriend.

"Enough!" he said, and the girl stopped screaming in mid-breath. She simply closed her mouth and all sound ceased, although the redness in her face and the shaking of her body made clear that her terror at awakening to discover a woman with a gun in the bedroom had not begun to abate.

The girlfriend began sliding toward the side of the bed, kicking at the covers, desperate to escape the threat. Her eyes remained glued to the gun with the feral expression of a caged animal.

Her feet hit the floor and she stood and backed away, but Tracie kept the gun trained on Gonzalez. She was certain that the second she directed her attention away from the man he would make a play for her weapon. Based on what she had seen and learned of the man first-hand, she doubted he would let a small matter like his girlfriend potentially getting shot and killed stop him from trying to save himself.

"That's far enough," she said, without even glancing at the young woman. "Stop right there."

The girlfriend kept moving, backing along the bedroom wall. Tracie had no idea where she thought she was going, since to get out of the room she would have to reverse course and walk past the gun she was trying so determinedly to escape, but she had had enough.

She was losing control of the situation and she had to turn things around.

She pivoted, moving quickly, turning the gun toward the girlfriend.

Then she fired.

A slug thudded into the wall and almost before it did, Tracie had returned her gun to its original position, aimed squarely at Juan Gonzalez of Omega 7.

All movement stopped, the girlfriend frozen in fear. "You shot me," she said, her voice a mixture of indignation and shock. "You actually shot me."

"No," Tracie corrected. "I shot *near* you. That's a key distinction, and one you'll learn about first-hand if you try to move again."

The girlfriend crinkled her forehead. "What?"

"Explain it to her," she told Gonzalez, her gun never wavering.

The man glared at her but directed his words to the frightened woman standing near the bed. "If you move again she'll shoot you in the head."

Tracie shook her head. "In the heart."

"In the heart," Gonzalez repeated.

Color rose in the girlfriend's face and she blurted, "Well, then *do* something! This is—"

"Enough!" Gonzalez shouted the word this time and once more the girlfriend shut her mouth instantly, although the look on her face made clear there was plenty more she wanted to say.

"You," Gonzalez said to Tracie, his eyes glittering and cold. "How did you—"

"Awww," she said, smiling tightly. "You remembered. Did you miss me?"

"How did you—"

Her voice turned cold. "That's not important right now. Let's try to focus, shall we, Juan? What's important is that you lied to me, and if you don't start setting the record straight in, oh, let's say three seconds, I'm going to start shooting, and guess who's going to be the first to eat a bullet?"

Gonzalez didn't answer and she said, "I'll give you a hint. It's not going to be Little Miss Victoria's Secret over there."

There was a short delay, during which nothing happened.

Nobody spoke. Nobody moved.

Then Gonzalez said, "What do you mean, I lied? I don't know what you are talking about."

"Come on, Juan, you can do better than that."

"You came charging into my office, ranting and raving about Castro murdering American citizens, and about me being an expert in the workings of the Cuban government. *You* came to *me* for help, remember?"

"All true," Tracie admitted. "And yet you sent me to Havana on a wild goose chase, knowing I'd likely never survive the night. And then, on the off chance I *did* survive, you had your men abandon me on the island."

Gonzalez affected an innocent look. Tracie had to admit, he was one cool customer; to be able to remain so calm and collected with the business end of a 9mm pistol pointed at his face was a rare gift.

"I only gave you what you asked for," he said, conveniently ignoring her point about being left in Cuba to die.

"But all the while, you knew Castro wasn't responsible for the murders at NCC, didn't you? You knew it because *you* were responsible."

"I don't deny giving you what you wanted—a ride to Havana. But me, responsible for killing the executive staff at National Circuit Corporation? Ridiculous."

She rapped the gun against the side of Gonzalez's head and said, "Don't play games, Juan. We're well past that point. I saw your little Omega symbol with the funky-looking stick figures inside it, *in Havana.* Care to guess where in Havana? Oh, wait. You don't need to guess, do you? Because Omega 7 was responsible, just like your organization was responsible for the NCC killings."

"That symbol doesn't prove the Castro government wasn't responsible."

"Oh, really?" Tracie scoffed. "You're telling me Castro sent a team over here to wipe out NCC after cleverly bombing more than a half-dozen of his own office buildings in order to build an air-tight alibi? You know, just in case we came sniffing around Havana? Is that really what you expect me to believe?"

Gonzalez didn't bother replying. Apparently even he realized how ridiculous his story sounded.

"Now," Tracie continued. "I know that—"

Out of the corner of her eye, she noticed the girlfriend beginning to shuffle backward away from the bed, and she bit off her sentence. Instead, she said, "Victoria's Secret girl, get your ass into this bed next to your lying boyfriend. Do it now, or the next shot I take is going to go right through you."

The girlfriend froze and Tracie said, *"Now!"* She barked it out with authority and the girl moved slowly, reluctantly, toward the bed. It was clearly the last place in the world she wanted to be. She climbed in and sat rigid, as far away from Tracie and the gun as she could get and still be on the bed.

"Where were we?" Tracie said to Gonzalez, who didn't answer.

"Oh, I remember. We were discussing your story, or rather your flimsy excuse for a story. I know that *you* didn't personally travel to Havana and blow up buildings, just like *you* didn't personally fly up to Washington and decimate the ranks of National Circuit. You're too big and too important to sully your hands by doing the dirty work, isn't that right, Juan?"

Gonzalez's eyes had narrowed and he was watching her closely, but still he said nothing.

"So what I want to know," Tracie continued, "is who *did* do the dirty work?"

The leader of Omega 7 remained silent.

"I'll help you out. I know it's a woman. It's a young woman, and pretty. Not in a slutty way like Victoria's Secret girl, here," she gestured at the girlfriend with her gun before returning it to bear on Gonzalez, "but in a sick, psycho, slaughtering-innocent-civilians way."

A flicker of surprise passed across his eyes and was gone in an instant. Tracie was watching closely for it, though, and didn't miss it. She had known—or at least, strongly suspected—that the hooker who had poisoned Allan Nesbitt was involved in the murder plot against the upper ranks of NCC. But her suspicion had been that the young woman in Nesbitt's room was nothing more than an accomplice, maybe even a hired gun, who had been sent to take out Nesbitt while the bombing was being carried out simultaneously by a different perpetrator.

She was beginning to suspect that wasn't the case.

She was beginning to suspect the young woman who had killed Allan Nesbitt by poisoning his cocaine with strychnine was the key to everything.

And Tracie wasn't leaving until she got some answers.

31

"We're wasting time here," Tracie said, fully aware that that was exactly Gonzalez's intention. If he could stall her long enough for the cavalry to arrive—in the form of the day shift security detail, not to mention whatever cooks, maids and groundkeepers he employed—he knew full well she would have to either beat a hasty retreat or risk a prolonged standoff.

She could not allow that to happen.

"I want answers," she said. "But first, you're going to restrain Little Miss Victoria's Secret, and then you and I are going to have a heart-to-heart."

"Restrain her? How am I going to do that?"

"Easy," Tracie said. She indicated an antique stuffed chair in the corner. It was plushly upholstered in maroon and gold velour, with rosewood legs and arms carved in an intricate Oriental pattern. The chair wouldn't exactly function as a jail cell, but it looked fairly solid. She guessed it would be strong enough to hold Gonzalez's girlfriend, who was even smaller than Tracie. "She's going to sit in that chair and you're going to duct-tape her to it."

Gonzalez's face tightened in anger and Tracie said, "The alternative is I shoot her now. She may or may not survive if we go with that option, but I guarantee she won't be running off anywhere, which would serve my purposes perfectly. It's your choice, but make up your mind because my patience is running thin."

The Omega 7 leader blew out a breath in frustration. He turned his head toward his girlfriend. "Do as she says," he said in a low voice, refusing to look at Tracie.

"*What?*" Her voice was shaking from fear and rage. She clearly had not expected those particular words to come out of Gonzalez's mouth.

"You heard what she said. I don't see that we have many options, do you?"

The young woman mumbled something under her breath that Tracie could not make out, but she slid off the bed and began padding across the room. When she reached the chair, she slumped into it and sat with her arms crossed under her breasts, a petulant look on her face. Tracie thought she looked exactly like a spoiled child who had not gotten her way.

"Get over there and tape her down," she said to Gonzalez.

"How?" He spread his hands in confusion. "I do not have any duct tape."

"Don't worry about that. By the time you get over there, you'll have duct tape."

She stepped away from the bed, giving the man room to get up, holding her Glock in two hands trained center-mass on his body. She backed up to allow plenty of clearance and then flicked the gun at his girlfriend. *Get moving.*

He clambered out of bed and lumbered past. When he reached the chair, Tracie knelt down and unzipped her backpack. She rummaged around in it with one hand while keeping her gun aimed in the general direction of her two prisoners until finding her roll of tape. Then she pulled it out and tossed it to Gonzalez.

"Do it," she said. "And don't be stingy with the tape. I can always get more."

He dragged the process out as long as he could, not even bothering to try to disguise his intentions. Still, within minutes his girlfriend's arms and legs had been securely fastened to the chair. Even from across the room, Tracie could see she wouldn't be going anywhere.

"Now, move back to your bed. Get all the way in, feet off the floor, and face me."

"Worried that I will attack you and take your weapon away, little girl?"

"Sure. Good luck with that. Just shut up and do what I tell you."

Gonzalez shrugged. Climbed onto the bed. Then he looked at Tracie expectantly. "I'm not going to give you any information. I cannot tell you what I do not know."

"Oh, you have the information I want," she said grimly. "And you'll give it to me. The only question you have to consider is how much pain I shell out before you talk."

He smirked, but Tracie's voice had gone icy and hard, and she thought she saw a flicker of fear pass through his eyes.

Not that it mattered.

"Who is the Omega 7 member you dispatched to murder Allan Nesbitt and blow up NCC's leadership in the Washington Arms Hotel? And more importantly, where do I find her?"

Gonzalez ignored the question. He ignored Tracie. He sat on the bed and stared at the wall, gazing serenely over her shoulder. He looked like an addict who had just gotten his fix.

She cleared her throat. "Last chance. Where do I find the young woman who killed Allan Nesbitt and blew up the leadership of NCC?"

Gonzalez continued to ignore her. Instead, he pursed his lips and spit on his own bedroom floor.

"Don't try to say you weren't warned," Tracie said. She crossed the room to the chair into which Gonzalez had taped his girlfriend. She reached down without hesitation and snapped the little finger on the young woman's left hand.

She screamed shrilly, a short gasp more of surprise than of pain, and then she sucked in a breath and shrieked again as the pain kicked in, this time the sound long and loud, and Tracie waited for her to take another breath before speaking.

"Remember anything yet?" she asked coldly.

Shock filled Gonzalez's eyes. He had expected Tracie to attack him, not his girlfriend, and he reacted instinctively. He began moving off his bed to come after her.

She raised her weapon and pointed it at him. "That's far enough."

He hesitated and then stopped, one foot on the floor and one still on the bed.

"Get back up there." She had to raise her voice to be heard over the young woman sitting next to her, whose screams had become shriller and more intense.

"Now," she said when the Omega 7 leader had reluctantly complied. "Tell me what I want to know."

He looked as though he was about to answer, but then he clamped his mouth closed, glaring at Tracie with cold, dead eyes but saying nothing.

She shrugged and reached back down toward the girlfriend's left hand. The young woman's little finger was bent grotesquely to the side, as if pointing at Tracie in painful accusation. She felt a moment of guilt and shame. The girlfriend was obviously nothing more than a plaything for Gonzalez, and the thought of injuring her further made her feel sick.

But she had chosen her path and would follow it to the end.

She would get the information she needed.

One way or the other.

She reached for the woman's ring finger.

32

"*Wait!*" Elena Maldonado screamed as loudly and with more conviction than she had ever offered regarding anything in her life. The pain in her ruined pinky finger was immense; it throbbed and burned as if the attacker in their bedroom had set it on fire, and it was swelling and turning purple before her eyes.

And now the crazy bitch was about to break *another* finger.

And Juan-Bear was doing nothing to stop her. Her lover, so much bigger than the tiny woman who had broken into his home while they slept, simply sat on the bed and watched with dead shark eyes as the intruder prepared to disfigure Elena finger by finger.

And even through the pain in her finger, even through the fear and the panic and the confusion, even through all of that, Elena knew he would do nothing to stop the lunatic with the gun.

She knew he wouldn't stop the bitch because she knew who had done the things the bitch was talking about. Maria Carranco was the one who had committed those horrible acts up in Washington DC, and even though she had killed all those people without Juan-Bear's permission—without even his *knowledge* until afterward—he would never turn Maria over to this obsessed bitch.

Because that was how much he loved Maria Carranco. He loved Maria like a father, had raised her from a baby and watched over her after her real father died storming Cuba in the long-ago days following Castro's revolution. Maria Carranco, almost exactly the same age as Elena, was Juan-Bear's weakness.

It wasn't that Juan-Bear didn't care that Elena's bones were about to be broken one by one in front of his eyes. Elena knew that Juan-Bear cared for her; she knew he cared deeply.

But he cared for Maria more. He cared for Maria in a different way. She was the one person he would never betray. Maria, who had gone behind his back and caused all of this trouble.

Elena wasn't one to pay much attention to Omega 7 business—her roots were in Cuba, too, but she had been born in the United States and loved it here and could not imagine ever living on the tiny island south of Florida—but she had not been able to ignore Juan-Bear's enraged soliloquy two nights ago, when he came home ranting and raving about what Maria had done and how it could jeopardize everything he had spent more than two decades working to achieve.

And yet, even after all of that, Elena knew her Juan-Bear would never open his mouth, no matter how badly the crazy bitch injured her.

Or even if the crazy bitch killed her.

Juan-Bear simply would not talk.

So she would talk instead.

She screamed *"Wait!"* through the tears and the pain, and just like that everything stopped. The crazy bitch's hand hung suspended over hers, and Maria looked at Juan-Bear and he was staring at her with eyes opened wider than she had ever seen and a face beginning to flush red with anger, and she didn't care.

She didn't care, because *he* wasn't the one being maimed while completely helpless and innocent. If Juan-Bear wouldn't save her, she would save herself.

By opening her mouth and telling the crazy bitch what she wanted to know, Elena realized she would be forever ending her relationship with Juan Gonzalez. He would no longer be her cuddly Juan-Bear, but rather he would be an enemy who would more than likely seek vengeance against her in ways that would make The Crazy Bitch seem like a Girl Scout.

But that was a worry for another time. Right now she had to make the pain stop. She had to. "Maria Carranco," she gasped.

From across the room, Juan-Bear shouted "NO!" and leapt forward off the bed, swinging his right hand in a roundhouse punch aimed directly at the crazy bitch's face. He moved more quickly than Elena had even seen anyone move, his big body coiling and striking like a rattlesnake.

But as fast as Juan-Bear was, the crazy bitch was faster, turning and ducking under the punch as if the whole thing had been choreographed for a Hollywood movie. Juan-Bear's punch whistled harmlessly over the crazy bitch's head and then he was ripe for the taking, off-balance and defenseless, and the crazy bitch swung her gun hand, a quick, compact strike with the butt of her gun that connected solidly with Juan-Bear's temple, and Juan-Bear dropped face-first to the floor without a sound.

The crazy bitch was on him immediately, her moves smooth and effortless and breathtaking. She started to hit him again and thought better of it, instead restraining herself and checking the unconscious man's pulse.

It all happened so fast, Elena hadn't even had a chance to scream, and now she sucked in a breath to do so and the crazy bitch seemed to realize what was coming and she lifted her gun and pointed it straight into Elena's eyes and said, "Don't do it."

Her voice was quiet and cold and impatient, and Elena didn't know whether the crazy bitch would really shoot her in the face but she *did* know she wasn't anxious to find out. She clamped her mouth closed and shook her head in a silent entreaty to the crazy bitch to let her live, and after a moment when the gun hadn't fired she realized she was holding her breath.

She forced herself to breathe and relaxed just a little when the crazy bitch turned her attention back to Juan-Bear. The attacker reached for the duct tape and wound it around Juan-Bear's wrists, which she had pulled behind his back. Then she taped his ankles together, and *then* she taped them to one leg of Elena's chair.

She did all of this in a matter of seconds. By the time she had finished, Juan-Bear was beginning to moan and twitch, blood leaking heavily from the side of his head where the crazy bitch had struck him with her gun.

"He'll be fine," she said as if reading Elena's thoughts. "He's going to have one hell of a headache, but he'll be okay."

Things had gone from bad to worse. About the only thing Elena could imagine being more dangerous than an angry Juan-Bear was an *injured* and angry Juan-Bear, but she had set her course of action and must now follow it through to the end.

So she continued speaking, surprising herself by the relative calm in her voice. "The name of the woman you are looking for is Maria Carranco. She is a member of Omega 7. Her actions were unsanctioned by Juan's organization"—she almost called him 'Juan-Bear' but stopped herself—"but she is the one who killed those people."

Elena looked down at Juan-Bear to discover him staring at her unblinkingly. He had apparently regained consciousness while she was speaking, and his eyes were filled with a smoldering rage she had never before seen. It was terrifying.

The woman with the gun saw it, too, but appeared utterly unfazed. "Where do I find this Maria Carranco?" she said softly.

"He needs help," she said, ignoring the question and nodding in the direction of Juan-Bear. She was afraid to meet his steady, angry gaze. Up until a few horrible minutes ago the man had been her lover. He was now undoubtedly a dangerous enemy, but she still did not want to see him bleed to death.

"The best way to get Señor Gonzalez the medical attention he needs—in fact, the *only* way to get him the medical attention he needs—is to cooperate fully now that you've started talking. Once I have what I came for, I promise I will allow him medical attention."

"Do not do me any favors," Juan-Bear said darkly.

"Shut up," the crazy bitch snapped, and then returned her attention to Elena. "This is the last time I'm going to ask," she said. "Tell me where to find Maria Carranco or the next move I make will be to break another finger."

As if to punctuate her point she reached down and grabbed Elena's wrist, steadying her hand, which had begun shaking uncontrollably from pain and fear. The woman reached for Elena's ring finger and her hand brushed against the broken pinkie and Elena screamed. It was as if a hammer had smashed down on the digit, the pain like fire blasting out of the knuckle.

"Okay, okay, I'll tell you!" she gasped, sobbing and breathless. "Just stop, please stop hurting me."

"I don't want to hurt you any more than I have to," the crazy bitch said. "But I am not leaving here until I get Maria Carranco's location. So if you want the pain to stop, tell me her address where I can find her, now."

"She does not have an address."

"What is that supposed to mean?" the crazy bitch began extending her hand again, reaching for Elena's finger.

"You can find her in the Everglades!" Elena shouted.

33

Tracie froze, her hand hanging inches above the mangled wreck of the girlfriend's left pinkie finger. She wasn't sure what she had expected the young woman to say, but that certainly wasn't it.

The silence in the room was deafening, and from the floor at her feet she heard Gonzalez blow out an angry breath. *He's pissed. She's telling the truth.*

"What did you say?" she asked.

"You said you want to know where to find Maria. She is in the Everglades."

"She *lives* in the Everglades?"

"No, you do not understand. She lives here, in this house, with Juan-Bear...with Juan."

Gonzalez became more and more hostile as his girlfriend talked, attempting to interrupt and intimidate her. After the second interruption, Tracie turned and raised her gun.

"Let me make something clear to you," she hissed. "I don't care whether you live or die. You and Omega 7 have been responsible for the deaths of dozens of Americans with your pipe bomb attacks. Castro supporters or not, they were Americans. So don't kid yourself into believing I won't just shoot you where you lie, right here and now. One more interruption, just one, and you will never leave this bedroom alive. Do we have an understanding, Señor Gonzalez?"

He looked down, angry but silent. The blood continued to flow from his head.

Tracie forced his hand. *"Answer me!"* she barked.

"I understand." He spit the words out like razorblades.

"Good. Don't forget it, because you won't get another warning."

Tracie turned back toward the girlfriend. "Don't play games with me," she said ominously. "Either she lives here or she lives in the Everglades. Which is it?"

"That is what I am trying to tell you. She lives here. But there is a hideaway in the Everglades that she uses to…think."

"You mean to get away and plan her attacks."

The girlfriend took a deep, shuddering breath. "Yes," she admitted. "When Juan learned of what Maria had done in Washington, how reckless she had been in potentially exposing Omega 7 to federal authorities, he became very angry with her. Juan is a good man, but sometimes he has…difficulties…controlling his temper."

"So do I," Tracie said. "Get on with it."

"Well, when Maria saw how angry Juan was, she decided it would be a good idea to get away for a few days, you know, to let him cool down. She knew he would, he always does where she is concerned. But sometimes it takes a little while. So she packed some things and she left."

"For the Everglades."

"That's right."

"She has a getaway on national park land? How is that possible?"

"The Everglades are massive, and mostly barren. Millions of acres, many hundreds of thousands of which have never been explored, even to this day. It is easy for people who wish to disappear to do so in the Everglades, provided they are not afraid of insects, snakes, bugs or alligators."

Tracie shook her head in confusion. "I thought the Everglades were all underwater. How can anyone live there, even temporarily?"

"Much of the millions of acres making up the Everglades *is* water, but there is dry land as well. More or less. Most of that land is tropical jungle, inaccessible to all but the most determined explorers."

Tracie pictured a young, beautiful woman camping out among panthers and crocodiles and billions of mosquitoes and shook her head. "It seems unlikely to me."

The girlfriend shrugged. "You said you wanted to know where

to find her. That is where."

Tracie was tempted to disregard her words as the statement of a person desperate to get rid of an intruder and doing so by sending that intruder off on a wild goose chase. If Gonzalez had said it, she probably would have done exactly that.

But this woman was not Omega 7 material. She was no hardened terrorist, committed to murder and mayhem and the overthrow of the Cuban government. She was just a frightened and injured young woman, probably younger than Tracie, and Tracie doubted the girlfriend, panicked and in pain, could have come up with such an unlikely story on the spur of the moment even if she had wanted to.

And Gonzalez's angry reaction to her words solidified Tracie's confidence that the woman was telling the truth.

Tracie glanced at Gonzalez. He was shaking his head and bleeding onto the carpet and muttering angrily to himself.

She crouched down until her face was level with the girlfriend's. Looked into her eyes and spoke softly. "Understand that if you're lying to me, I'm going to come back for you. And when I do, a broken finger is going to be the least of your problems."

The young woman stared back, wide-eyed and white-faced.

Tracie said, "Tell me you understand what will happen if you're lying to me."

She licked her lips and sobbed once and said, "I understand, but I am not lying to you. I swear it."

"Then tell me how to find Maria Carranco in the millions of acres of Everglades National Park."

"I don't have to tell you. I can give you a map."

Tracie felt her pulse begin to race. "Where is it?"

"It is in the second drawer of Juan-Bear's desk in his office downstairs."

"*That is enough!*" Gonzalez shouted suddenly in a volcanic eruption of fury.

Tracie turned and fired, and a 9mm slug whizzed past the Omega 7 leader's ear and embedded itself into the floor.

The concussive blast assaulted her ears and they began to ring as the girlfriend screamed next to her.

The gunshot had succeeded in refocusing Gonzalez, though.

He froze and clapped his mouth shut, looking as though he would like nothing better than to strangle his girlfriend with his bare hands. Based on what Tracie had seen of the man, she believed there was every possibility that was exactly what he was thinking.

She turned back to the girlfriend. "Stop screaming or the next bullet goes right between his eyes."

Tears were rolling down the young woman's cheeks but she did as she was told. "Now," Tracie said. "Does Juan-Bear lock his desk?"

She sniffled and sobbed and said, "No, there is no reason to. Or, at least, until tonight there was no reason to, not with armed security patrolling the property."

Tracie asked a few more questions but quickly realized the girlfriend was in no position to give any more specifics about Maria Carranco or Omega 7 because she was not involved in their operation.

Hopefully, everything the girlfriend said about Carranco and the map was true. Tracie would be staking everything on her conviction that the terrified young woman was telling the truth.

She rose and turned to Gonzalez. Surprisingly, he had not attempted to interfere after Tracie's warning. She hadn't really expected her threats to have much effect against a terrorist like Juan Gonzalez. It was one thing to intimidate a frightened, injured young woman, but quite another to do the same to one of the leaders of Omega 7.

But apparently, Gonzalez had accepted the fact that he was in no position to convince his girlfriend not to talk. Instead, he lay quietly. He stared at her unblinkingly, rage radiating off him in waves. Tracie felt she could almost reach out and touch the man's anger.

She rose to her feet to find Gonzalez's desk. Turned toward the door.

"What are you doing?" the girlfriend said anxiously. "He is bleeding heavily, he could bleed out!"

Tracie grunted. "He's not going to bleed out. The skull is skin and bone and not much else. Any head wound is going to bleed like that. He'll be fine, believe me."

"But...you said if I gave you the information you wanted that

I could take care of him."

"No I didn't," Tracie said. "I told you that if you gave me what I wanted, I would ensure he got the medical attention he needs, and I'm going to do that. It might not be what you had in mind, but I'm going to keep my word to you, which is more than he did with me."

"But...what does that mean?"

Tracie ignored the girlfriend and spoke to Gonzalez. "Turn over and sit up," she said.

Gonzalez chuckled darkly but did as he was told. He rolled onto his back and groaned as he lifted his torso off the floor. His hair was soaked in blood.

She had seen worse. Her own shoulders had bled much more heavily after getting shot atop the Minuteman Insurance Building in D.C. last spring, and she had recovered just fine, although the wounds still ached more often than not.

"Where do you keep your clean clothes?" she asked.

"Why?"

"Because I'm holding a gun and you're not. Just answer me."

He nodded his head at a large dresser on the other side of the room, his eyes glazed. He was going into shock.

Trace stepped to the dresser and began opening drawers and rifling through them until finding what she was looking for—a white cotton t-shirt. She lifted the shirt out of the drawer and ripped it in half. Then she knelt and wound the material around Gonzalez's skull, pressing it firmly against the bleeding wound. She picked up her duct tape and secured the shirt to the injury, forming a makeshift bandage.

Gonzalez winced as she worked. "Bitch," he muttered under his breath.

"Is that any way to talk to your nurse?"

By now she had finished working. The gash was sealed and the blood flow had stopped. "That's the best I can do," she said, "and more than you deserve."

She stood once more and Gonzalez said, "I am going to kill you," his voice cold and hard and furious. "I am going to find you, wherever you are, and cut you up into little pieces. Then I am going to pack your dismembered body into a trunk and bring it back to

Miami, where I am going to go out in my boat and use every last piece of you as shark bait. I will take great pleasure in doing all of this, do you hear me?"

Tracie smiled sweetly at him, her amusement genuine. "Thank you for the reminder, *Juan-Bear,* I almost forgot something."

She bent and lifted her duct tape.

Wound it around Gonzalez's mouth and then secured it behind his head. Repeated the exercise with his girlfriend, who babbled promises about keeping her mouth shut and not screaming, right up until she could no longer speak.

Tracie slapped the tape down, ensuring solid adhesion, and then winked at the leader of Omega 7. "Thanks for the dance, Big Boy, but I expected more of a challenge out of you. Better luck next time."

She turned away and took a couple of steps before turning back to him, pretending to think of something. "Oh, wait. That's right. There won't be a next time, will there? You'll be doing hard time in federal prison for terrorism."

She locked eyes with the furious man, holding his gaze without blinking until he finally looked away. Then she picked up her backpack and walked out of the bedroom.

34

Tracie waited impatiently as the secure telephone installed in Aaron Stallings's home office rang over and over. He was an early riser, and on most weekdays would have been up and on his way to Langley by now. Today was Saturday, but depending on what was going on in the world of international espionage, he might be working on the weekend as well.

Finally the line was picked up and she breathed a sigh of relief. A short pause was followed by a raspy voice fogged with sleep. "Stallings."

"Director, I have a situation."

A short pause. "Of course you do, Tanner. Are you on a secure line?"

"No sir, but I'm alone, at a public telephone. There is virtually no chance this call is being intercepted from my end."

"What do you want?"

"I have a situation and I need your help."

"Where are you?"

"South of Miami, in Coral Gables."

"Gonzalez."

"That's right."

"You haven't gone and killed him, have you?"

"No, he's alive, but he's injured, and I need a team to remove him and two others from his property ASAP. I need him out of commission for awhile."

"What the hell have you done, Tanner?"

"You said you wanted the NCC Killer stopped at all costs. I'm trying to make that happen."

Stallings sighed more than a thousand miles away, the sound loud and clear through the payphone handset pressed to Tracie's ear. "How soon do you need these people removed, and why?"

"I have a line on the killer. It's not a Castro rep at all, rather a member of Omega 7 that went out on her own. She went to—"

"Wait a second. The killer is a woman?"

"Yes. The hooker that Dr. Kiley saw leaving Allan Nesbitt's Washington Arms hotel room is the mastermind of the whole thing. I'm almost certain she ran the entire op on her own, but I won't know for sure until I can interrogate her."

"Maria Carranco."

Tracie felt her jaw drop. It was an involuntary reaction based on utter shock. "How do you know Maria Carranco?" She spoke the words slowly.

"We've worked with Juan Gonzalez in the past, remember? He made very clear to our people that no matter what else happened while he operated as a mole, Maria Carranco was not to be harmed in any way."

Tracie worked to recover her bearings. "Well, sir, she's a mass murderer of American citizens. Are you telling me to back off? Because I have a real problem with that if you are."

"Goddammit, Tanner, be quiet for a second and let me think."

Tracie bit back the reply she wanted very badly to make and waited. Finally the CIA director spoke. "No, your mission has not changed. Make every effort to bring Carranco in alive, though. Gonzalez has a lot of followers in Omega 7, and we don't need to make an enemy of him any more than *you* already have."

"Frankly, sir, I'm not terribly concerned about the feelings of a terrorist and murderer."

"Frankly, Agent Tanner, *I'm* not terribly concerned about your opinion. Just get out there and do your job."

She swallowed heavily, choking back the rising tide of anger that threatened to blow the top of her head off. "Yes, sir," she said tightly.

"Now, give me the details on what you need out of the cleanup team, starting with how soon you need them at Gonzalez's home."

"I need them at his house ASAP. If Gonzalez's staff start showing up in the morning and find him before our people are able to get him out of there, the first thing he's going to do is warn Carranco I'm coming for her. She'll disappear and I'll never find her. At least not until she's killed who knows how many more innocent people."

"Fine," Stallings said.

"His street address is—"

"I already have it."

Again Tracie fought to control her temper. If Stallings had simply given her Gonzalez's home address, she could have saved a lot of time and trouble. And if she had known about "Juan-Bear's" position in Omega 7, she might have approached her whole assignment differently, too. That was probably why Stallings had kept the information to himself, she realized.

The CIA director continued. "How exactly is Gonzalez injured, and is he the only injured party?"

"More or less." She gave a quick rundown of the injury to the Omega 7 leader's head, as well as the girlfriend's broken finger and the fact that a security guard had been left trussed up in the woods next to the property with a likely concussion. "Oh, yeah," she added. "Gonzalez probably has a concussion as well, now that I think about it. I hit him pretty hard."

"Jesus Christ, Tanner, you're like a bull in a china shop, you know that?"

"You told me you wanted results, and I'm trying to get them for you."

Stallings sighed. "Yeah, yeah, whatever. I'll have a team dispatched to the Gonzalez house immediately. They should be there within half an hour and all trace of the subjects will be gone before sunup. How long are we going to have to hold them?"

Tracie considered the question. "I believe the information I was given about Maria Carranco's whereabouts to be accurate, but there's no way of knowing whether she's going to be there when I arrive. My guess is that she will. It seems unlikely she's had time to plan another attack yet, so she'll probably be holed up doing exactly that."

"And?"

"And I hope to have her within twenty-four hours. If that changes I'll let you know."

"Wonderful." The insincerity of the word came across the phone line loud and clear. "Now, if there's nothing else, it's the middle of the night and I'd like to get back to sleep before dawn."

"Yes, sir."

She prepared to disconnect the call and Stallings's voice came through the earpiece as she lifted the handset to hang it up. His voice sounded tinny and insubstantial but strident. "Oh, and Tanner?" he said.

She brought the phone back to her ear. "Yes, sir?"

"Try not to fuck this up any more than you already have."

She started to answer but he was gone. She sighed deeply and replaced the handset on its cradle.

35

Tracie was stunned at how fast the geography changed once she had left the Miami area behind and begun moving west on the Tamiami Trail in her newly rented four-wheel drive truck. The densely populated urban sprawl gave way to wet flatlands as if someone had flipped a switch, with more than a million and a half acres of swampland and subtropical wilderness ahead. Virtually all of South Central Florida, between Miami on one coast and Tampa on the other, was nothing more than uninhabitable jungle.

The truck droned along the pavement, one lane of traffic moving east and one moving west. The abundance of wildlife was breath-taking. Colorful birds soared in massive, complex formations high above huge crocodiles sunning themselves on the side of the road.

It was all she could do to keep her attention on the traffic and on the job that lay ahead.

It was a job she was ill prepared for; she knew that.

The mass murderer Maria Carranco had been raised in this area. Had been using the vast wilderness of the Everglades as her own personal retreat for virtually her entire adult life.

She was undoubtedly armed, likely possessing firepower far in excess of the 9mm Glock, backup revolver and combat knife Tracie sported. But Tracie possessed one advantage that she hoped would trump all of Carranco's: surprise.

Juan Gonzalez and his broken-fingered girlfriend were the only people alive besides Aaron Stallings who knew Tracie was coming for Carranco, and within an hour after Tracie's phone call yesterday, the two of them would have been swept into custody by a CIA cleanup crew.

Tracie eased down on the accelerator and drove on.

Forty minutes after leaving the Miami city limits behind, Tracie spotted her first marker: a wooden sign on the right side of the road bearing the words CRYSTAL LAKE CAMPGROUND. The sign had been professionally carved, the lettering painted white against the redwood background. Crystal Lake Campground was clearly part of the National Park system.

She slowed and continued past the campground. Immediately after passing a large body of freestanding water—Crystal Lake, presumably—she slowed even more, grateful for the lack of traffic on this side of the Tamiami Trail. A hundred yards later another wooden sign told her it was time to leave civilization—what was left of it—behind.

SLOUGH ROAD, this sign said, and it was notable for its contrast with Crystal Lake Campground's. The Slough Road sign was weathered and battered and looked as though it had been handmade and erected by a hermit, which, given the history of the Everglades, may have been the case.

Tracie had spent a couple of hours this morning sitting in a carrel at the Main Branch of the Miami-Dade Public Library, doing as much as she could to prepare for what was coming. Her knowledge of Everglades National Park was practically nil, and in the world of covert ops, ignorance would get you killed faster than anything else.

So she had studied and scanned books, magazines and newspaper articles relating to the Everglades. She learned that despite the forbidding nature of Everglades National Park, over the decades a number of hermits had made the desolate area their home.

She strongly suspected the cabin Carranco was using as her retreat was the abandoned home of one of those hermits. Tucked away inside the map book she had taken from Juan Gonzalez's desk outlining the travel route to the shack were a couple of photos. They were yellowed with age, but showed a tiny log cabin in the middle of a small clearing that had been hacked out of the thick, jungle-like vegetation. The cabin was perched atop a foundation of cement blocks.

The purpose of the blocks was obviously to keep the rest of the structure elevated off the spongy ground, preventing—or at least slowing—the inevitable wood rot that the area's moist, humid subtropical climate promoted.

The photos were clearly old and even at the time they were snapped it was obvious the cabin had been in its location for a long time. If Maria Carranco was in her mid-twenties, there was simply no way she could have built it herself. She had appropriated it after the hermit living in it had passed away or moved on or disappeared.

Or had come to his senses and gotten the hell out, Tracie thought to herself uneasily. She continued slowing, and then turned onto Slough Road and began moving north. Another thing she had learned from her research was that Carranco's cabin wasn't technically located in the Everglades; it was sitting on the marginally drier land of Big Cypress National Preserve.

Every bit as wild and subtropical as Everglades National Park, Big Cypress National Preserve consisted of nearly three-quarters of a million acres that had been set aside and given protected status by President Gerald Ford thirteen years ago, in 1974. When added to the 1.5 million protected acres of Everglades National Park, which had been established nearly a half-century earlier, a vast swath of well over two million acres of South Central Florida was now untouchable by developers and the protected habitat of thousands of birds, animals and insects.

And Tracie was driving into the middle of that wilderness.

Alone.

To flush out a mass murderer.

And nobody knew where she was.

If she wasn't on top of her game, she knew she would disappear and her body would never be found.

She checked her map and kept going.

36

The condition of Slough Road deteriorated as she drove, until within five miles of leaving the Tamiami Trail even the most optimistic of souls couldn't have classified it as "paved." Probably not even as a road.

Tracie didn't consider herself as being even close to the most optimistic of souls, especially right now. The vegetation crowded in on her rental truck, slowly but surely overtaking Slough Road. Massive weeds grew through cracks and holes in the pavement, vines and tree branches scraped the sides of the truck, deep potholes—most filled with water—pocked the trail.

Perhaps the occasional hunter came up here, or poacher, or terrorist. But whatever Slough Road's original purpose had been, it was plain to see that the road was now nothing more than a forgotten relic that would be completely reclaimed by Big Cypress in just a few more years.

She slowed and stopped, leaving the truck in the middle of the "road." Pulling to the side would be impossible, given the thickness of the vegetation. And it would be pointless as well, since the likelihood of another vehicle coming along out here was about as great as of Tracie Tanner being elected to Congress.

She wiped the sweat off her face and swatted at a swarm of mosquitoes that had appeared the moment her forward progress stopped. She considered rolling up the windows and maxing out the truck's air conditioning but nixed the idea immediately. It was critical she acclimate herself to her surroundings.

She consulted her map and then shifted the vehicle into four-wheel drive. The paved portion of Slough Road was now little more than a pleasant memory, and the potholes had continued to develop until now it was virtually impossible to find more than a couple of feet of flat driving surface anywhere.

She waved her hands in a fruitless attempt to scatter the mosquitoes and hit the gas, plunging deeper into Big Cypress National Preserve.

*   *   *

Tracie squinted and concentrated on the map. If it was accurate, Maria Carranco's cabin should be located approximately four miles northwest of her current position. She had cut the engine and finally rolled up the windows, raising the white flag in her losing battle against the onslaught of mosquitoes.

Now, sweat rolled off her in waves and the insects trapped inside the cab were feasting on her with enthusiasm. She slapped at them and tried to concentrate, cursing Maria Carranco and questioning her own choice of careers.

After shifting the truck into four-wheel drive, she had followed the steadily deteriorating Slough Road for another four to five miles, occasionally losing all sight of it before eventually picking up the faint trail again. The only reason she was even able to find it was because Slough Road ran straight as an arrow. Why anyone would have constructed it and what its original purpose may have been was a mystery.

The terrain was rough, and getting rougher, and she was unable to maintain a speed much over five miles per hour. The heat was nearly unbearable, even though the thickness of the jungle canopy almost totally blocked the sunlight. The air seemed saturated with humidity and Tracie forced herself to drink plenty of water.

And the mosquitoes. The mosquitoes were everywhere.

At one point she stopped and stared in wonder at the sight of a massive crocodile sunning itself on the remains of Slough Road. It was a beast, easily twenty feet long, with creased, leathery skin and an utterly disinterested demeanor.

Tracie inched the truck forward, hoping to frighten the animal into retreat, but the croc only lifted one eye, unconvinced the vehicle posed a threat.

She pictured razor-sharp yellow teeth tearing one of the truck's tires apart and then attacking the sheet metal of the driver's side door. She decided she wasn't willing to bet against the big beast in such a confrontation and imagined the powerful jaws clamping down on her body, tearing her apart as he made a midday snack out of her.

She continued moving forward until the front wheels were almost on top of the animal. Any closer and the truck would drive right onto its back, which didn't strike Tracie as the smartest move to make. The big crocodile didn't seem interested in attacking the truck but wasn't showing any signs of abandoning its position, either.

It was a standoff, one she didn't think she could win.

She shifted into reverse and backed slowly away from the stubborn animal. When she had put enough distance between them, she spun the wheel hard to the left and hit the gas, plunging into the vegetation, praying she could maintain enough momentum to fight through the thick jungle cover until she had gotten past the croc and could regain the semi-road.

The truck screeched and groaned as vines and branches scraped its sides, scratching the paint, likely destroying the finish. Tracie bounced and jolted in her safety harness as the truck plunged into deep depressions in the jungle surface and clawed its way up the other side.

She didn't dare slow and couldn't afford even a half-second's glance in the rear view to see if she had gotten past the croc yet. Given the thickness of the underbrush, she doubted she would be able to see it, anyway. But the truck's forward progress was slowing badly and she knew she had to get back onto what was left of Slough Road right now, or she was going to be stranded.

Just a few feet away from a twenty-foot-long predator.

She wrestled the steering wheel and punched the accelerator to the floor, sweating and cursing, and the truck's four drive wheels whined, kicking up mud and muck and the detritus of an ancient wilderness. Waterlogged dirt splattered the windows, the engine screamed in angry protest, and Tracie realized she was muttering, "Come on, come on, come on," repeating the words like a mystical talisman.

And then the truck broke free of the jungle. It slammed up onto the remains of Slough Road, getting airborne and then nearly bottoming out before careening toward the equally thick jungle on the other side of the ancient trail.

Tracie stood on the brakes and the truck ground to a halt. She was panting and shaking and had almost forgotten about the mosquitoes.

Almost.

She sighed deeply and raised her eyes to the rearview and smiled despite herself.

The damned crocodile hadn't moved an inch. It lay across Slough Road, still ignoring the truck, utterly confident inside its lizard brain of its status at the top of the local food chain.

Fine, Tracie thought. *You win. Hopefully I'll be alive for Round Two on the way out of this godforsaken jungle hellhole.*

She took a moment to regroup.

Gulped water.

Slapped at the ever-present horde of mosquitoes, knowing it would do no good but unable to stop herself.

Consulted the map again.

Hit the gas and kept moving forward.

37

Eventually, a nearly invisible trail appeared to Tracie's left. Slough Road had long since become nothing more than a vague rumor, and Tracie prayed she hadn't accidentally left the primeval track behind.

Still, the faint trail looming in the windshield seemed to be in the approximate location of a turn indicated on the map, so Tracie said a quick prayer and veered left, keeping steady pressure on the accelerator.

The jungle vegetation seemed marginally less dense here than it had been during Tracie's showdown with the crocodile, and the truck was able to fight its way through the brush for a longer distance than she had initially feared would be possible.

Following the trail was a problem. Often it was nothing more than a tantalizing hint, a potential depression in the sawgrass that might have been nothing more than her imagination. Sometimes it disappeared entirely. Tracie was well aware of her limited experience as a tracker and hoped she hadn't missed Carranco's cabin.

She forged ahead, picking her way forward, reversing course when she got off track. The thought occurred to her that even if she was successful in recovering Maria Carranco, unless she could convince the young terrorist to help her navigate back to Slough Road she might never make it out of here alive.

She forced that disturbing thought to the back of her mind.

First things first.

She had to get Carranco.

* * *

Tracie was surprised to discover that she could probably continue most of the way to Carranco's cabin without getting out of the truck if she chose to do so. The vegetation was uniformly dense, enough so that making forward progress was a challenge, but not so much so that it became impossible to accomplish.

Of course, whether she could do so or not was irrelevant, because even the most dimwitted of fugitives would be spooked by the sound of an approaching engine way out here at the end of the world. And Tracie didn't think "dimwitted" would be an apt description for the Omega 7 terrorist. "Cold-blooded" definitely, "dangerous" certainly, but she doubted "dim-witted" would apply.

She drove as far as she dared, then stopped the truck and killed the engine. She didn't need to worry about hiding the vehicle, because unless Carranco happened to come along the other way and run into it, *everyplace* was a suitable hiding place.

The terrorist would have to get within ten feet of the truck to have any chance of seeing it, and her cabin was still at least two miles of rough terrain from here. According to Gonzalez's girlfriend, Carranco had planned to stay out here several days, maybe as long as a week, to allow the Omega 7 leader time to cool off. It had only been two days so far, so barring a stroke of the worst kind of luck the truck would be just fine where it was.

She opened the door and stepped to the ground, feeling the squishiness of water-saturated soil the moment her feet plopped onto the earth. Immediately, a cloud of mosquitoes surrounded her. She had prepared by wrapping a spare blouse around her head and had secured it by tying the sleeves together, leaving just a tiny slit in front of her eyes to see through.

Immediately, sweat began to soak the material and she knew the protection it offered—minimal to begin with—would decrease markedly within just a few minutes. Still, it had to be better than nothing.

She started walking, gun in hand, backpack slung over one shoulder. She imagined a crocodile behind every tree and an alligator submerged in every section of standing water, and wished fervently she were back in Washington, tracking down a Soviet collaborator.

Get your head straight, she told herself sternly. *Maria Carranco is just as deadly as any alligator. More so, probably. Allow yourself to be distracted, and getting eaten by an overgrown lizard would be a better fate than the one you'll suffer.*

She swatted at the hordes of mosquitoes and moved on.

38

Maria Carranco's hideaway looked to be in much better condition than it had appeared in the yellowed snapshots Tracie had found in Juan Gonzalez's map book. Someone had obviously done a fair amount of maintenance on it—likely Carranco, since there couldn't be many other lunatics anxious to spend time out here.

Tracie had slogged through the damp, marshy terrain for nearly two hours after leaving her vehicle behind. The cabin was located exactly where it appeared on the map, its position marked with a ball point X. But despite the fact it was less than two miles away in a straight line from where she abandoned the truck, the hike had been a grueling one.

Between climbing over or moving around fallen trees and standing water, sinking ankle-deep into the muck with every other step, and moving carefully in order to keep a sharp eye out for predators, Tracie felt wrung out and exhausted by the time she realized she was getting close.

She slowed her progress even more, forcing herself to ignore the ever-present mosquitoes, and fifteen minutes later the tiny one-room log cabin she had seen in the photographs presented itself in a clearing in the distance.

Tracie moved as close as she dared, careful to avoid giving herself away by stepping on and snapping a twig or tree branch. Then she hunkered down, determined to gather as much intel as she could on her foe before finalizing a plan to deal with Maria Carranco.

For nearly two and a half hours Tracie remained unmoving in

her surveillance position, screened from view of the cabin—she hoped—by trees and Big Cypress scrub brush.

She was close enough to observe the front of the shack without binoculars. There was a door squarely in the middle, flanked by a small window on either side. She couldn't be sure, but Tracie guessed neither of the windows actually contained glass. It looked as though a pair of screens—one fastened to the cabin's exterior, the other to the interior—served to protect its inhabitant from the mosquitoes and snakes and other Everglades/Big Cypress animals and insects. Each window also featured a set of heavy wooden shutters that could be closed to seal the cabin.

How Carranco had gotten here from Miami—and whether, in fact, she was even here at all—was a question Tracie could not answer. There was no vehicle parked in the vicinity of the cabin. No Jeep, no four-wheel-drive truck, nothing. Tracie guessed there must be more than one arrival route here from the Tamiami Trail, and even with as close a relationship as the young woman had with Gonzalez, she would protect herself by keeping knowledge of at least one of those routes to herself.

Of a more immediate concern, though, was Carranco's whereabouts. Tracie had kept her attention glued to the little shack and had been rewarded with nothing to indicate the presence of another human being. No figures moved behind the screens covering the windows. No footsteps sounded from inside the cabin.

Nothing.

The mosquitoes continued to swarm and Tracie found she was able to ignore them—more or less—by adopting a Zen-like focus on her mission. She had duct-taped her jeans to her ankles and worn a long-sleeved blouse to complement the shirt tied around her head and face, offering the insects as little exposed skin as possible at which to aim their relentless attacks.

But the drawback to all that clothing was obvious: the midday heat and humidity pounding down on Big Cypress and the Everglades was stifling, worse by far than anything Tracie Tanner had ever experienced. Sweat flowed from every pore, soaking every article of her clothing and making dehydration a very real concern despite the bottled water she had been sipping virtually nonstop.

And she was getting hungry. She had packed little food,

preferring to include mostly water in the limited space of her backpack.

All of these problems were manageable, though. With the exception of the brutal heat and humidity, Tracie had faced worse—much worse—in her career as a covert operative. She estimated the temperature to be close to one hundred fifteen degrees, with humidity at least seventy percent, but even those blast-furnace temperatures were marginally easier to endure when she thought back to some of the bitter cold temperatures she had faced on assignments in Soviet Russia.

The sun would begin setting soon, which in turn would lower the temperatures, at least marginally. But nightfall would bring its own set of problems. While she felt relatively safe from attack by crocs, alligators and snakes during daylight hours, she knew she would become a sitting duck once she could no longer see.

One way or the other, she would have to take shelter before sunset. She would either have to force her way inside the cabin or hike back to the truck. And the second option was becoming less feasible by the minute, given the fact it would take at least two hours to accomplish.

And she still had no idea whether Maria Carranco was even here.

She sipped her water and watched the cabin and considered her steadily dwindling options. She decided she would give it another forty-five minutes. An hour at the outside. If by then she had not gotten a line on Carranco's whereabouts, she would begin making her way toward the cabin with the intention of breaking in.

It wasn't the best of plans. She couldn't even convince herself it was a *good* plan, but at least—

Ch-chunk.

She froze. The sound was distinctive. There was only one thing it could be.

Someone had racked a shotgun.

Someone behind her.

How far behind and from what range was impossible to say. Not that it really mattered. With a shotgun, precision aim was a luxury, not a necessity.

She debated spinning and firing a blind shot—she was still

holding her Glock, by this time more as a defense against an attacking crocodile than out of any real expectation that she was going to see Maria Carranco—but she had been crouched in the same position for so long, the odds of turning smoothly and cleanly and getting a shot off without falling on her ass were slim.

The odds of doing it without being blasted by buckshot were nil.

"Turn around slowly and show me your hands," a female voice behind her instructed.

Carranco.

Tracie dropped her gun onto the spongy turf, hoping the terrorist's view would be screened by Tracie's body and the terrorist wouldn't see her do it. She didn't think the woman would be foolish enough to believe she had come all the way out here unarmed, but she couldn't imagine any drawback to trying, either.

The gun plopped to the ground and she raised her hands, fingers splayed, as she turned slowly.

And saw Maria Carranco for the first time.

The woman was young, breathtakingly beautiful, and tiny. From this distance, perhaps twenty yards, she looked more like a twelve-year-old girl than a woman in her mid-twenties, a fanatic capable of murdering more than a half-dozen innocent people in cold blood.

Carranco held the shotgun down by her hip almost casually, although Tracie noted the two-handed stance: right hand on the pistol grip, finger resting on the trigger guard, and left hand on the foregrip.

She looked comfortable, like holding the shotgun was the most natural thing in the world, and despite the brutal heat Tracie felt a chill in her bones she wouldn't have believed possible just a moment before.

"Who are you and what do you want?" the woman asked in Hispanic-accented English.

Tracie smiled brightly. "Avon calling. Beautiful place you have here. Nice and private."

Anger flashed in Maria Carranco's eyes. Tracie could see it even from where she stood, and the woman spat, "Do not play games, or you will die where you stand."

Tracie cleared her throat, thinking hard. She needed to buy some time, wait for Carranco to make a mistake.

And judging from the way the terrorist was handling herself, a mistake didn't seem likely.

"I need to talk to you," she said, speaking loudly enough to be heard through the material of the shirt wrapped around her head, but calmly and levelly. Taking even the chance of spooking Carranco struck Tracie as a very bad idea.

"Who are you?"

"My name is Holly."

Maria Carranco tightened her grip on the shotgun. "How did you find me, Holly, and what do you want? You should know this is the last time I will ask these questions."

Tracie cleared her throat and took a chance. "I have a message from Juan. He needs you back in Miami as soon as possible, and since he had no other way of contacting you, he sent me."

Uncertainty showed in Carranco's expression face. She paused a moment and then took a couple of hesitant steps forward. "Juan needs me? Why?"

Tracie shrugged, doing her best to affect a lack of interest. "Beats me," she said. "He didn't tell me. He said to bring you back, so here I am."

Carranco stopped walking and raised the gun to her shoulder. Tracie couldn't be sure, but it looked like a Mossberg 500 pump-action 12 Gauge that had been fitted with a pistol grip and fold-down stock. At the moment, the stock was locked in place. "That is bullshit," she said.

Tracie spread her hands innocently. "What are you talking about? You think there's any other reason in the world why I would come out to this godforsaken mosquito-infested swamp?"

"Omega 7 is not that big. I know everyone in the organization, at least by sight. Take off the shirt you have wrapped around your head. I want to see your face. If I do not recognize you, you die. Right here, right now."

39

"Who says I'm a member of Omega 7? I never made that claim." Tracie struggled to keep her voice steady and felt she managed it fairly well under the circumstances.

"Take the shirt off your face. Do it now." Carranco held the shotgun steady. It looked as big as a cannon to Tracie, staring down its barrel.

"Fine," she said. "But you're not going to recognize me because I'm not a member of Omega 7. And Juan is going to be even angrier at you than he already is if you kill me." She untied the sleeves she had wrapped around the back of her head and let the shirt fall to the wet ground, waiting for the shotgun blast that would pepper her body with pellets and end her life.

For a long moment, nothing happened. Tracie stood arms spread, her sweat-soaked flame-red hair framing her face in greasy strings.

It felt like minutes later that the terrorist spoke, although it was probably only seconds. "If you are not Omega 7, what are you doing working for Juan?"

"You think a man as important as Juan Gonzalez only works with people you know? You think someone like Juan doesn't have a trusted group of contractors, to whom he farms out certain jobs? Jobs that for whatever reason, he doesn't want Omega 7's name or reputation attached to?"

Carranco was clearly skeptical, but she hadn't squeezed the trigger yet, and Tracie considered that a win. The beautiful young

223

woman said, "Is that so? And what sort of contracting services do *you* provide for Juan?"

"I'm a tracker. I find people."

"And he sent you to find me." It should have been a question, but Carranco phrased it flatly, like a statement.

"That's right."

"Why didn't he use an Omega 7 member?"

For the second time, Tracie took a calculated risk, one that could cost her life. "Look around you," she said, making a show of gazing at the Big Cypress panorama. "What Omega 7 member would have been able to come out here and track you down?" She took a deep breath and continued. "None of them have ever been here. They're revolutionaries, freedom fighters, not trackers or wildlife experts."

"And you are."

She shrugged. "I found you, didn't I?"

"And we come right back to my question. *How* did you find me?"

"Simple. Juan took a map book out of his desk drawer and handed it to me."

Carranco lowered the Mossberg again, pointing it at the ground. She continued to hold it in her two-handed grip, though, and regarded Tracie suspiciously. "What is so important he cannot wait a couple of days for me to return? I have been coming out here since I was a little girl and he has never before sent a… *tracker*"—she spit the word out distastefully, like she had bitten into rancid meat—"to bring me back."

"I told you already, I don't know what Juan wants. He hired me to find you and bring you back. That's really all I can tell you."

"Are you armed?"

"Look around you," Tracie said, putting an element of exasperation into her voice. "Of *course* I'm armed. What kind of lunatic would come out here unarmed?"

Carranco seemed to consider Tracie words. Then she shrugged and said, "Well, if Juan wants me back in Miami so badly, we should probably be going right away, yes?"

"Absolutely," Tracie agreed.

"Fine. But before we leave I must retrieve a few of my things from the cabin."

The terrorist walked forward a few more steps. By now she could see Tracie's backpack, as well as the small pile of empty water bottles she had been steadily draining throughout her surveillance.

What she still could *not* see, Tracie hoped, was the Glock she had blocked from view with her body and dropped onto the ground when first challenged by Carranco. Now that she had allayed Carranco's suspicions—she hoped—the next step would be to find a way to retrieve the gun and regain the advantage against her captor.

But it wasn't going to happen. Not yet, at least. Carranco moved a little closer and said, "Step away from your things. Back up at least fifteen feet."

Dammit.

Tracie stood her ground and Carranco's eyes narrowed. She began to raise the Mossberg.

Tracie knew her only play was to keep up the fiction that Juan Gonzalez had sent her here. Be patient and wait for an opening. If she could convince Maria Carranco that they were not working at cross purposes, sooner or later she would get the break she needed and could take the terrorist down.

She nodded slowly and began backing up, hands at her sides, palms out, fingers spread. "Fine with me," she said. "But we really need to get moving if we're going to hike back to my truck before sunset."

Carranco made no reply. She reached the spot Tracie had just vacated and picked up the backpack, sliding it onto one shoulder.

For just a moment Tracie thought she was going to miss seeing the Glock, but then she bent at the knees and plucked the gun off the ground with her left hand, all the while keeping the shotgun trained more or less in Tracie's direction. She examined the handgun quickly, glanced at Tracie once, eyes shrouded, expression neutral, and then slid it into a pocket of her camouflage fatigues.

Carranco inclined her head in the direction of the cabin and Tracie began trudging across the clearing. She still had her backup gun in its ankle holster and her combat knife in its sheath on her leg, but with her jeans taped to her ankles, there was no way to quickly access either one.

Besides, based on what she had seen of Maria Carranco thus far, she doubted they would remain in her possession very much longer. And in any event, she couldn't do anything while being covered by the Mossberg, so she moved toward the cabin and waited to see what would happen next.

She didn't have to wait long. When she reached the shack, she climbed a set of three cement block steps and stopped at the rough wooden door, hoping Carranco would climb up behind her and then reach past to open it. There would be no way for the terrorist to do that and remain balanced, and Tracie would make her move then.

Again she was disappointed. Carranco stopped at the base of the stairs and said, "Open it." She didn't move until Tracie had complied.

Tracie sighed and pushed the door open. It was heavier than she had expected. She walked inside the little cabin and immediately scanned for something she could use as a weapon. She would have to grab it, turn and—

No luck. In barely more than the time it took for her to enter, Maria Carranco bounded up the steps and into the cabin behind her.

Tracie resigned herself to waiting until they had returned to her truck before attempting to disable the terrorist. In some ways, waiting was a better idea, anyway. The two-mile hike through Big Cypress's rugged terrain would be much easier to navigate with someone who was coming willingly than with a captive.

She moved into the middle of the cabin, taking in her surroundings. On one side was a cot, rickety and very basic but neatly made. A gas cook stove was set up on another wall, next to a rudimentary counter upon which had been placed a gas lantern and Carranco's store of food supplies. Next to the counter sat a small table and a single rough-hewn bamboo chair. The chair was obviously handmade and she wondered if Carranco had constructed it.

The other two walls were stocked with weapons. Rifles, shotguns, handguns, knives, bombs and bomb-making supplies shared space with chemicals and unmarked wooden crates filled with God-knew-what.

Tracie's pulse quickened. The killer was even more dangerous than she had realized, and that was saying something given the havoc Carranco had wreaked back in D.C.

Stallings was right. This psychopath had to be removed from the picture, one way or the other, before she murdered more people, ruined more lives.

She put a smile in her voice, trying to keep things light, determined to make an ally out of the terrorist until the time was right to make her move. "How long will it take you to get your things together?" she said. "We really should get going."

She turned to face the woman and barely had time to flinch. Her peripheral vision caught a blur of motion and she tried to jerk out of the way as Carranco swung the shotgun like a baseball bat at her head.

The barrel caught her flush on the temple and she dropped straight down. The last thing she remembered thinking before the darkness rushed in was, *Mossberg. Just like I thought.*

40

Tracie's head pounded relentlessly. The blasts of pain radiated through her skull with every beat of her heart, and she became aware of them even before realizing she had woken up.

Heartbeat/pain.

Heartbeat/pain.

Heartbeat/pain.

Her mind felt fuzzy and confused. She was almost positive she hadn't had too much to drink last night because she almost never had more than one drink. A drunk covert operative was a covert operative living on borrowed time.

Heartbeat/pain.

Heartbeat/pain.

She reluctantly opened one eye, bracing for the explosion of discomfort that she knew would follow. Waited a moment. When the pain wasn't as bad as she expected, she eased her other eye open and everything came rushing back.

She was in the middle of nowhere: Big Cypress National Preserve, hard by Everglades National Park. She had come here to bring a cold-blooded female terrorist back to Langley, or to kill her if necessary.

And she had been blindsided by that terrorist.

Her head was resting on her shoulder and she could feel dried blood crusting the right side of her face. She tried to look around, to take in as much of her surroundings as she could, without alerting her captor to the fact she had regained consciousness.

Carranco had duct-taped her into the homemade bamboo chair she had seen upon entering the cabin. The chair was placed in the center of the tiny structure and she guessed she had been secured into it with her own tape. It was crudely constructed, solid but splintering in places, badly in need of sanding. Razor-sharp slivers of bamboo poked at her and made an already painful situation even worse.

She deserved it. Deserved every last scrape, scratch and head-ache for allowing this disaster to unfold the way it had.

And unless she could figure a way out of this mess, and quickly, she was going to die out here alone. She would simply disappear and no one would ever know what had happened to her. Even if Aaron Stallings sent another operative to South Florida after Carranco, that agent would never find this place, would never find her body, would never...

No.

She wouldn't do this.

She had to stay positive. Negativity would get her killed just as surely as a gunshot to the head.

A deathly silence hung over the cabin, and Tracie wondered where Maria Carranco had gone, and why she had left Tracie alive. If she didn't believe Tracie's story about Juan Gonzalez sending her out here to bring Tracie back to Miami, why not just kill her and be done with it?

Sweat rolled freely down her face, mixing with the dried blood and leaving pinkish-red trails as it dripped onto her already-soaked blouse. As stiflingly hot as it had been outside, it was even worse inside the little tinderbox sitting in the middle of a clearing under the brutal subtropical sun.

The two small screen-covered windows flanking the front door were complemented by identical windows in the rear of the shack, theoretically allowing for the flow of air. But a breeze would be required for that to happen, and the air outside the shack was as dead and still as a corpse.

Convinced she was alone, Tracie lifted her head off her shoul-der in a tentative experiment to see how much pain she was going to have to endure from the gash above her ear.

An ice pick stabbed through her skull, the pain hot and

sickening, turning her stomach and making her feel like she might puke. She squeezed her eyes shut and concentrated on compartmentalizing the pain like she had been taught years ago during her training at The Farm. She had learned that once the initial shock of a blow to the head—or anywhere else on the body, for that matter—wore off, managing the resulting pain was as much a mental issue as a physical one.

What most people called "a high threshold for pain" was really nothing more than the ability to take that pain and file it away in a tiny portion of the brain, to acknowledge it but move past it, to understand it was going to be present no matter what, and to accomplish what one needed to accomplish *in spite of* the pain.

She held her head steady and counted to one hundred, refusing to let it drop back onto her shoulder.

Breathed deeply.

Reopened her eyes.

And saw Maria Carranco standing directly in front of her. The terrorist's own eyes were narrowed and she held Tracie's Glock steadily, aimed at her chest.

Tracie tried to hide her surprise. She had assumed she was alone, and Carranco had obviously been standing or sitting right behind her; that was the only way she could have been inside the cabin without Tracie seeing her.

Tracie nodded at the gun in Carranco's hand and said, "What's the matter, did I bend the barrel on the Mossberg?"

Carranco smiled thinly. "Do not give yourself that much credit," she said. "The Mossberg is an effective weapon under the right circumstances, but for close quarters, a 9mm handgun is more than sufficient. But of course, you know that already."

Tracie took a deep breath and forced herself to ignore the steady drumbeat of pain in her skull. "Juan is going to be very unhappy with you when he learns what you've done to me."

"Give it a rest," Carranco replied. "Juan Gonzalez did not send you here. I know you are CIA."

Tracie snorted. "You're delusional, babe. Why the hell would you think I worked for the CIA?"

"Obviously you do not realize what kind of relationship Juan and I have," she said. "I am not a typical Omega 7 member, and the closeness with which he guards information when dealing with other members of the organization does not apply to me."

"What's that supposed to mean?" Tracie said. The sick feeling was building in the pit of her stomach and it wasn't entirely due to her head injury. She thought she knew what Carranco was going to say and didn't like it one bit.

"It means that Juan told me about the beautiful, red-haired CIA operative he sent off to Cuba on a wild goose chase. Congratulations on your safe return, by the way. I, of all people, understand how difficult that is to accomplish."

The terrorist paused and then smiled again. "Not that it matters now, of course."

There was no point trying to continue selling the fiction that she was working for Gonzalez. To do so would only anger Carranco and likely make things worse than they already were.

If that was possible.

The only chance she had now was to keep Carranco talking, to drag things out and hope for an opening she could take advantage of. It seemed unlikely, but she wasn't going down without a fight. She said, "So you knew who I was the minute you saw me."

"More or less," Carranco said, "although I wasn't completely certain until you unwrapped the blouse from your head and I saw that hair. Then I knew for sure."

Tracie flexed her hands in an effort to determine whether there was any play in her bindings.

Nothing.

She tried moving her ankles and discovered them secured tightly as well.

Carranco clearly knew what she was doing when it came to immobilizing a prisoner.

Things were going from bad to worse and the question she really wanted to ask was, *Why didn't you just kill me when you had the chance and get it over with?*

But suggesting her own death to a psycho with a gun didn't seem like the smartest move, so instead Tracie said, "How many more Americans do you plan on killing? I assume, from looking at the munitions you've stockpiled here, that you don't intend to stop with the NCC massacre."

"You assume correctly."

"What can you possibly gain from this? Murdering people over something that may or may not have happened a quarter-century ago?"

"Oh, it happened alright. But how could I expect you to understand the concepts of honor, and of accountability?"

"Honor and accountability? Are you kidding me?" Tracie knew she should shut her mouth now, knew that by continuing the discussion she was probably accomplishing nothing besides hastening her own death.

But she couldn't help it. Listening to the twisted logic this black-hearted soul was using to destroy innocent lives was making her angrier and angrier.

Her head pounded and her stomach flip-flopped and she ignored it all. Said, "How is there any honor in killing Allan Nesbitt, NCC's CEO, a man who wasn't even out of college when the Bay of Pigs happened? How can you consider that 'accountability' in any way, shape or form?"

"I wouldn't expect someone like you to understand," Carranco said, her voice tight with emotion.

Tracie nodded at the stockpile of munitions lining one wall of the cabin. "And how did you get all this stuff out here, anyway?"

Tracie's goal was to keep Carranco talking, to drag everything out. But by the same token, she really was curious to learn the answer to that particular question. Even with a decent-sized box truck, it would have taken more than one load to transport all of the deadly weapons and materials stacked in front of her, and no box truck in the world would have been able to get all the way out here in the muck and the soft, wet terrain.

"A person dedicated to the cause of justice can accomplish much if she is willing to work at it," Maria Carranco answered serenely. "And I have worked extremely hard for a long time to put myself in a position where I can begin getting retribution for the injustice that was inflicted on my people."

"Justice?" Tracie scoffed. "You think you're getting justice? Is that what you consider the murder of more than a half-dozen innocent people to be?"

"I would not describe them as 'innocent,'" Carranco said coolly.

"And in any event, we are not here to debate the point." She removed a combat knife from a scabbard at her ankle and moved around behind Tracie's chair.

The terrorist began sawing through the tape securing her right ankle to the chair, and a moment after that, she freed Tracie's left ankle as well. Then she stood and said, "I am going to remove the tape from your wrists now. I suggest you do not forget who is armed and who is not."

Tracie smiled. "Aren't you forgetting something?"

"What do you mean?"

"You forgot to mention the qualifier."

"I do not understand."

"You should have said, 'Do not forget who is armed *for now.*'"

Anger clouded Maria Carranco's pretty eyes and she tightened her grip on the combat knife. She raised it as if to slash at Tracie and then regained control of her emotions. "You do not concern me," she said. "Before our little encounter, you had in your possession two handguns and a combat knife. Now you possess none. So you tell me, Miss CIA Agent: who should be worried?"

Tracie ground her teeth in frustration, but there was no good comeback for Carranco's taunt. Everything she said was true.

The terrorist sliced through the tape binding Tracie's wrists to the bamboo chair and then stepped back. "Get up," she said brusquely.

Tracie rubbed her wrists together in a mostly unsuccessful attempt to get the blood flowing again. "About time," she said. "What happens now? Are we going for drinks? Is it Happy Hour already?"

"You talk too much, do you know that?"

"That's hurtful, Maria. And I thought we were really starting to bond."

"Shut up and get out of that chair. Now."

The lightning bolts of pain continued blasting through her head, originating at the ragged gash the Mossberg had put in her skull and radiating outward. Her vision was intermittently blurry and she was as thirsty as she thought she had ever been.

And she didn't know what this crazy, homicidal terrorist had planned now, but she was pretty sure she wasn't going to like it much.

She pushed up with her legs, wobbled a moment, and then dropped heavily down into the chair. It rocked on its rear legs and Tracie nearly pitched backward onto the floor.

Carranco braced the back of the chair with her gun hand and shoved it forward. The front legs dropped down with a *thud.*

"I SAID GET UP!" She was getting angrier and angrier, about to blow her stack, which was exactly what Tracie wanted.

Tracie felt her gorge rising and swallowed heavily. "I'm going to throw up," she said.

"I do not care," Carranco answered. "For what it's worth, your pain will be over soon. *Now get up."* The last three words were shouted.

Tracie closed her eyes and concentrated on not puking. She said a quick prayer that what she was about to try next would not get her killed.

Then she pushed with her legs again and began rising. As she did, she hooked her right ankle around the right front leg of the chair and began falling heavily onto her side, jerking her ankle hard to topple the chair behind her.

She landed hard and her head felt as though it was going to explode, like it might just fly apart and scatter her brains all over Carranco's lonely cabin. *It'd serve her right,* Tracie thought. *Good luck cleaning up that mess.*

A split-second later the bamboo chair crashed to the floor behind her, exactly as she had hoped it would.

Carranco was screaming in fury now, her words partially garbled, half in English and half in Spanish. "Get up! Get up right now," she shouted, "or you will die where you are!" and Tracie hoped she had gotten the unstable woman angry and distracted enough for what she was about to try.

She pushed herself onto her hands and knees and turned around, facing the toppled chair. Then she braced herself on the chair frame and rose unsteadily to her feet.

She stepped on the chair leg to anchor it and wrapped her fist around a long, splintered piece of bamboo. Then she pulled hard as she rose to a standing position. The sliver of bamboo released from the warped, splintered chair with a crack that was lost in the sound of Maria Carranco's angry rant.

Tracie wobbled on her feet as she extended to her full height, the action only partly meant as a distraction. She really did feel weak and disoriented. She stumbled to the side and as she did she palmed the thick splinter—it was at least six inches long and as sharp as any kitchen knife she had ever used—behind her forearm.

She dropped to one knee, shielding the right side of her body from Carranco. As she rose again, she hitched up her jeans, sliding the splinter down the waistband at her hip. She felt it slice her skin as she shoved it under the denim, opening a gash down her right side, the pain bright and sharp and strong enough to make her momentarily forget the lightning bolts piercing her skull.

Her actions were desperate, hurried, and as she turned to face Maria Carranco, she prayed the bamboo shard would remain anchored against her side and not simply slide down her leg where it would become inaccessible. Her blouse tumbled down over her waist, covering the half-inch or so of bamboo that poked up over the top of her jeans.

She hoped.

Carranco was still ranting at her, worked up to the point Tracie could understand little she was saying, even in English. Tracie sighed deeply, swaying on her feet, and spread her hands. "What do you want me to do?" she said quietly.

The words seemed to snap the terrorist more or less out of her rage, and she stood in front of Tracie, breathing hard. Her face had turned bright crimson during her tirade and her eyes glittered with the unfocused fanaticism of the true believer.

For the first time, Tracie realized the full extent of Maria Carranco's obsession with avenging what she believed to be the American treachery at the Bay of Pigs so long ago. Capturing or killing Carranco would be the only way to bring her murderous rampage to an end; failure to do so would mean the violent deaths of many more innocent Americans before she was finally stopped.

The young woman stood in front of Tracie, gun in her right hand aimed more or less at Tracie's midsection. Her combat knife she had returned to its scabbard. For a moment Tracie thought she was going to simply shoot her where she stood.

Then she smiled, her eyes cold and hard. "What do I want you to do? I want you to come outside with me. It is time for you to dig your own grave."

41

Tracie blinked in surprise. "You kept me alive so you could make me dig my own grave?"

"You have a problem with that? Would rather be dead already?"

She shrugged. "For such a motivated woman, you're kind of lazy, aren't you?"

"Laziness has nothing to do with it. I want to watch your eyes as the pit you dig gets deeper and deeper. I want to see your fear as you realize every shovelful of dirt you throw out of the hole might be your last, that I might shoot you at any moment and cover your cooling remains with waterlogged soil." Her voice turned icy. "I want you to suffer, Miss CIA Agent."

"Tracie."

"Excuse me?"

"My real name is Tracie, not Holly. We're getting so close, and I know so much about you, that it only seems fair you should at least know my name. Besides," she added, letting her voice trail off, waiting for the inevitable.

Finally it came. "Besides, what?" Carranco asked.

"Besides, it's only right you know the name of the person who's going to kill you."

Maria Carranco laughed in delight, the sound high-pitched and jarringly innocent, like a ten-year-old who's just discovered she got a horse for her birthday. "You are very funny, I must give you that," she said. But then her voice turned cold again. "Let us see if you can keep your good humor when you are knee deep in your own grave."

She stepped back and gestured at the door with Tracie's gun. "Get moving," she said.

"What am I supposed to dig with, my hands?"

"Shut up and walk. I have tools behind the cabin."

Tracie moved unsteadily past the terrorist and walked out the door into the still-bright South Florida sunshine. It was late afternoon but the temperature and humidity seemed every bit as brutal now as it had been at noon.

She briefly considered making a run for the cover of the jungle but realized to do so would only result in certain death. Injured and unsteady, she would be easy prey for the petite, nimble terrorist to catch.

Besides, even if she somehow managed to escape, doing so without accomplishing her mission would be unacceptable.

She climbed down the cement block steps and waited at the bottom to be joined by her fanatical host. It only took a second, and then Carranco said, "Move around behind the cabin and grab a shovel."

Tracie walked to the rear and discovered a series of gardening tools lined up in a neat row against the back wall of the shack. She selected a long-handled spade and turned to face Carranco, mentally comparing the length of the handle with her distance from her enemy.

Escape wouldn't come that easily, however. Carranco had stopped walking at the rear corner of the cabin and remained well out of reach.

Cold fingers of terror clawed at Tracie's insides and she forced herself to ignore them. Panicking would do nothing to help her save herself. The blazing sun ratcheted up the pain in her skull, and her vision blurred and cleared, blurred and cleared.

She made a show of shrugging as if she hadn't a care in the world. "Where to, boss?"

Carranco grinned evilly. The act contained not an ounce of humor and was terrifying. "Where would you like to spend the rest of eternity?"

"Rural Virginia," Tracie said without hesitation, refusing to give this crazy bitch the satisfaction of seeing her fear. But it was building.

"Try again."

She sighed, the breath coming out just a little bit shaky. Then she nodded at the edge of the clearing, along the side of the tiny shack. "Out there, I guess."

"Then get to work."

*   *   *

Every shovel full of loose, moist turf she lifted out of the hole felt heavier and more cumbersome than the last. Tracie realized she should have given more thought to the location she had selected. Not because she had any intention of making it her final resting place—at least not without one hell of a fight—but because had she pointed at the other side of the clearing, she would be working in the shade right now.

As it was, the sinking sun continued to blast her with its damnable rays, the humidity every bit as high as it had been all day, and she could feel herself becoming more and more dehydrated. The speed at which she was losing fluids was shocking. Spending most of her career working in the typically cooler temperatures of the Soviet states had done nothing to prepare her for this.

She knew that her mounting dehydration was aggravating the pounding in her injured head, but she refused to give in. Maria Carranco was clearly waiting for her to ask for water and she was determined not to give the sadistic bitch the satisfaction of doing so.

Which was foolish.

Self-destructive, even.

If there had ever been a time she needed to conserve her strength absolutely as much as possible, this was it. She was only going to get one chance to take this fanatical killer down; if she failed she *would* end up at the bottom of the shallow pit she was digging. So electing not to ask for water was the most counterproductive thing she could do, short of telling the terrorist to shoot her in the head.

She didn't care.

She would win this battle of wills.

"Let me ask you a question," she croaked.

"Shut up and dig."

"I can do two things at once," she said, although given her rapidly weakening state she wondered how much longer that would be true.

"What is it?" Carranco said, exasperated.

"Why bury me at all? Why not just shoot me and leave me in the clearing? With all the predators in this swamp, my body would be long gone by morning. Or, if it wasn't, all that would be left would be a pile of bones, picked as clean as a Thanksgiving turkey."

The effort of asking the question left her out of breath and dizzy. But it was critical she distract the terrorist, try to get her off-balance, and what better way to do that than by feeding into her obvious need to feel superior?

Carranco was silent for a moment and Tracie kept digging, tossing shovelful after shovelful of sandy wet terrain into a rising pile next to the hole. She thought the young woman was going to ignore her question, but then she surprised Tracie by answering.

"Three reasons," she said. "First, I was raised a Catholic. I still go to Holy Mass every week."

A number of retorts sprang to mind, but none of them would do anything to improve her situation if she voiced them, so Tracie bit them back and said, "So?"

"So, a person who has died should not be left lying on the ground like a piece of trash. A person who has died deserves a proper burial, even someone like you. And while I cannot provide you with a funeral mass—" she spread her arms wide to indicate the vast Big Cypress Preserve and said, "No priests out here!" then continued—"the least I can do is bury your corpse."

"So murdering me in cold blood is okay, but leaving the carcass above ground is a deal breaker? That's where you draw the line?"

Carranco ignored her comment and continued as if she hadn't spoken. "Second, and perhaps more importantly, once you are gone, I fully intend to continue using my little retreat to get away and plan my incursions. Leaving such a delicious meal for crocodiles and alligators and leopards—yes, there are some out here—would not be a wise thing for me to do. It is important not to draw the predators' attention to this area any more than it already is drawn."

Tracie was surprised by the thoughtfulness of the answer. Maria

Carranco might be a vengeance-addicted psycho—*no "might be" about it,* she thought—but she certainly wasn't dumb.

She tossed another shovelful of sandy dirt onto the pile and noticed that she was sweating much less than she had been when she started digging. The temperature and humidity had not noticeably diminished, so that could mean only one thing: she was becoming dangerously dehydrated. A faraway buzzing had started in her ears, coming and going like the circling of a swarm of mosquitoes. For a while she thought it *was* the mosquitoes until she realized the noise was coming from inside her head.

Breathing heavily, she said, "You said there were three reasons. That's only two. What's the third?"

Carranco laughed, the sound like the *pop* of a firecracker. Or a gunshot. "The third reason I am making you dig your own grave? Because it is fun."

Tracie shook her head in disgust and regretted it immediately as the pain in her skull spiked. She continued to dig, carving out a hole maybe six feet long by three feet wide that continued to grow steadily deeper.

The buzzing sound inside her head was getting louder and she knew she was almost out of time. It was becoming hard to concentrate. She badly needed rest and water. Her vision continued to blur and clear, although the blurry periods were beginning to outnumber the clear periods by a significant margin.

Still she dug, wondering how deep the little pit would have to get before Carranco would shoot her while she worked and then lift the shovel off her corpse and fill in the hole.

She had tried to maintain a continuous awareness of the terrorist's location, waiting for the right time to strike. And given the extent of her injuries and her deteriorating physical condition, she thought she had done a pretty good job of it.

But Carranco had not come close to giving Tracie an opening. She was smiling like a kid in a candy store, obviously enjoying Tracie's misery, but she'd been far too wary to wander close enough to allow Tracie the chance to strike at her with the spade.

The loose, sandy turf was easy to shovel, a situation for which Tracie was grateful. But that was a curse as well as a blessing, because the job went quickly. Too quickly for Tracie's taste. The pit was now at least two feet deep and she guessed she had no more than another foot to go before the psycho with the gun and the bombs and the poison decided to finish her off once and for all.

She drove the spade into the ground and leaned on it tiredly. "Water," she finally rasped. She was surprised at the sound of her voice. It was weak and gravelly and sounded like someone else's.

Someone who should be on her way to the hospital.

"Keep digging."

"I need water or you won't have to shoot me. I'll just drop where I stand."

"Fine with me," Carranco said. "One more bullet I can use on someone else."

Tracie shook her head. Her vision swam, the ground tilting crazily, like camcorder video taken on some bizarre amusement park ride.

"Just one sip," she said, "Please." And then she stepped out of the hole, catching her toe on the lip of the pit and stumbling forward. Her feet felt incredibly heavy, and she almost caught herself but then sprawled face-first onto the ground.

"Get up!" Carranco screamed. "Get up! Get back in that hole and finish digging!" Her temper was on a hair trigger and her anger had returned in a heartbeat, and even though Tracie could not see her face, she knew it was red and tight and furious.

She pushed herself up to her hands and knees, her sweat-and-blood-soaked hair hanging in her face in ropy strings. Lifted her right foot and placed it beneath her body. Pushed up and sprawled forward again, smashing her face into the ground again, this time at Carranco's feet.

The terrorist was swearing and threatening, once again half in English and half in Spanish. She advanced on Tracie, brandishing her gun. Stopped next to her. Reached back and kicked her in the ribs.

Tracie dropped. Then she groaned and forced herself to her hands and knees once again. Put her right foot underneath her exhausted body and pushed.

This time she didn't fall forward. This time she shot to her feet, unsteady but determined, yanking the razor-sharp bamboo shard from the waistband of her jeans, waiting for the gunshot that would rip into her and end her life.

But the shot never came. Carranco was too angry or too distracted or had been lulled into a false sense of security by Tracie's apparent helplessness.

Before Tracie had even stretched to her full height, her arm was already coming forward, the six-inch-long shard of bamboo protruding like a dagger from her hand.

She aimed for the eyes and missed, but felt and saw the improvised blade dig deep into Carranco's cheek. It struck bone and veered left, digging a furrow under her eyes, breaking bones in her nose and then reappearing out the other side as blood flew, splattering across Tracie's face and nearly blinding her.

Carranco screamed and staggered backward, her hands clutching at her ruined face in an instinctive attempt to protect herself. Tracie's Glock dropped to the ground and bounced, tumbling into the shallow hole with a wet, muffled *thud*.

Tracie ignored the gun and pressed her advantage with a rabbit punch to Carranco's bloody face, dropping the terrorist.

But the moment Carranco hit the ground, she was moving, rolling away from the attack and toward the gun, somehow retaining the presence of mind to track the weapon with her eyes despite her shock and the gouts of blood spurting from her cheeks and what used to be her nose.

She hit the edge of the hole, still rolling, and dropped in. Tracie dived in after her, landing on the woman and knocking the wind out of her with an audible "Ooof."

Still Carranco fought, kicking her legs and punching at Tracie's throat with her left hand while feeling desperately around the hole for the gun with her right.

Tracie lifted Carranco's head and smashed it against the ground, trying to knock her out or at least disorient her. But the soft ground cushioned the blow, and the terrorist grunted in pain but continued to struggle.

Carranco located the gun and she lifted it and fired wildly. A searing pain creased Tracie's left leg and she nearly blacked out, the world caroming wildly in her vision.

She jabbed at Carranco's injured face and then dove left, desperate to wrench the gun away before the woman could get off a kill shot. She wrapped two hands around the butt of the Glock and yanked, twisting viciously, and the gun barrel veered toward Carranco's bleeding, mutilated face.

The terrorist's finger snapped like a dry twig, caught between the trigger and the trigger guard, and as it did it engaged the trigger, and the gun roared and spit fire, and Maria Carranco's head exploded in a spray of tissue, shattered bone and even more blood.

And Tracie felt the darkness closing in even though the sun was still shining.

And the buzzing in her ears became a screaming, and she realized the screaming was coming from her.

And then the world disappeared and the pain was gone.

42

Tracie's head hurt.

And her leg hurt.

Every part of her body hurt.

But unlike a little while ago, when she awoke duct-taped to Maria Carranco's homemade bamboo chair, she knew the moment she regained consciousness exactly where she was and exactly what had happened.

The terrorist lay unmoving at the bottom of the gravesite, her body partially covered by Tracie's. The left side of her face was a ruined, pulpy mess. Blood covered the dirt under and around her head, most of it having soaked into the ground thanks to the loose, sandy turf.

Instinctively Tracie reached up and placed two shaking fingers against Carranco's carotid artery. They slipped in the blood and she tried again. Felt for the pulse she knew she would not find.

The woman was dead.

Tracie realized she would suffer the same fate if she didn't get moving. The buzzing in her head was gone for the moment, but she had no doubt it would soon return if she didn't take care of the gunshot wound in her leg and begin to rehydrate.

The sun had dipped below the horizon and night was approaching like an onrushing train. The predators Carranco had talked about were undoubtedly close by. If she didn't get to the shelter of the cabin—soon—she would probably wish she had been shot.

She rolled off the dead terrorist and reached for her gun. She had lost her grip on it when she lost consciousness, but it was still firmly in Maria Carranco's grasp, the trigger guard caught on her hideously misshapen finger.

Tracie pried it out of Carranco's hand and heard/felt another bone break in the dead woman's finger, not that it mattered now. Then she shoved it into the waistband of her jeans where she had so recently hidden the makeshift bamboo dagger.

She breathed in deeply and took her first look at the gunshot wound in her leg. The slug had struck the meaty outer portion of her thigh, and while it looked as though a lot of blood had soaked into her jeans, she guessed the bullet had passed through without causing any major damage.

Hopefully.

She flexed the leg experimentally, bending her knee. A searing flash of pain blossomed where she had been shot and a gush of blood jetted out the entry wound. The pain was intense but manageable. If she could get to the cabin and patch up the wound, she wouldn't be in any danger of bleeding to death.

She wondered whether Carranco kept any first-aid supplies inside her cabin, but realized the answer was mostly irrelevant. She could use her duct tape to seal the bullet wound, and then use her combat knife to cut the wooden handles off some of the tools lined up behind Carranco's shack to fashion a makeshift splint.

It would take some time, and would seriously limit her mobility in hiking back to her rental truck, but with Carranco dead, time had ceased to be an issue. And with nightfall nearly complete in Big Cypress National Preserve, she wouldn't be going anywhere tonight, anyway.

But all her plans depended upon making it to the shelter of the cabin. She was completely exposed at the moment in a wilderness vaster and more untamed than almost anywhere else in North America. Getting her hands on her gun had made her feel immensely better, but the fact remained that she was easy prey in her current condition, injured and almost immobile.

Tracie gritted her teeth and struggled to a sitting position, jostling her left leg and forcing more blood out the bullet's entry wound. She wouldn't be certain until she reached the cabin and had the chance to examine the wound, but she thought she felt the sticky wetness of blood on the back of the thigh as well.

If true, that would mean the slug had indeed passed through her leg, which was mostly good news, but which would also mean she had just dragged the open wound through the damp, mucky earth. Infection would become a near-certainty.

It was too late to worry about that now. All she could do was keep moving. She leaned forward and braced her forearms on the soil next to the hole. Then she dragged herself up and out of the gravesite, using her good leg to push off and propelling herself forward with her arms. She crashed down face-first into the clearing, moaning from the pain in her leg and the pain in her skull and the raging thirst that losing consciousness had done nothing to assuage.

She lay face down, breathing heavily, wanting nothing more than to rest.

To take a break.

She had earned a break, goddammit. But she wasn't going to get one, not unless she wanted to die trapped between the jaws of a crocodile, screaming and wishing she had been murdered by Maria Carranco instead.

Remotivated if not refreshed, Tracie used her arms to raise her upper body off the ground like she was doing a pushup. Then she flexed her good leg underneath and lifted, doing her best to raise herself to a standing position while bending her injured leg as little as possible.

It worked. She stood, swaying precariously, and tried desperately not to drop back to the ground. It wasn't easy. The earth tilted and yawed as she tried to remain balanced. Nausea bloomed in her belly and she clamped her mouth shut and swallowed heavily. There was no way she would be able to remain standing if she puked, and no way she would be able to rise again if she fell.

After a moment she began working her way toward the shack, taking little bunny hops on her good leg, gasping as the effort jarred the bullet wound and her injured skull. The pain in her leg had leveled off, but her headache had returned and her vision seemed to be narrowing. She focused her gaze on her goal—the front door of the cabin—and a frightening blackness that had nothing to do with sunset began to appear around the edges of it.

The buzzing had started up again, returning with a vengeance inside her head. Her good leg felt like jelly and she had resumed sweating, although she felt suddenly freezing cold.

She gritted her teeth and continued moving grimly forward, telling herself she had to be getting closer to the shack even though it didn't feel like it. She thought about Marshall Fulton, picturing him as he looked at the Congressional Steakhouse, big and muscular and handsome, confident enough in his masculinity to let his tiny redheaded date handle the two Neanderthals who had taken it upon themselves to register their disapproval of inter-racial dating.

She liked Marshall a lot, had known immediately she wanted to see him again but had committed to nothing because of the dangers inherent in her career, and even more because of what had happened to the last man she had allowed herself to fall in love with.

The vision of Shane Rowley appeared unbidden in her memory, Shane falling backward in slow motion off the roof of the Minuteman Mutual Insurance Building in DC, his eyes locked onto hers as he sacrificed his own life to save her, doing so after knowing her for only a few days.

She kept moving, tiny hop after tiny hop, dimly aware that she was crying now, for sacrifices she had made as well as for the ones that had been made on her behalf, suddenly desperate to survive if only to make that second date with Marshall, to visit the Congressional Steakhouse again, or a fast food restaurant, or anywhere at all, and to look into that ruggedly handsome face and tell a joke so she could see that dazzling smile again and this time maybe see if Marshall wanted to stay with her at the end of the night.

And then she discovered she had arrived at the concrete block steps leading to the doorway of Maria Carranco's unlikely cabin in the middle of nowhere. She turned and slumped down on the cement block stairway, exhausted and shaky, too tired even to try to climb the three steps.

Night had fully fallen during her short trek from the improvised gravesite to the old hermit's shack, the inky blackness tempered by the light of millions of stars beginning to appear in the vast, cloudless Everglades sky. A faint rustling sound in the distance told Tracie the jungle of Big Cypress was giving itself over to the nighttime predators, and she breathed a sigh of relief she had regained consciousness in time to make it to the shelter of the cabin while there had still been sufficient daylight to see it.

The blood leaking from her bullet wound seemed to have slowed almost to a stop, but there was no real way of knowing how much blood she had already lost, and the awful lightning bolts of pain in her injured skull were getting worse, not better.

And she was still thirsty. Maddeningly, distractingly thirsty.

Tracie lifted her butt off the bottom step and sat back down on the next.

Rested for a moment.

Moved one more step up and sat again.

One more time and she found herself seated on the small landing. She reached inside for one last reserve of strength and forced herself to her feet. The nausea that had receded for the last few blessed minutes came rushing back and she wished she had never stopped moving.

She leaned against the side of the shack to avoid losing her balance and tumbling back to the ground, and waited for the nausea and the blackness that had again begun blossoming in her peripheral vision to disappear.

Thirty seconds later it hadn't disappeared and she knew it wasn't *going* to disappear until she had taken care of herself. She twisted the tarnished brass doorknob and shoved on the wooden door and tumbled into Maria Carranco's cabin, dropping onto the floor with a bone-jarring thud.

The darkness inside the cabin was even more complete than outside. Tracie struggled not to lose consciousness, fearing she might never awaken if she passed out again.

She took deep breaths and blew the air out forcefully. Began crawling toward where she remembered seeing a Coleman gas lantern. Treating her bullet wound would not wait until morning, and doing so would be impossible without artificial light. A heavy Maglite flashlight had been among the supplies inside her backpack, but Carranco had taken the pack after slugging Tracie with the shotgun and Tracie didn't know where the terrorist might have hidden it.

Her progress across the little cabin's interior felt agonizingly slow, but eventually she bumped up against what she hoped was the kitchen counter—which was nothing more than a roughly-constructed shelf, really—upon which she had seen Maria Carranco's supplies and the lantern.

She felt around in the dark until banging her knuckles against one of the counter's wooden legs, and then she wrapped both hands around the leg and began dragging herself painfully upward.

When she reached the countertop, she grabbed onto it with both hands and lifted, using her good leg to brace herself, until somehow she had gotten into a standing position one last time. Her head pounded and the nausea bloomed and her leg throbbed and she did her best to ignore all of it.

She thought she remembered seeing a box of waterproof matches next to the lantern and she felt around blindly, banging into gallon jugs of water and scattering food and other supplies across the counter. At last her fingertips brushed what she thought might be the matchbox and she wrapped her hands around it with all the fervor of a miner who has just struck gold.

She was weak and sweating and freezing cold again, but she managed to open the box and pull out a match. Somehow she even managed to strike the match without it falling from her shaking fingers and setting fire to the tinderbox of a shack.

The tip of the match flared and Tracie smiled with delight. That tiny yellow glow was the sweetest sight in the world. She set about lighting the gas lantern, saying a prayer that the reservoir contained at least enough fuel to allow time to treat herself and to figure out where the lunatic terrorist had hidden more fuel.

A moment later the twin mantles flared inside the glass globe. Tracie breathed a sigh of relief and realized she was crying again.

43

Sunrise came early in the Everglades, and with it, oppressive heat and humidity.

Tracie didn't care. She was anxious to get moving.

After rehydrating last night with fresh, sweet water from one of the gallon jugs on the counter, she had stripped her clothes off and prepared to begin cleaning her bullet wound. She swallowed a handful of aspirin and gritted her teeth against the pain she already felt and the pain she knew was to come.

She searched until finding her backpack—one advantage to the cabin's minimal interior square-footage was that there weren't many places to hide anything—and then pulled out her trusty duct tape. The roll was getting a little thin after all it had been used for, but she thought there would be enough left for what she needed to do.

She sat on Maria Carranco's cot and began wrapping the tape as tightly as she could stand around her thigh. If cleaning the wounds with soapy water had been painful, this was agonizing, and she gasped as she worked, squeezing her eyes shut and moaning through clenched teeth when the pain became almost unbearable.

The hike would be long and difficult, and she knew she could not afford to take the chance of the bullet wounds beginning to gush blood when she was halfway between the cabin and her truck.

By the time she finished with the makeshift bandage, her hands were shaking so badly she almost could not keep hold of the roll of tape. Her plan had been to get some food in her stomach before trying to sleep, but the prospect of fighting her way one more time to the other side of the cabin was more than she could bear.

Instead, she lifted her backpack onto the cot and adjusted it until she could use it to elevate her injured leg. Then she closed her eyes and was asleep—or perhaps unconscious—almost before she had any idea what was happening.

Now, with the sun rising and the jungle predators banished—more or less—for the next fourteen hours or so, Tracie was ready to move. She still needed to fashion a splint to immobilize her left leg, so the first order of business would be to cut the handles off two of the shovels or other gardening tools Carranco had lined up behind the shed.

Tracie's backup gun and combat knife had been hidden among the weapons Carranco had squirreled away in the cabin. There was no doubt her knife could handle the job of hacking the handles off the tools. It might destroy the blade, but that seemed like a small price to pay.

She struggled to the door and then opened it. Stepped out of the shack. Looked at the hole in the ground where a life-and-death struggle had taken place last night.

And gasped, this time in surprise rather than pain.

Maria Carranco's corpse was gone.

Just gone.

If Tracie didn't know the full story of what had happened in and around that hole, she would never have known Carranco was even there. The blood from her fatal head wound—at least, the small amount of blood that hadn't soaked into the sandy ground—was still there, but it was the only remaining evidence of the life-and-death struggle that had taken place last night.

She shivered. It seemed unlikely the alligator or crocodile or whatever monster had dragged Carranco's body away would have differentiated between a dead human and a live one, and she wondered how long it had taken after nightfall for the corpse to disappear.

She thought about the dead black eyes of the croc she had encountered in the truck on the way here and shivered again.

Then she did her best to put it out of her mind. There was a lot left to do and she had a long way to go; it was important she get a grip. Without the proper focus, even with Carranco out of the picture it would still be very easy to die out here in Big Cypress National preserve, especially given the extent of her injuries.

She forced her gaze away from the now-empty gravesite and moved carefully down the concrete block steps, using Maria Carranco's Mossberg as a cane and holding her Glock firmly in her right hand. The omnipresent horde of mosquitoes found her almost immediately upon stepping outside, and she waved at them out of habit, knowing the action would do nothing to disperse them but trying anyway.

She sighed deeply.

She couldn't wait to get the hell out of here.

44

Tracie entered CIA Director Aaron Stallings's home on crutches and clumped down the hallway toward his office. As always, Stallings's wife was nowhere to be seen, although it was entirely possible she was elsewhere in the massive home.

She had reported straight to Langley, as instructed by Stallings, after her flight touched down at DCA, more than a little concerned about what would happen at the front gate. Since her employment had been officially terminated shortly after the kidnapping of U.S. Secretary of State J. Robert Humphries, she had become persona non grata at the agency.

Even after recovering Humphries and returning him to DC unharmed—more or less—she had been refused entry into agency headquarters and then steadfastly ignored when she had delivered the secretary of state.

This time, though, a pair of agents had been waiting for her cab when it pulled to the curb, and one had whisked her inside the complex in a wheelchair while the other paid the driver and took charge of her few personal items.

Tracie hated hospitals. Hated being admitted to them, hated driving past them, hated *thinking* about them. So the news that her bullet wound could be cleaned, disinfected and bandaged and her head injury could be sutured, all on site and all by the agency's medical staff, had come as a pleasant, if not entirely unexpected, surprise.

Treating patients without asking too many questions—or any

questions at all—was routine for CIA doctors, and Tracie was thrilled she would not have to deal with the DC police, who would certainly have been notified immediately had she appeared at any area hospital with a bullet wound in her leg.

She was treated professionally and courteously, and four hours after being ushered inside, she exited the complex on a brand-new set of crutches, with a freshly bandaged left leg and freshly sutured right side of her head, not to mention freshly *shaved* right side of her head.

She found herself worrying more about what Marshall would think of her now odd-looking hairstyle than about recovering from the bullet wound. All things considered, she supposed that was a good sign.

The diagnosis regarding her still-throbbing headache was that she had suffered a concussion—no surprise there—and the consensus of the medical staff seemed to be that the headaches would begin to subside over the next few days.

They offered prescription medication to minimize the pain, which she turned down flat. Anything that could serve to dull the senses or slow reaction time was potentially deadly to a covert operative, and while Tracie doubted she would be sent into the field on crutches, she couldn't entirely discount the possibility, either. Aaron Stallings was that unpredictable.

At no time while inside Langley did she see anyone she knew, which was probably another good sign. It seemed unlikely any employee of the Central Intelligence Agency would ask the obvious question of why an ex-operative with no current ties to the CIA would be receiving treatment for a gunshot wound, but still, her preference was not to have to discuss the issue at all.

And she couldn't deny feeling a certain sadness at being back here as an outsider. The CIA was the only employer she had ever had as an adult, and her entire identity had been tied up in her work as a covert operative—a NOC, which stood for non-official cover.

She was doing the same type of work now, and she supposed her current position—working for the agency on the blackest of black ops missions while not even officially being *employed* by the agency—was as NOC as NOC could get, but she missed the camaraderie of fellow intelligence employees.

Before her official termination, she would have felt a sense of belonging, of shared commitment, when walking the halls of CIA Headquarters, even though she might not see a single face she recognized. The bond of shared commitment and sacrifice toward a common goal was that strong.

But now, despite the fact she had been treated well and cared for in the most professional manner possible, that camaraderie was gone. That sense of shared purpose was missing.

She was the outsider.

Still, she knew she was doing important work, work critical to national security, and although the history of the CIA was that once terminated, an employee—especially an operational employee—would never be rehired, Tracie held out hope that her case might be different.

If she performed her duties as Aaron Stallings's personal Black Ops agent to the highest level possible, if she made herself so valuable he would have no choice in the matter, maybe he would see his way clear to returning her to the CIA's roster of operatives on an official basis.

She knew she was probably kidding herself. Hell, she was *definitely* kidding herself. But she had to have something to hold on to. She needed that little bit of hope, even if it was unreasonable hope. She needed it like an addict needed his next fix.

The sound of her crutches echoed down the hallway as the rubber stoppers moved along the meticulously polished hardwood floors. As always when she visited her boss, Tracie marveled at the exquisite furnishings, wondering how even a decades long civil servant could possibly afford the expensive taste Stallings exhibited.

She arrived at the director's closed office door and before she could raise her hand to rap on the door, he bellowed, "Come in!" He had heard her less-than-stealthy approach.

Tracie turned the knob and struggled inside, leaning on her right crutch to keep it from clattering to the floor while she opened the door with her left hand. She clomped through and then paused just inside the office, using her crutch to push the door closed.

Stallings glanced up from the ever-present pile of paperwork cluttering his desk, grunted something that may or may not have been "hello," and then dropped his attention back to his work. He didn't bother to offer her any assistance, which was just as well. She would never have accepted. Not from him.

The usual hard-backed chair had been placed in front of his desk, and Tracie crutched her way across the room and eased into it. The boss paid her no attention after his brief glance as she was entering, and Tracie took advantage of the opportunity to lean her crutches against the desk as Edison Kiley had done during her last visit here.

Stallings showed no signs of being prepared to interrupt his paperwork, so she lifted her injured leg with both hands and propped it onto the surface of the desk and then leaned back in the chair with a sigh of satisfaction.

Stallings lifted his eyes from the desk, made a point of staring at her leg, and then raised his gaze to meet hers, his forehead wrinkled and his entire demeanor screaming, "What in the hell do you think you're doing?"

Tracie smiled brightly in response. "Gotta keep it elevated," she said, although the doctors had told her no such thing. It only made sense, though, and she decided they had probably *meant* to give her those instructions, but that it had just slipped their minds. *Better safe than sorry,* she thought. *Especially if I can tweak the boss.*

Stallings cleared his throat and said, "So, you weren't able to apprehend Maria Carranco."

"The threat has been eliminated, yes. Those were your instructions, correct?"

"I would have much preferred you to bring the young woman in, so we could interrogate her and perhaps gain intel that would be of use to the agency down the line."

"And also so you could wait a sufficient amount of time and then release her discreetly back to Omega 7. You wouldn't want to jeopardize your working relationship with Juan Gonzalez, now, would you?"

Aaron Stallings's temper was legendary around Washington, DC. It was never far from the surface, and now anger smoldered in his gaze. "Thanks to your heavy-handed tactics, we'll never have a 'working relationship' with Gonzalez again. And before you try to justify your methods, let me remind you that the 'working relationship' you denigrate so easily has resulted in the prevention of numerous felony crimes, including murder."

"So you have no problem with this supposed 'ally' sending me to Havana on a wild-goose chase and then leaving me there to die."

"I never said that."

"You didn't have to." Tracie had by now dealt with the legendary spymaster long enough that she had convinced herself she would be able to keep her temper in check, that she was used to his manipulations and the unending mind games. But once again, she felt her anger rising to match his own.

Her voice had begun rising in volume and now she lowered it but continued to speak. "Your instructions to me were very clear: I was to remove the burgeoning threat to defense-related industries ASAP, and to do so by any means necessary. Those were your exact words. 'Any means necessary.' Given the opportunity, I would have brought Carranco back with me, but I have to tell you, if there was any chance at all she would have ended up back on the street, where she could have killed or injured more innocent people, I don't apologize for being forced to kill her. And for the record, it was either her or me in that goddamned hole in the ground. I *was* forced to kill her or die myself."

Stallings glowered at her but said nothing, and after a moment she continued. "This woman was a Grade-A, first-class psycho, Boss, and protecting her in order to maintain connections with Gonzalez would have been the wrong move. Trust me on this."

He continued to stare her down and she returned his gaze defiantly. Finally he changed the subject.

Sort of.

"We have a team of agents removing all the weapons, bomb-making materials and other evidence from her shack in the middle of the Everglades even as we speak. That place was a treasure-trove of extremely dangerous substances. It was a minor miracle she never blew herself sky-high while constructing explosive devices out there. It's a tremendous win to get those materials off the street."

Tracie realized this was as close to an apology as Aaron Stallings would ever allow himself to come. It was also as close as he would come to admitting she had done well, and she smiled—sincerely, this time—at her boss. Of course, a return smile was unthinkable, but she thought the hard set of his face might have softened just a bit.

Maybe.

Stallings cleared his throat and said, "We can only hold Gonzalez for so long. He's going to be released from custody down in Miami very soon, probably by the end of the day if our recovery team can get everything out of Carranco's shack by then. Once that happens, he's going to discover Maria has gone missing, and once *that* happens, he *will* come looking for you."

Tracie chuckled grimly. "Let him look. He'll never find me, and even if he does, good luck to him. I handled him once, I can handle him again."

"I know this man. He'll never give up."

"I'm not worried."

"I'm not saying you should be. But you should definitely be wary."

"I'm always wary, Director."

"Good. Now, how long did the medical quacks say you were going to be laid up?"

"They didn't say, specifically. But the slug went through and through, and caused no structural damage to my leg. My head injury—aside from the sewing job required to close the gash—is just a concussion. They say the headaches will begin to diminish soon, and I'm a fast healer. By the time I get the stitches out of my head and my leg I should be fine."

Stallings looked at her dubiously.

"What?" she said. "You don't like my new hairstyle? Buzz-cut on one side, long on the other?"

The CIA Director grunted in what may or may not have been a chuckle. With Aaron Stallings, it was hard to tell; he might just be suffering from heartburn. He shook his head and said, "Is there anything else, Tanner?"

"No, sir."

"Then get your leg off my goddamn desk and get the hell out

of here. Rest up and feel better, but stick close to your phone. You can expect a call from me five minutes after you're ready to return to work."

"I'm ready right now." That wasn't entirely true, of course. Her head continued to pound and she wouldn't be winning many footraces any time soon. But it was close enough as far as she was concerned. She'd be damned if she was going to show any sign of weakness to Aaron Stallings.

He expelled a blast of air in what she knew this time *was* a chuckle and said, "Yeah, right. Get out of here, Tanner."

Tracie eased her leg off the desk and struggled to her feet. She leaned onto her crutches and began clumping slowly toward the office door. Again Stallings declined to offer any assistance and again she was unsurprised.

She exited the office without saying goodbye.

Called a cab from Aaron Stallings's empty kitchen.

Began working her way to the end of his long driveway to wait for her ride.

It would be a few minutes before the taxi's arrival, and she passed the time thinking about Marshall Fulton and that second date. She wondered what he would say when he got a glimpse of her half-shaved head.

She found herself smiling at the thought. She didn't think he'd mind too much.

Looking to enhance your enjoyment of *The Omega Connection*? Check out the official *Omega Connection* soundtrack album, consisting of three long "soundscapes," music written and recorded by Steve Buick of Evokescape specifically to accompany this book.

The album consists of nearly two hours of original music designed to act as a background for the expressed purpose of adding suspense and excitement to your reading experience. The tracks are outstanding, and can be enjoyed no matter what point you find yourself in the book, and I cannot recommend the album highly enough. Give it a listen and see if you don't agree.

Tracie Tanner will return soon in her fourth exciting thriller. To be the first to learn about new releases, and for the opportunity to win free ebooks, signed copies of print books, and other swag, take a moment to sign up for Allan Leverone's email newsletter at AllanLeverone.com.

Reader reviews are hugely important to authors looking to set their work apart from the competition. If you have a moment to spare, please consider taking a moment to leave a brief, honest review of *THE OMEGA CONNECTION* at Amazon, Goodreads, or your favorite review site, and thank you!

I learned a lot about the Florida Everglades and its companion, Big Cypress National Preserve, in researching THE OMEGA CONNECTION. It's an area of unparalleled beauty and raw danger, and provided the perfect setting for the final showdown between Tracie and the beautiful and cunning Maria Carranco.

It probably goes without saying, but there is no real-life Crystal Lake and no Slough Road jutting into the wilderness off the Tamiami Trail, although there *are* any number of lonely, overgrown trails that do just that. The name – Slough Road – comes from the tiny town where I grew up in Massachusetts, and I though it fit perfectly into the remote Everglades setting.

The same is true of Woodchuck Hill, the road Dr. Edison Kiley lives on. Believe it or not, the address of the house I spent the first seventeen years of my life in was Woodchuck Hill Road, I swear to God. Ever since I began writing, I've been waiting for an opportunity to use such a cool name, and I'm glad I finally got the chance.

The Bay of Pigs Invasion of Cuba in 1961 drives the plot of THE OMEGA CONNECTION, and is a fascinating event for history buffs. It – along with the Cuban Missile Crisis – illustrates perfectly the uneasy relationship between the United States and the Soviet Union during the Cold War. It's hard to imagine now, more than a quarter-century after the fall of the Berlin Wall, that a Communist country and satellite of our sworn enemy was located so close to the U.S. mainland.

I tried something new with this manuscript, submitting *THE OMEGA CONNECTION* to Amazon's brand-spanking-new Kindle Scout program.

As I write this, the Kindle Scout campaign is ongoing and I don't know whether the ebook edition will be picked up for publication by Kindle Press or not. But what I do know is that a hell of a lot of people have nominated it during the campaign, and I wish I could thank you all personally. I truly appreciate the support of my loyal readers, and I promise I will never take you for granted.

Thrillers from Allan Leverone

Parallax View : A Tracie Tanner Thriller
All Enemies: A Tracie Tanner Thriller
Final Vector
The Lonely Mile
The Organization

Horror/Dark Thrillers from Allan Leverone

Mr. Midnight
After Midnight (coming April 2015)
Paskagankee
Revenant
Wellspring

Novellas from Allan Leverone

Flight 12: A Kristin Cunningham Thriller
The Becoming
Heartless (currently out of print)
Darkness Falls (currently out of print)

Story Collections from Allan Leverone

Postcards from the Apocalypse
Uncle Brick and the Four Novelettes

www.ingramcontent.com/pod-product-compliance
Lightning Source LLC
Chambersburg PA
CBHW060533260626
47161CB00003B/876